# The Swan Maiden

**Book Two of
The Surface and the Deep
Story of Anna of Cleves**

By G. Lawrence

Copyright © Gemma Lawrence 2024
All Rights Reserved.
No part of this manuscript may be reproduced without Gemma Lawrence's express consent.

To Terry and Julia,
For walks in the sun at Hever
For wanders through the Tower under grey, cloudy skies
And for all your support
Every day before and after.

## Chapter One

### Near Antwerp
### Flanders
### The Low Countries

### November's End 1539

"Hold!"

I sighed, gritting my teeth, as our wagon shuddered to a halt, wishing I could simply expire, cease to be, be done with life, just so I might put an end to this interminable journey. I fought down a sudden urge to bash my head against the side of the covered wagon I sat in with my women, all of whom looked just as miserable as I felt, but I knew I could not release my feelings in so obvious, crass a way. A lady, a born Duchess of the houses of Cleves and Julich on her way to become Queen of England, did not act without decorum or mastery of her emotions, no matter how sore she was tempted. *Courage, Anna*, I told myself.

I straightened my shoulders and smiled gently at the glum faces before me. "Arrange the blankets better, so you all are all covered," I said to my companions, noting that some of my more senior, and elderly, ladies appeared to be trying to keep all the woollen blankets to themselves. "I am sure this stop will be of short duration."

I could see glances, lights in eyes which spoke of intense weariness. This had not been the first time I had said something of this kind and although I was doing my best to use a different phrasing each time, I was sure it was not to be the last, either.

We had hardly been travelling fast as it was. Remaining at a standstill was in truth only slightly slower than the agonizingly sluggish pace we had been travelling at. Had I thought to walk to England, I might be there by now.

*Hold*. That word, so simple it was, yet it had become so hateful. *Hold*. How could that one instruction have become so very irritating that now whenever I heard it all I wanted to do was scratch my own skin off and pluck out my own eyeballs?

How can a word become this hated? Overuse. *Hold* had been the command I had heard more than any other on this journey, more than "ride on", more than cries of celebration when a city promising hot fires and food and cool ale came in sight, more than the sound of my own breath, I was sure I had heard *hold*. More than anything, *hold*, had marked this journey from my home into the Low Countries.

In some ways this word, which was trying even my famous patience, should have been a good one, for it was an instruction intended to keep us together. My party was large, an escort worthy of a princess, and it was therefore somewhat unwieldy, for rather than a steady march of say, trained soldiers, or a constant stream of merchants driven to market by lust for gold, we were a gaggle of guards and soldiers, courtiers and ladies all on our way to take me to England, to my new husband.

And neither road nor weather were feeling obliging or generous to my journey.

Autumn was never a good time for travel. In summer months the roads would be dry and although dust could be an irritant it did not delay one overly. In winter it was true sometimes the ways to cities and towns could become blocked by snow, or dangerous because of ice, but generally, if one went when paths were frozen hard and solid it was a good time to travel. But autumn, autumn was the season of rain and wind, and mud was their child, and mud was our most decided and determined enemy, in large part the reason for every single ghastly cry of "Hold!" I had heard for what felt like an eternity. There had been also roads which were flooded, or crossings where the water was too high and we had to go around, but it was the muck on the roads which was causing the most problems for us.

The days were shorter at this time of the year too, the hours we could travel safely in light getting briefer every day as autumn plunged headlong and reckless into winter. As we sat there waiting for the command to ride on that day, I could already see the evening sun setting in the skies, a haze of red and pink, of azure and gold igniting in the skies, birds black as the coming night winging as silhouettes against the tumbling brilliance of the light, making pretty spirals in their elegant flight. We had made it three miles that day. It would soon be time to shelter for the night, time to find a lord or, more usually, an abbey, where we could be taken into guest quarters to rest our aching backs and heads, and then we would rise before the dawn once more just to set all those pains formed of discomfort and inaction back into our muscles all over again.

Sometimes as we travelled, when I dozed off in the wagon or in my litter, I would dream that this was indeed an endless road, that I had not been promised to the King of England as his wife and was on my way there, but instead had died, and this was purgatory. I had never been able to imagine what purgatory was like before this journey, but I felt as if I had a fine idea of it now.

We had left Dusseldorf and my family in early November and had made slow progress, which had got slower, and slower ever since. The roads were clogged with mud sometimes so thick it felt as though we were being pulled through a barrel of oats sodden with thick honey, the paths were running with water from rain causing poor horses to slip and wagons to slide in the mire, and the occasional storm struck, which had forced us to remain within a castle held by this lord or that – their names blurred now, there had been so many. This had led to us covering little more than five miles a day, an achingly slow pace. I was carried for much of it, either by litter or in a covered wagon, my mother having sent instruction I was not to ride much due to fears for my safety, in case some lord or the Emperor or vagabonds on the road should think to try to carry me off, but also so my complexion would not be damaged. I had not gone by sea in order to preserve the paleness and smoothness of my skin, so the thought of ruining that by having me on a horse for a month in the wind and lashing rain was not something my mother tolerated with any joy.

In my secret heart, though, I was dying to get on a horse and ride. Being cramped in a chilly, draughty, confined wagon day after day with women who were, through no fault of their own, growing more and more miserable and fractious every day, was not aiding my flagging spirits. Staying true to promises to my worried mother, however, I had not obeyed my, at times violent, compulsion to climb into a saddle and ride away the cramping pains in my body or the stiffness in my back. I tried to remind myself that I was one of the fortunate; the men heaving wagons along, the soldiers standing outside in the mist and hail all night and day, they were the ones who truly suffered.

I stared through the gap in the curtain, a light pattering of rain striking the oiled cover over our heads. It was a pretty sound, a gentle tap as if sharp-fingered elves sought to gain our attention. There was shouting coming from behind us, whatever it was that was delaying us, there were men working on it, some of them were swearing but I could hardly blame them. If I knew any curse words beyond 'God's teeth!' as my father used to exclaim in times truly dire, I might well have muttered a few of them. My eyes roamed the countryside, and I felt a hunger, a now familiar urge resonating deep within me to escape this wagon, find a horse and ride. To where, I knew not.

*Courage, Anna,* I said. *And behave!*

Far off, mist was swirling over long, flat expanses of fields. The countryside was different here, flatter than Cleves. It seemed like an endless vastness of fields and fields and more fields, and the horizon did not stretch up to touch the sun with hillsides or mountains, as it did at home. In some ways it seemed as if here in the Low Countries the sun fell down to touch the earth when night came. The occasional cottage struck up from the land, here and there, smoke billowing from chimneys, joining the dance of greyness in the air above. The houses looked a little different to those we had passed in Cleves. Every difference I noted, and it made my heart hurt a little more. I was leaving all I knew behind. I could smell wet earth, wet air, and a tang of iron on the wind telling me that snow was thinking to come. I put a hand to my scar, in my eyebrow, but it did not ache that day. Cold weather certainly was on its way, but it would not snow that night.

We had passed through many towns and cities, and, since our pace was so slow, advance warning of our arrival was had by these studs of civilisation stuck upon the landscape weeks before we got there. Perhaps because any event becomes more interesting in the dull, grey months of the year, crowds of people had gathered at each new place, throngs lining up along the roads, some to cheer and wave, many to bow, taking their hats from their heads and many more to stare at me in pity. The antics of the mad King of England, he who was to be my husband, were well known to most people. In some ways the lines of people waiting to see me reminded me of my father's funeral procession. I wondered if they thought that too, if they wondered if they were indeed seeing me to my grave, a tomb hollowed out within this marriage.

At Antwerp, a city we had just passed – and if I looked back, I could still see the spires of churches within its walls – there had been so many people turned out to welcome us that our cavalcade had been almost swamped. Flemish nobles had told my men that never had they seen so many people gathered, "Even for the Emperor's entrée to the city, there were never this many," they said. I could well believe it. Although at first I had opened my curtain to the outside, waved at people and accepted gifts of posies and dried herbs, bread and honey and flasks of ale, I had been forced to close it quickly enough, the press of people too great and my guards fighting to hold them back too few.

"God's eyebrows!" Mother Loew, my companion had sworn as the litter rocked perilously. I had glanced in shock at her for never before had I heard her swear. "They will have us over, my lady."

Although I had reassured her, it had been a hard fight to control my own fear, for hands banged on the litter and it jolted this way and that as my men struggled to maintain control of it as well as their feet, as the crowds jostled in, so close I could smell their sweat. "God bless you, Your Grace!" they shouted to me, some so close to my ears their greeting came as roars of beasts in the darkness.

"Stand back! Stand back!" shouted the good men of the Antwerp watch, and thankfully the press of people had receded. I could still, however, and for some time after, feel my heart hammering in my chest, a silent echo of remembered fear.

That night we had been escorted to a castle by fifty English merchants in a torch-lit procession, but even there I was not safe, for my house had been thrown open to the public, with Englishmen and foreigners coming one after another, after another to pay homage. The night was long, and my head ached, pounding with all the names and flowery addresses of esteem I had received. I sat before them unveiled, feeling quite naked to be so before so many men, but they had come to see their new Queen and give report of me to others, so I had to be seen.

"They all praised your beauty and graciousness, Your Grace," said Olisleger, my translator, as the night finally ended and I could retire to my bed.

"Then it was worth the pain in my head and my back," I said, and he smiled.

"Courage, my lady," he said. "Courage."

Courage indeed. That was all I had been telling myself since we left my home.

I was glad when we made it out of the city the next day, but once there, the mud had found us, again.

"Just a moment more, Your Grace," said a voice by the side of the litter. I opened the curtain and looked up at Count von Overstein, one of my party. He was the highest-ranking man present, sent by my brother to give me away, a proxy. The count, who was of a mature age certainly, but not old, seemed nonetheless to have taken it upon himself to have become a surrogate father to me, and it was he and Olisleger I saw the most. Poor Olisleger. I felt for him in many ways. I had already begun to cling to him like a man lost at sea who spies a branch in the water. He was, at my intense urging, trying to teach me English. At the moment I felt as mired in my own incompetence with the language as our baggage carts were in the sludge upon the road.

"Another wagon stuck, my lord?" I asked the count.

He inclined his head, offering a smile that held understanding and annoyance in equal measures. It was mostly the wagons that were inhibiting us. They were heavy, carrying my clothes and furniture, and the possessions of all my ladies too. Some were carrying my other ladies, of course. The mud would cause them to slide, or one wheel would bounce off a rock and end up in a ditch, getting stuck, then men had to dismount and push, sometimes unload chests or people to make the wagon lighter, and drive the poor horses to pull until it was free again. Horses all, and my men with them, were already tired from the ill weather and long, hard journey, so every time we became stuck it took longer and longer to get us out and get us moving again. We were all tired of this.

"We will be on our way soon enough, Your Grace," the count said, his face displaying just as much weariness as mine even as his voice attempted a false lightness of spirit.

"I have no doubt you all are doing your best," I said. "Give the men some ale when they have the cart out, would you please? So many times they have had to heave a wagon out of the mud on this journey I think they will be exhausted by the time we reach Calais. And something extra of meat for them tonight, if we can manage it."

"It is hard work," he agreed, "and they will thank you for such generosity, my lady. There are not many who would be as understanding as you are."

"I feel tired merely listening to all their effort, so they must be wearier than I can possibly imagine," I said. "I feel as if we have been on this road forever."

"We'll get you to your husband, my lady," he said. "It might take time, but we'll get you there."

"Thank you, my friend."

I closed the curtain, and the call to ride on came not long after. Watching rain pour down upon us once more, turning the landscape from hazy green to solid grey, I wondered if it was not a blessing we were so delayed, and so often. In truth I had no wish to reach our destination, and perhaps God, hearing my fears and taking pity on me, was holding us back. Certainly at times it felt that way, that something, a power we did not and could not understand, was intervening.

At times in the night, as I settled into one unfamiliar room after another, in a castle, in a monastery's guest quarters, where the walls echoed silence, I felt I could hear something in the wind, some voice warning me not to go on, something trying to hold me back. There was a whisper in the breeze and a shriek in the storms, warning, always warning, trying to tell me I was in danger.

Perhaps the voice thought I was unaware of the peril I was heading towards with this marriage to this already so-married King, but I was not. Had I had the choice, I would have done as God and the weather, as the mud and the warning voice riding the wind wanted, and turned back, turned for home, for safety, but I could not. I had made a promise to marry this man, to protect my country from the Emperor and prevent my sister from having to wed this King. To keep so many safe, I was walking into danger, and although I knew some of what I might face, the great unknowns were what I feared the most.

And my husband. Him I feared more than anything. Three wives married, three women dead and only one by truly natural means, and here was I, the fourth. Would England be my future, or would it bring my death?

I turned to my ladies, trying to keep my mind occupied so I did not linger in terror. "Come," I said. "Let us tell tales to pass the time. Who has a story to tell us?"

Mistress Loew gazed at me with grateful admiration. She, the Mother of the Maids, was finding it hard to keep the young ladies of Cleves, women sent with me to be my travelling Frauenzimmer, occupied. Frequently they lapsed into bickering.

One struck up a tale of the Swan Knight, and I tried to listen to her version of the story, tried to set from my mind the fearful imaginings of what would come when finally we reached our destination. The wagon rocked into life once more and our slow trundle towards England resumed. *Courage*, I told myself. *Courage, Anna.*

# Chapter Two

**Gravelines and Calais
English Territory
France**

**December 1539**

It was the sound of gulls which first caught my ears, a guttural cawing shattering the skies just for a moment. First there were but one or two calling from the clouds and then more and more until the wind ceased to breathe and all there was, was the cries of raucous gulls swooping like fast-moving fog in the heavens above us. I pulled up my horse. I had finally succumbed to my urge to ride, given into the necessity of getting out of the wagon. It had, in the end, been a choice of sanity, to either lose mine inside the wagon with my bickering ladies or leave and preserve at least a few of my wits by riding on a horse. For many miles I had ridden with my hunting mask on which obscured my vision and was sweaty and clammy, but it preserved my complexion, and then for some miles I had ridden bare of face, only a veil between me and the world. I felt most daring, as if I was some wild woman of the old tales riding into battle. Very few noted much of my daring escapade, however, and it came to me that we can suppose at times that the whole world notes immediately all that changes about us, all we do, all we say, and yet it is not true. The men were more concerned with the smooth running of the wagons and the cavalcade, the women more interested in the pains in their backs. Mistress Loew made one comment on the removal of my mask, that my mother would not like it, but did not go further. This act, riding almost bare of face, which to me was so freeing to my soul, meant little to others.

It was remarkable in a way, to understand that the events or times that can hold the most meaning for us, to others are meaningless and pass unnoticed. Other people are more interested in the concerns of their own lives, in their own pains and adventures, than they are in ours. We think we are so observed as we move through the world, but we are not as watched as we think. It made me feel even more at liberty, until a thought, in that voice which seemed to be within the wind, came to me. *Soon, you will be noticed, for you will be Queen,* it said.

*But not yet,* I reminded it. *Not yet am I so seen, so let me this moment enjoy.*

I did not mind feeling unnoticed for a moment. I was sure, as the voice pointed out, it was a pleasure that soon would pass, and as towards Gravelines we came, the last town before Calais, and as gulls started to shriek overhead gathering in vast clouds of thousands, I heard another noise and I knew this short time of feeling wild and free and daring was done.

It was a blast of trumpets, blaring in the distance. The English were announcing their Queen had come to them, at last.

"I wonder they did not think me lost, or taken on the road somewhere," I mentioned to Count von Overstein as we stilled our horses and looked along the road to where the crowds were, milling groups of hundreds of men.

"We have, of course, been sending messengers ahead, Your Grace," he said.

"It was a jest, my friend."

He chuckled, a little late, but it was still appreciated. "Of course, my lady."

"Hold here, for I must change my clothes before they see me for the first time. I cannot appear before them splattered in mud and filth in my riding clothes."

"Of course, Your Grace."

A tent was hastily erected, and in the damp interior I changed clothes, the canvas sides of the tent snapping wet and angry in the wind. My women brought water, warmed on a fire, for me to wash my hands and face. I had done little more than this on the entire journey. My underclothes of linen had been changed daily, my hair combed, my face and hands, sometimes arms washed, but we dared do no more. Bathing in winter was not usually a done thing, for there were wandering spirits of sickness in all winter winds, and out on the road we were utterly exposed to them. My ladies dabbed me with lavender oil and helped me into a gown suitable for meeting the English for the first time on their native soil. This was part of their remaining pocket of a long-lost empire. Once the English had owned much of what was now France, but over time and through war, they had lost it.

"Your Grace." Von Overstein was at the door, but did not venture inside. It would not have been seemly for him to spy me in a state of undress, after all, and he was a highly respectful man. I suspected this had been the main qualification for my brother choosing him in particular; Wilhelm knew Overstein could be trusted. "Lord Lisle, who is the first Viscount Lisle, and bastard uncle of the King of England as well as Deputy of Calais, is here to escort you to Gravelines and thenceforth to Calais."

"The bastard uncle of the King?" I asked through the door to the tent. "I thought the King's father had no brothers?"

"Lisle is the bastard son of Edward IV, Your Grace, father of the present King's mother."

"His name?" I asked as my women pinned my headdress into place.

"Arthur Plantagenet."

I turned to my women as they finished. "All is in place?" I asked. We had no mirror here, so I had to rely on their eyes to check all was well.

"Your skin is a little ruddy, my lady," said Mistress Loew, frowning. "Let us put some cooling balm on it."

"Very well," I said, grateful that she did not point out it was my fault if my skin was a little beaten by the weather. Had I stayed in the wagon, I would have maintained my complexion, as my mother had wanted.

Eventually they were satisfied, and I stepped from the tent, my women in procession before and behind me. Pearls rattled on my headdress and my skirts shimmered silver and crimson. I was taken to Lord Lisle. "My lord Viscount," I said, as Olisleger translated. "I understand you are the uncle of the King, which makes you now my uncle too."

He bowed long and deep, a most respectful gesture. "I am honoured, Majesty," he said, "to welcome you at last to English soil. We have heard of your journey and are most sorry for all the trials you have encountered. I hope now to offer you all comforts, to appease your temper and calm your mind."

I smiled. "My temper is already appeased to be here, and to be already with family, my lord," I said. "And I shall call you uncle, if you are pleased to be named so. In leaving my own family I was most sorrowful, but now I am to enter a new one, headed by my loving and devoted husband, and I would embrace every one of my new kin."

Olisleger nodded to me, the very slightest inclination of his head as Lisle's smile beamed out at me. My translator was indicating my public declaration of an intimate relationship with this man was appreciated, and accepted as a sign of great favour, although I could have told this myself from the look of pleasure on this royal bastard's face.

I found myself escorted to the town on horseback in a huge procession, with trumpets blaring and men cheering my name. "God save you, Queen Anna!" I heard more than once, and wondered fleetingly what God should be saving me from. I waved to all of them, stopping here and there to accept a present, or have my ladies do so for me, since my horse could not carry all the coins and posies of dried herbs – it being winter there were few flowers for them to hand me – which they offered.

"The men of England are handsome, generous, merry of spirit and well formed," I said and Olisleger translated this to Lisle. From my new uncle my compliments trickled out and made their way through his men, leading to more cheers.

A mile from the gates of Calais, not to mention the enormous walls, the Admiral of England came to greet me, clad in purple cloth and gold. His name was William Fitzwilliam and he was also the Earl of Southampton. He was an older man, perhaps around the age of my new husband, with a jowly face and a rather large nose. When his face was still and settled, he looked quite grim, but the moment something interested him all those grave features became most animated and bright. He had known the King almost all of his life, as he informed me himself, having been brought up in the King's household when my royal spouse was but a prince.

There were others there to greet me too. Lord William Howard, a relative of one of the premier nobles of England, the Duke of Norfolk, though in the introductions I missed exactly what kind of relative he was, was there too along with two men both called Seymour, who I swiftly ascertained were related to the late Queen Jane. There was also a rather wild-looking man wearing an eyepatch glittering with gems called Sir Francis Bryan. His eyepatch shimmered so in the dull light it looked as if he was winking and when I later learned his reputation I wondered if that was the point. "Once he marched into a brothel, Your Grace, asking for a soft bed and a hard harlot," I was told by Carl Harst, my new Clevian ambassador, who had caught up with us at Calais. He had been acting as ambassador to the Emperor in Spain, but had been sent by my brother to take care of me in England, a thoughtful gesture. Our father had trusted the word of Harst as few others, for the man had been an apprentice of Erasmus, and he knew England well for when working for Erasmus he had been sent there.

"Bryan sounds like a wit," I said. "Albeit a rude one."

"There are many such in England, Your Grace," he said, and he had been there so could speak with some authority. "Their humour tends towards the crass."

Four hundred gentlemen stood there too, cheering me. The noise was magnificent. "This is Master Culpepper," Lisle said as we reached the end of the line of important, titled gentlemen I was to meet. I was struck by the fact this one unlike the others had no title and was more struck by his looks; he was a most handsome lad. "Culpepper is one of the King's favourite men of the Bedchamber," Lisle explained, "and has come, Majesty, to give you a gift from the King."

I smiled as the lad handed me a little purse of coins, with a few gemstones twinkling within them. "The King sends his most passionate greetings to you, Majesty," said Culpepper, bowing with fluid, liquid grace. "And hopes very soon to see you with his own eyes."

"I too am eager to meet my new husband," I said. "But already I am assured he is the greatest of princes, for only such a king could have men as welcoming and gentlemanly as those I have seen here today."

As Olisleger translated for me all the men's faces there broke into smiles so bright they could have been the sun.

In truth, I had never seen so many men. My world had been one of women for so long that I felt here as if I was a sole chicken set amongst geese. I was fighting to remain in control and not become jittery as I found myself more and more surrounded by strange men. Fortunately, my women were always close by. There is something reassuring to a woman, about the presence of women.

As we rode towards the gates of Calais two hundred yeomen of England saluted me, their coats resplendent in blue and red with the royal arms of England stitched upon them. As I rode through the gate, cannon fired, announcing the Queen of England had come to English soil.

When I entered, I was handed a solid gold C by the town mayor, and finally met noble ladies of Calais, led by Lady Lisle, the wife of Lord Lisle. I had been wondering where they were, half-imagining Calais was a place where only men lived. There were a wealth of them, and all these women flowed into gracious curtsies as I approached.

"We were to take you to see the ships, those bound to take you to England, Majesty," said Lord Lisle, glancing at the Admiral, "but the weather is fast closing in."

It was indeed, rain had begun again and it was hard and persistent. The wind was rising too. I looked to my men and to the English before me and I laughed a little. "I would see the ships," I said boldly. "Let us not be daunted by a little rain and wind. The King is most fond of his fleet, so I hear, and although I never have been on the sea, I wish to fall in love with them too. This cannot be, unless I set eyes on them."

When this was translated, the Admiral looked so pleased I thought he might explode with pride, and the rest of the party gazed at me with admiration for not being intimidated by the weather.

In unyielding wind and lashing rain, my tour went ahead. I exclaimed much about the things I was shown, though in truth I had not a single idea as to why one particular rope was more important than another, or why the men were so proud of the guns which looked wildly unstable to me, or why the wood used to make these vessels was superior to any other. The wind tore at our clothes and the rain soaked me to the skin, despite the great cloak I wore, but I did not complain once or ask for the tour to be cut short. I must have examined a hundred lengths of rope and wandered through every cabin of the cramped ships, and after had to go in procession through the streets of Calais, where the world and his wife as well as his mistress and her maid came out to see me, but my resolution had benefits.

"The Admiral is most impressed with you, Majesty," Olisleger told me later. Since the English were calling me Queen already, my people had altered their speech to use the highest of my titles, even though I was still in truth only promised to the King. "He has told all that he thinks you lovely, gracious and charming, and says you are so obviously pleased with all things English that you will settle into the country in no time. He admits he had reservations about the match with Cleves, but now he has met you, he has none. You are a woman worthy of their King and country, he tells me, and since he knows the King so well, this is a grand compliment."

"Then it was worth it," I said, watching my gown drip on the floor. I had entirely ruined a pair of shoes, I was sure, for there were puddles slopping about my toes. But clothes can be changed, and shoes mended. Finally, we were in the Exchequer Palace within Calais, having entered to yet another giant crack of gunfire which seemed to be a requisite of my arrival anywhere, and I could remove my wet things and get warm. "Let me to my chambers now, Olisleger, for I am so wet I cannot tell where the sea ends and Anna of Cleves begins."

Olisleger's happy chuckle ran down the corridors as I turned to my women, who hastened me to a chamber with a roaring fire, where, shivering, I could rid myself of my soaked clothing.

*So, I am a woman worthy of the King of England?* I thought to myself as they dried me.

*He has met many worthy women,* said that voice. *And he has destroyed them all.*

# Chapter Three

### Calais
### English Territory
### France

### December 1539

I watched the shutters, drawn tight against the rain and wind. They were as tiny cracks of light, splinters of dimness against a carpet of black about me. Darkness was outside the chamber and inside it, yet there must have been a little light for I could see where the window was, the wooden shutters drawn tight against it, trying to keep out the wind and the rain, boon companions of yet another storm lashing Calais. The soft breathing of my maid at my side, in my very ear, could hardly compete with the noise of this latest, fresh tempest hitting this one last piece of English soil standing alone on the Continent, but the soft noise at my ear, the tickling whisper of her breath, I found reassuring. I was a little jealous too. I would like to be as soundly asleep as she was, not lying awake worried about what might come during another day where I would be pandered to, paraded about, and stared at by a million inquisitive eyes, all trained on me. I had been right to enjoy the time when no one watched me, for that time had now passed.

Everyone had been polite, I had little to complain about except the weather and the skies were not servants of the English, theirs to command, so they could not stop the rain, and yet, whilst mouths smiled eyes assessed. Everything I did, from greeting an official to smoothing my gown, was observed with a scrutiny which was starting to unnerve me. I could sense minds taking note of all my actions and ascribing something to those actions. Simple things, a cough into a handkerchief or a smile to a lesser person brought before me, were all becoming indicators of my personality, my values, my character, to the eyes that watched. All my actions were taking on meaning to these people sent to welcome me in the name of the King.

I knew not what personality they were attributing to me, but I felt each notch and tally in their mental books, accounting and weighing the value of my character. It was exhausting. I never had felt so observed. I had not known it weighed on one so. Not for the first time I pitied my elder sister. Sybylla had been so observed all her life and I had thought it gave her power, but now I understood. It had taken all the power within her not to cave in under the crushing weight of all the eyes and expectation upon her. She had been powerful to resist this, not been made powerful because of it.

Stunning, at times, are the lessons of life, that what we think, what we assume, is not always what is true.

I had already made one small mistake. I had invited the Admiral and his men to dine with me one evening in my private quarters, not understanding that as a lady engaged but not yet wed this was unusual. In truth I had thought the English so carefree about so many rules I had not thought this would be a problem but had later been told by Olisleger that it was. "But why did they all come to dine, then?" I asked and had been told that apparently the good Admiral had been too embarrassed to explain this was not done for a lady in my position, and also too embarrassed to refuse my invitation. I only hoped that when this got back to the King he would not decide me a scandal and send me away.

Although part of me wanted to be sent home.

Rain driven by wind hit the wall, the window, a thousand fingertips of wetness striking at once. The maid at my side stirred, mumbling in her sleep, then into my back she nestled again, her face burrowing deeper into the covers where she could be protected in slumber from the noise of the storm. It was before dawn. Light was growing outside, the light through the shutters taking on a softer grey than the deep blackness inside the room, but I had a little time alone with my own thoughts yet.

I had been taken to see the ships, the walls of Calais, all the grandest houses. On one good day we had watched jousting. I had dined with the Admiral, with Lord and Lady Lisle, and had lost track of the number of gentlemen I had greeted and who had kissed my hand. In truth, I suspected my party of welcomers had started to run out of things for me to see, or do, as they had not expected I would still be here by this time. I was supposed to spend no more than a day or two in Calais, but we could not sail. Every time they thought of it, another storm fell upon us.

There was, too, a strange feeling to this place. That voice which had followed me all the way on the road seemed to be whispering louder here, and there were other things. I would walk along a corridor here and feel as if there was someone behind me. In truth there often was, my ladies or the people of the palace dogging my every footstep, but yet it felt as if it was something else. I could almost hear laughter, deep and throaty, ringing with triumph here, far away down some passageway. Sometimes I felt as if a hand had brushed mine, yet when I looked down there was nothing. Sometimes I looked up, thinking I had seen a person in a doorway, but again there was nothing. Yet I felt some presence here, something coming closer to me and although it was uncanny I did not fear it.

There was a rustling at the door, and in the darkness, I saw a figure enter and steal on soft feet to the fire. Her skirts whispered against the rushes on the floor, and I smelt the perfume of herbs flow into the air as her feet crushed them. The scent, not unlike the smell of the chambers of home but at the same time not the same – because the herbs were not the ones my mother had ordered lain down – made a wash of homesickness sweep through my heart and up, into my mouth. I could taste my own sorrow, the bitter tang of missing my family. At home, when I had heard such a noise it was usually Sybylla or Amalia sneaking into my room, some terror of the night having come to them, they sought me out for always I could banish their bad dreams. Sybylla was married and far away now, of course, but even to the last week I was in Cleves, on the last night Amalia had come to me. Who would she go to now, when nightmares tumbled into her sleeping mind to trouble her? My heart ached to think of her alone, in her bed, fearing to sleep without me to snuggle against.

I watched the figure sneaking through the chamber without fear. It was one of the chamberers, girls set below the maids of honour who would serve me, who did menial tasks about the rooms of the Queen, such as clearing plates or tidying up. She had been sent to ignite the fire without waking me, or anyone. More of my ladies were asleep in pallet beds on the floor. The chamberer did her task well. I doubt, had I been asleep, she would have wakened me. *Good assassins women would make,* I thought as I heard the little *chip-chip* sound of her flint in the corner, watched as she gently woke the banked fire from dull slumber to a little blaze then a bigger one, and as heat began to slowly smooth through the air, like honey upon bread, I roused my sleeping companion so we might get on with the day. I did not want reports, no doubt being written by every person here and being sent on to England by fast ships bold enough to set sail in this inclement weather, reaching anyone that their new Queen was lazy, lying in bed past the dawn.

In faded light and candlelight, the sun still unwilling to illuminate the chamber, I washed my hands and face in warm water. Little petals of a flower I knew not bobbed in the glazed bowl. It was pretty, a faded blue with a white centre, small and delicate. Thinking to ask what it was – I was doing that a lot so I could learn all I could before we reached England – I made sure my face and hands, especially the nails, were clean as I was bound to be inspected by all I saw that day. By my bed we knelt, my maids and I, thanking God for the blessings He had granted, asking for His grace in all our works.

"Grant me courage, Lord," I whispered to myself and to the God whom I hoped heard me. "Let me do well today." Today was all I could manage. I did not want to think of tomorrow, or the next day, or what came after. One day, that was the span of my hopes.

They dressed me in gown and kirtle, as well as a cape lined with fur to keep out the chill. My hair was combed and flowing down my back, before I insisted on it being bound up in plaits and set into a reticulated hood. The women here in Calais, they wore clothes entirely different to my own. I had thought, though I knew this land was not part of the Holy Roman Empire, that there would be some women dressed in the same style I wore, but there were not. All the women here wore French hoods, freer and more daring than the ones I had worn all my life, and to own the truth, I could see why the English favoured them for they were prettier than mine, even though my headdresses were richer, encrusted with gems and covered in golden lace. A few wore a style known as the gable headdress, which, like mine, hid the hair of the wearer and was a little boxy to look upon, but they were fewer than those in the becoming headdress of France.

The same rebellious hunger as had come upon me when I wanted to ride a horse rather than be dragged in a wagon had risen in me when I looked on their pretty dresses and becoming hoods. I wanted to try one, wanted to see how the long train they all wore would look on me, to see whether the French hood would suit me and to know whether I had the courage to wear such scandalous clothes before others, as they all did without any sense of shame or even the notion they should feel that emotion at all. A hunger yes, a temptation rising, was within me.

But I had told my mother I would continue to wear modest clothes, especially in this court so known for scandal, and when I met my new husband for the first time, I would meet him as Anna of Cleves. In truth, I was a little wary of becoming so bold as to wear such clothes as the English women of Calais did. Many were audacious, wearing gowns that were cut so a little, just a suggestion, of bosom could be seen. There was lace or sheer silk covering their chests, of course, but still, there was enough there so something of their charms, many of them *great* charms, could be seen. I had always been taught to cover everything of my body, from toe to neck. It was a shock to see so many, all in truth, here, wore clothes so alien to mine.

I had the impression the women of Calais thought my clothes the alien ones. Although some had complimented me, noting gemstones or the fabric of this gown or that hood, many others had worn widened eyes and open mouths upon seeing my clothes. I knew I looked different to them already, the widening of eyes or a gaping mouth was not needed to tell me I stood out here.

I had also caught more than one person staring at my plucked forehead, as this too was not something they did in England anymore, I was told by my maids. It was considered a little old-fashioned. The women of this land were proud of their hair and that was the glory they wanted to allow men a peek of. To my eyes they all had quite thick eyebrows, too, for they did not pluck them almost bare as we did in Cleves, but only tidied stray hairs from the edges.

When I was ready, we walked to Mass in the chapel where we asked God to forgive our trespasses and bowed our heads as the priest spoke in Latin over us, giving a sermon later in English about the ills of women. Women were wicked, easily corruptible and corrupting of others, he droned as maids of Calais giggled quietly at the back of the church. Women were doomed since Eve to tempt men, and had to be controlled, he said. It was the place of men to ensure we did not run out of control.

I heard my gown rustle and felt soft fur on my skin as a cat snaked about my ankles. I smiled but said nothing, not wanting to draw attention to the little feline, who would be tossed from the door and into the storm if found, and that was no doubt what she had come in here to avoid, poor thing. Calais was a port town and therefore there were lots of rats, and therefore there were a lot of cats. They were everywhere, welcome in many of the buildings, especially storehouses, since they caught vermin who pillaged food and would spread sickness. Sometimes as I had walked the town, being shown around, I felt angled, almond eyes upon me, a glittering of green or yellow in the shadows, and I wondered if the cats of Calais found me as fascinating as all the people here seemed to.

I looked up at a noise to the side of me, older men trying to get younger ones to behave. The young were lounging about, leaning on pillars, ogling my ladies, no doubt trying to see what they looked like under the veils I had instructed them to wear. Just because I had all eyes on me did not mean my ladies had to endure it too. I think it was a relief to them, to retain a whisper of cloth between the eyes of the world and their faces.

These young men, standing on the other side of the church, did not look particularly interested in following the priest's commandments or the instructions of older men telling them to stand straight and behave as gentlemen. They were more interested in what the girls were doing. I had the impression that unlike in Cleves, where religion and faith were matters taken most seriously, England was not the same. There were some, the older generation of course and others, who looked devout and interested, but many of the young were more interested in attending church as it gave them a chance to see others, what they were wearing, what they were doing, rather than trying to reach God.

I wondered if the King's changes of religion and the ever-altering practise of that religion had led to some of his people not taking their faith as seriously as they did in other countries. Perhaps his swift changes had left some confused and others blasé about the faith. After all, God had not struck the King down for all his abandonment of the papacy and Rome, or for dissolving the monasteries. Indeed, God had not taken action when the King had separated from one wife, casting her out, then beheaded another. Perhaps the King was teaching his own people, particularly young and impressionable ones, that they did not need to take the faith seriously, for their King was their leader and he did not.

I prayed for Sybylla and her sons, for my mother, for the soul of my father and for peace and joy for Amalia and Wilhelm. As I prayed for them, my heart seemed to want to stretch, an endless ache which tried to become as a band wrapped over sea and land and shore, trying to reach my beloved family. I swallowed hard, attempting to contain the sorrow within me, yet it rose and kept rising, joining with the song of the choir at the end, lifting as pleading hands into Heaven itself. Would there come a time when I would not grieve for losing my family? I doubted it. I still mourned my father and suspected I would every day for the rest of my life, and leaving my family in Cleves, though they were alive, was as another kind of death, a sorrow which felt the same and perhaps worse, for they were alive in the world, yet I could not touch them. My father could not hold me either, but at least the reason in his case was that he was gone from this life. It felt worse, somehow, to know that there were people who truly knew me, who truly loved me out there in this wide world, but I could not get to them. I was held here, soon to be sent further away still, and in part this was to secure England as our ally so I might aid these people I loved so well, so it had to be done. My pain of missing them, not to mention fear of what might come, it was set upon me because I loved them.

When God was done with us, we broke our fast on bread and fish, it being Advent, making sure to say a prayer and make the sign of the cross upon our lips before eating. It was eleven when the chapel bell rang over the palace, and we went to the great hall to eat. The other nobility were on tables below mine, servants of court on lower tables still, and I ate at the head with the dignitaries there to guide me. There, I was shown how to wash my hands in the bowl brought around before the meal, the custom only slightly altered from what I had known in Cleves, since now the bowl came to me first, and I knew, of course, how to sip pottage quietly, was well aware I was not to belch or scratch, and was to wipe my mouth carefully before drinking from the shared ale-cup. I knew how to dip my knife daintily into the salt cellar, taking only a little. The English customs of feasting appeared to be the same as ours, but one trouble was I was always served first, so if I made a mistake all would see it. I was careful therefore, never taking too much of anything, and as others started to eat I ensured I was doing the same as they, starting with the same foods, wiping my fingers on my napkin as often as they did. Lady Lisle was kind, sometimes pointing out something, a dish or drink, if I found it unfamiliar. The English were fond of sweet dishes, that I worked out swiftly, and some of the flavours were odd to me, but I did not find them unpleasant. I tried many, asking which were the King's favourites.

"He dotes on aleberry pudding," Lord Lisle told me. "We do not have it here, today, I am sorry to say, but I will ask the kitchens to make some for tomorrow, perhaps. And lamprey is another favourite. He adores good venison too, Your Majesty."

"Aleberry pudding," I said. "This I never have heard of."

When the recipe was recited to Olisleger, he tried to conceal a grimace. "It seems to be a liquid kind of sweet dish, my lady," he said, and from his tone I could tell he found the idea of the pudding unappetising. "Made of ale, sugar and stale bread. Some might call it a beverage, but it depends how much of this stale bread, which they apparently toast, is added. They say it is good for a cold."

"I am sure it tastes better than it sounds," I said, but told him to say to Lisle only that I could not wait to try it.

"I thought you might like to tour the ships again this afternoon, my lady," said the Admiral, and though my heart dropped to think of walking on those creaking, groaning contraptions again I smiled brightly as if I had longed to do nothing more in my life than attempt to balance again on those slippery decks which stank of fish and seaweed.

"And perhaps after," Lady Lisle said, "I could beg you away to meet with my ladies and my daughter. We have much admired the embroidery on your gowns, Majesty, and would know how the stitches of Cleves differ from ours."

"I would be pleased to show you," I said when this was translated to me. "For I made these gowns with my own hands."

Later, Lady Lisle would announce to all she knew that she had never seen another woman who produced embroidery as good as mine, and much as I was grateful for that, I was even more so for her suggestion I go to her fire and sew that afternoon. She saved me from many more hours than I could imagine of staring at rigging and sheets and sails with the amiable, albeit entirely blind, Admiral, who thought I loved ships just as much as he did.

# Chapter Four

**Calais**
**English Territory**
**France**

**December 1539**

"Tell me, what gentle diversions does the King of England enjoy?" I asked one of his men that night, through my translator. Rain whipped the windows again. We were listening to musicians play – it was a song the King had composed, I was told – but no amount of noise could drown out the storm. "Something which is not jousting or sword play, but that he might do on a day like today?"

Cards, I was told. Cent was a popular game at the English court. I sent Olisleger to Admiral Fitzwilliam, asking him to come to me and, "Go to cards with me, with some game that the King uses."

"Will you teach me?" I asked the Admiral when he arrived.

"My lady…" my translator began, looking shocked. "It is not done for ladies of our country to play in public with men at cards." Evidently Olisleger had thought I would watch the game be played, rather than engaging with it.

"I am to be Queen of England," I said to him, a stern but soft expression on my face. "I will always of my country be, good friend, but I am, too, to be of this country, and must know its customs."

Looking not unlike a shocked partridge meeting an unexpected fox in the undergrowth, Olisleger revealed to Fitzwilliam that I wanted to learn this English game. The man glanced at my translator then at me, and whilst he did not understand the words between us, he did see the conflict. A mischievous smile arrived on his lips and played there a while as he called for cards and taught the game to me. That smile faded somewhat an hour later when I soundly beat him and won his, not insignificant, pile of coins stacked in the middle of our table, but I laughed and gave it back. "Consider it payment, for teaching me this game so fine," I said to him. Three other English men who somewhat spoke my language, their interpretation variable in skill, laughed along with me.

"The Queen had you by the nose, there, Fitzwilliam," chuckled one. "Were she not a gracious lady with a kind heart, you would have lost all you had tonight."

I smiled when this was translated. "I would never suffer any man of England to lose all he had to me," I said to them, "not when I want so much to grant my people all I am able to give."

"Our Queen is gracious and generous," said Fitzwilliam, gazing with some suspicion at my hand, as if he thought I had not only learnt the game well enough to beat him in one hour, but to know how to cheat too.

"It would appear you have made yourself popular with these strange men, my lady," Olisleger said later as my companions at cards walked off in a fine mood, no doubt to find some women of the Calais night who would also offer all they could to them, for a few coins of course. "You seem to understand them well, though they are so different to the men of our court."

"Everything here is so different, friend," I said. "And so, it seems to me that all I must do in order to understand my new people is to be the opposite of what we are in Cleves and be open to learning all that is new. This much, I can do."

"You will make a fine Queen, my lady," he said.

"And with that in mind, you must not try to stop me taking on these English customs. I understand you are trying to protect me, and you have all my thanks for that and every other pain taken, my friend. I will not do anything to expose myself to censure, but the people here, and the women, what they do and are allowed to do, they are different to us, and I must be like them if I am to fit in. You must take a step back and trust me."

He nodded. "I do understand, my lady, and it is indeed only for love of you I have intervened, but you are right, the customs here are dissimilar to ours and you must adopt many of them, although I hope you will bring something of our great country to this place too."

"We will see," I said. "But if that is to be done, it must be softly so. We must understand, my lord, that here, to these people, we are the strange ones. We are the foreigners, the interlopers and outlanders, and I would have the English and their prince forget that as soon as possible, or an outsider in a foreign land I always will be, and that would not be a fate welcome, I think."

Later, one of my maids came to me to tell me, a smile dancing on her lips, that English lords were saying I was turning a little rebellious on my over-protective men. "And they said it was a good thing for their new Queen to have courage enough to face her own men. They were marvelling, too, at your skill in the game, Your Grace," she said, "and said to each other it was a fine thing to have a new Queen who, although from a land so different, was already immersing herself in the culture of her new country. They said you were obviously English at heart, Your Grace, a true compliment."

I smiled, feeling my heart settle a little for the first time.

Perhaps I could do this.

# Chapter Five

**Calais
English Territory
France**

**December 1539**

"If ships passing all these messages to England can get through, why cannot we?" I asked the lady to my side, as Olisleger translated swiftly.

We were standing in a corridor of the Exchequer Palace, watching the distant sea. It was windy and the waves were high, but a ship had got out of port only that morning, carrying all the news, gathered by so many people, of me to England. I have no doubt it was carrying other things, spices perhaps, but the taste buds of the English were presently more titillated by gossip of their new Queen than by offerings of nutmeg or mace.

Lady Lisle smiled gently. "For love of Your Majesty, they would not want to make the attempt, you are cargo most precious to the King, to all of England."

I smiled as the words were gabbled back to me. I was starting to understand a few words here and there, words used often. *Your Majesty, love, the King*, these things I was starting to pick up, but much of the rest still just sounded like noise to my untrained ears, and the English spoke fast. Perhaps all people of all countries do, but to the one trying to learn, swift-spoken words become a haze of noise. Perhaps the delay in Calais was a good thing, for it was enabling me to learn a little English as well as a few diversions that I hoped I could share with the King without need for much talking, like cards. I was getting rather good at Cent, much to the chagrin of the men I played each night. I had ceased giving the coin I had won back, you see.

"I know you never have been on the sea, Majesty," my companion went on when she was sure I had heard all of the last sentence properly. Unlike many, Lady Lisle did not simply prattle on, leaving my translator trying to think fast in two languages and convey everything, no matter how complex, to me. Lady Lisle paused, and that pause was a blessing. In truth I had come to think that some of the English, the men most particularly, were rather like children. The Admiral gabbled like a shocked hen when he was excited, and usually his excitement had something to do with a ship, but any man explaining things to me here took on an animated, childlike expression to his face when they became stimulated. I found it quite endearing, although I would have welcomed them slowing just a touch. Count von Overstein found the English a baffling kind, although he did seem to enjoy the company of the elder Seymour brother, Edward, who was of a more staid and dignified nature than the rest of them.

"And as you never have been on the sea," Lady Lisle continued, "you do not know the horrors of the waters when it is a bad trip. The stomach can rock and cause one to bring everything back up, even water, and there is of course the danger of drowning. The King would never forgive us, and we would never forgive ourselves if we took you across in inclement weather."

I liked Lady Lisle, she was a gentle soul, and although she had those enquiring eyes that everyone here possessed, she tried harder than many to be not only an observer but a companion, and her effort was most appreciated. One of her daughters was in England, already at court, and was to be one of my maids of honour when I arrived. I understood, from my maids who seemed adept at gaining information despite only few of them having any English, that Lady Lisle had tried for years to get one of her daughters into a coveted position within the Queen's household. She had repeatedly petitioned Queen Anne, then Jane Seymour. The latter Queen had eventually offered Lady Lisle's eldest daughter a post, but on the condition that she dressed in modest English fashion rather than the French styles which were so popular here. "How did you learn this?" I had asked my maids and was told there was a chamberer within the palace who had been born in Saxony and could tell them all. I had instructed them to find out as much about England, and the King, and everyone else I was to meet as possible.

"Do you tell your daughter Anne of me?" I asked Lady Lisle. She had told me she had a letter on that ship heading for England and her missive was bound for court, for her daughter had asked her to send information on England's new Queen as soon as possible, so my new household could be prepared.

"Of course, Majesty," she said with another charming smile. "All of court, and especially your women, are keen to know the kind of mistress they will serve, but fear not, for I have told them how gracious and munificent you are and now they will be even keener to meet you, it is ever a reassuring thing to servants to know that their new master or mistress is clement and kind."

"Tell me of recent diversions in England," I said. "I wish to understand the culture better before I arrive. I hear the King is fond of jousting and pageants?"

Lady Lisle told me of an odd event, but one which told me much about the country I was to join, as well as its King. It occurred during the summer just passed, a pageant upon the waters of London.

"The Thames is the great river which through London flows," Lady Lisle told me. "And this pageant was a favourite of the King's for it took place on ships upon the Thames, as a game of war."

"A game of war?"

"A mock-battle, Majesty, such as the Romans once performed for their people."

It started because of a death. The Empress Isabella of Spain had died, as I already knew of course, weakened by fever after a miscarriage, and although – according to the English, for I had not heard this – her husband the Emperor was apparently considering invading England on behalf of Rome, the customs required for a royal death were upheld in England still. The court was ordered into mourning for fifteen days, and there was a service at St Paul's, which I was told was the great cathedral of London. Five heralds carrying banners of the Virgin Mary and Saint Elizabeth, the Empress's patron saint, entered the cathedral and the service was led by the archbishops of Canterbury and York. Surrounded by hangings in hues of night displayed about the church and illuminated by the fire of thousands of candles, dark-robed lords of England stood together that day, mourning the wife of England's enemy. Each church in London was ordered to light candles for Isabella, to ask God to carry her swifter to Heaven, and requiems were sung.

But beneath all this pageantry was tension, I could hear it in Lady Lisle's voice. French and Imperial ambassadors had turned up for the ceremonies together in a display of troubling unity, and the King had sent his man Thomas Cromwell, the very man who had advocated for my marriage and brought about the end of two other marriages of the King, to represent him rather than attending in person.

And then, came the pageant.

Eleven days after the service at St Paul's, two galleys took to the Thames to enact a mock battle. Rowing up and down the waters, the galleys blazed against one another with all their guns.

"They were firing at each other?" I asked, amazed. I had heard and occasionally seen tournaments of sword or jousting, although my father had ever thought such things inane entertainments, but never had I heard of men firing guns at each other on ships just for the sake of entertaining a crowd.

"Oh, indeed," said Lady Lisle in an off-hand way, as if this was not lunacy but the most normal thing in the world. "The King is much enamoured of such diversions, for he always has loved war, as a young man and... as a mature man."

I smiled, certain she had been about to say an *old* man, which, if it got back to the King, would not be a welcome compliment.

On one ship, she went on to tell me, were the King's men, resplendent in Tudor green and white, the colours of my husband's house, and in the other were players dressed as men of Rome in papal purple. The King and his court watched from the water stairs of Westminster, cheering on the men of England.

Two more barges floated on the water, pennants of England fluttering from their masts, and sails snapping and cracking in the wind. A man playing Saint George cried out words of victory to gathered masses on the slippery banks, and musicians played songs of glory, battle and triumph over the enemies of God.

At the end, the players dressed as the Pope and his cardinals were thrown headlong into the river.

The message was clear. The King cared not a fig for the Pope or Rome. This was a public insult.

"After that event, there was much fearful talk again of the Emperor invading our lands," said Lady Lisle, "and for many of us, Majesty, that was the first time we heard your name. It was said by many, but Cromwell most of all, that this marriage was England's chance to finally unite with the Schmalkaldic League. He tried, years ago, to persuade the King to join with them but the King did not like the League's demands. But it was said, when your marriage was first discussed, that if England unites with Cleves, we will have a connection to the League and will be better protected in Europe."

"Cleves is not of the League," I told her.

"But your sister's country, and indeed her husband, are close linked, leaders of the League," she said, looking confused.

"That is true," I replied, worrying anew that the English did not fully understand. Cleves had links to the League, but never had joined. The distinction seemed lost on the English. We could not call on the League as allies, and neither could the English. I wondered if they were truly aware of this.

That was not the only thing troubling me. There were many slight misunderstandings, such as how they proudly displayed the Black Lion of Julich, not understanding that was the sigel of my mother's house, not my father's. They kept calling it the Black Lion of Cleves, and I had not the heart to correct them. There also seemed to be many in Calais who believed I was a Lutheran, for some had politely and carefully warned me that the King was not enamoured of Luther and thought him a heretic. I had told them many of my country did too and had gazed then into baffled faces.

"The King's only reservation was about your looks, my lady, but once he saw your portrait he was entranced," Lady Lisle continued as we strolled down the corridor. "He carries it everywhere, you know, a miniature of your portrait on a chain at his waist, and in his apartments there hangs a full size one. He tells people to look upon your face and asks them if you are not the most perfect creature ever God made."

I smiled uneasily.

"You must not fear the King," said Lady Lisle in a soft voice, regarding the fragile stretch of my smile with understanding. "There are many tales told of him, most of them by enemies of England, but he is in truth a gentle man, learned and cultured, a knight in the true sense of the word. He is good to his people, to those who serve him well, and to his children he is an excellent father."

I forced my smile to look more convincing.

"Tell me more of your daughter, Mistress Anne Bassett," I said, changing the subject. "I would know more of the women who are to be my good friends."

I hardly heard a word she said after, as she raved about her daughter who was apparently most well educated and graceful. The Lady Lisle might tell me not to fear the King, and that I could almost do, but I did fear his expectation of me. I was not perfect, I was well aware of that, and if the King was expecting one who was, he would be most disappointed.

*

Christmas Eve came and there was no news that we could travel, the winds still wild. I was told the King distracted himself from the pain of missing me – although how he could miss someone he never had met I knew not – by planning the marriage of Lady Mary, his daughter, to Phillip of Bavaria who had come to London for the negotiations. Lady Mary was refusing to countenance the match, saying she would rather die than marry a heretic, for Phillip was Lutheran, but her father insisted she meet him, so apparently the King did not object to all Lutherans. The Admiral told me there had been whispers of plots to put Mary on the throne and knowing of this gossip and the danger it presented to her, she had submitted to her father and signed a document which stated he was Head of the Church and her mother had never been truly married to him, all for fear he might hear these rumours and arrest her. I wondered if Lady Lisle would still name the King a good father, if he actually sent his daughter to the Tower, where he had already sent one wife.

But although she had bowed to her father over much that was important to her, it seemed Lady Mary did not want to submit in all ways, and one of those was her choice of husband. To my mind, she had ceded her past to her father, perhaps the present too, but the future she wanted to keep her own. I admired her spirit in this matter.

"She has taken to her bed," Lady Lisle told me. "Lady Mary heard that Duke Phillip is most eager to marry her, so she is pretending to be sick and has retired from court. Some say she will flee to Spain if the King insists."

"Poor lady," I said, "To be forced to marry where she loves not, that is a sad fate."

"That is the fate of most people, Majesty," said my companion.

My head snapped up as wind shrieked past the window. It sounded as though there were a white bear of the north scratching the panes, looking for food within, and I shuddered.

"The King slapped Cromwell about the chops one afternoon this week, my daughter told me," mentioned Lady Lisle, evidently heading off to another branch of gossip. "Shouted that it was his fault that you, Majesty, were not at court, for Cromwell should have sent sturdier ships to bring you to England."

"Cromwell is my husband's Chancellor, is he not?" I asked, wondering for a moment if Lady Lisle was speaking of another man with the same name.

"Indeed, the most powerful man, under the King, in England," she said.

It was common for servants to be hit or slapped by masters, but I was somewhat shocked the King would do so to one of his best men, his highest advisor in many ways. Lady Lisle however seemed to find the tale amusing. I gathered she did not like Cromwell, and also that she seemed to think I should take his being slapped as a compliment.

I was not sure the King's inability to restrain his hands, on my behalf or anyone else's, could have been ever considered a compliment to me.

# Chapter Six

**Calais
English Territory
France
and
Dover Castle, Kent**

**December 1539**

On Christmas Day we woke to fresh skies, no more troubled with grey iron. The weather had broken, the skies a brilliant, glaring blue. "The Queen can to England go!" was the cry about Calais. My heart panicked for a moment, beating so hard I thought I might collapse. *Courage, Anna,* I whispered.

*Courage, indeed,* said that voice, not mine, in my mind. It sounded sardonic, amused, but not entirely unsympathetic.

We left the next day, and although I thought the crossing treacherous, I was assured it was calm enough. In truth, although the ship made my stomach jolt and tumble, although I took fright when the vessel moved and rocked upon the waves and I realized we were far from land and all that was solid, I relished the feeling of adventure. I had never been upon the sea, had never even seen it before I reached Calais. Heading out into the vast ocean, I was as full of trepidation as excitement, and both fought inside me, writhing in my belly and heart, until they mingled to become one glorious sensation of energised, elated terror, igniting some spark in my soul which set my mind afire. Suddenly I understood why the King loved these ships so, why the Admiral had gone on endlessly about them; these were the vessels which allowed them to stand upon the sea, which released this feeling of freedom and boldness and energy so boundless to rise up within a person, to consume them, so that they became as a part of the writhing waves and the sparkling horizon. It was a sensation both mighty and humbling at the same time, and I was intoxicated by it.

I stayed below deck for most of the journey, upon the ardently given advice of those accompanying me. My ladies, many of them green – something I had always thought a myth until I saw the colour of their faces – lay sweating and groaning on crude beds in the cabin chambers. We were surrounded by the noise of creaking timber and slapping rope, shouts from above as the captain gave orders and others followed. I came above board for a few moments, when I was permitted, and marvelled at the sight of small lads, barefoot and clad in slight clothing, racing up rigging to adjust sails, of aged men devoid of teeth and many of the odd limb here and here, or eye, barking orders at others, at men rolling goods fast down the deck, if the ship was unbalanced in some way. I was reminded of once spying a nest of ants in my father's gardens, all of them busy with a task and all seeming to know exactly what they were to do and when. I envied these men this, this sense of understanding and purpose in life. I hoped I would know all I was to do, soon.

As we neared England, however, the blue skies vanished, and grey came rolling over us. Another storm hit. We were not more than a league away when the winds came screaming at us. Taken below deck I was, almost by force, as rain and hail started to lash the boat. About us the ship groaned as if it was a thing living and in pain and my ladies cried out in fear that the wind or the waves or giant monsters living under the water would tear the ship and then us apart. A man half-fell down the stairs and came with a message. We were to land at Deal, I was told, which meant nothing to me, and then would ride from there to Dover Castle, where I was to stay.

When we reached the shore, the rain was heavier still, lashing us with hard pellets of ice hidden amongst liquid. Water spewed up from below too, waves crashing on the ship's sides as hands bent on tearing it apart, and so as we were brought up from the cabins we were pounded with water from all sides. The light was fading and the path off the ship was treacherous. Planks had been set out so I could reach the dock from the ship, but they were slippery, and my boots were not made for such terrain. I almost fell once, almost tumbled right into the sea where waves were foam and ice, but my hand was caught, and I was taken safe to the wall of the dock. My ladies were unloaded too, many bundled out of the belly of the ship, green as young parsley.

I could barely hear the greeting of the Duke and Duchess of Suffolk, who had come to meet me, and could not see them either for they were clad in thick, hooded cloaks. The rich, embroidered canopy held over them, meant to protect them and my party from the rain, was sodden and leaking. Thankfully I was hastened quickly upon a horse and to a great castle we rode. Even in the darkness, or perhaps because of the darkness it looked more ominous and impressive, a giant looming from the night, than it might have in daylight. It was dark, the night coming on fast, and by the light of torches held aloft, valiant against the wind and rain, I was ushered in. I was soaked through. Stumbling to the fire in the Great Hall, trying to maintain any snippet of dignity I had left, I gazed down ruefully at my glorious gown, one chosen to impress, which was not impressive anymore. I thought how I must resemble some kind of drowning rodent as I stood before them in the hall, by the fire, dripping water onto the rushes, my hair soaked under its headdress, and all I had on me limp.

"Warm clothes for her Majesty!" the Duchess called, with such authority that I almost stared at her. She reminded me of Sybylla, that confidence of character so obvious and forthright.

"You are kind, Your Grace," I said to her in my broken English, and she started a little, taken aback that I knew a little English. "In Calais, I am learning English," I stumbled slowly, trying not to let my teeth chatter, and she smiled broadly, as if I had said something most intelligent.

Blankets came, so they could warm me, and wine heated in the fire with a poker was set into my shivering hands. The Duchess took me to a room where my clothes had been brought, thankfully protected by good oak and wrappings, and with the aid of my ladies I changed out of yet another set of soaked clothes. I was starting to think that many of my fine gowns and shoes might well be in tatters by the time I met the King.

The Duchess kept up a stream of both conversation with me, through Olisleger – who had his back turned of course – and commands to the maids and other servants. I found myself watching her with great admiration.

Katherine Willoughby, the Duchess of Suffolk, and wife to the rather notorious Charles Brandon who was best friend to the King, might have been called interesting to look upon, rather than beautiful. Mistake me not, there was no hardship to any eye which came to rest upon her face, but Katherine was not a classical beauty of England. I had seen enough of those now, so I thought, to understand what an English rose was; pale of face and fair of hair, large of bosom and hip, although slim enough of waist to present a pleasing contrast. Katherine was a little different. Her hair was fair, but of a honey-colour, rather like that of my sister. Her eyes were blue, and sharp. There was intelligence in her conversation and her gaze, which was quite penetrating. She had a strong wit, which was often playful, and her upturned nose, small and delicate, held a suggestion of mischief. Ask me not how a nose might convey such, but hers did.

She was much younger than her Duke, that I could see without needing to guess. He must have been around the age my new husband was, and although Brandon was a large, strong man still, his muscle had turned to fat and his hair to snow. His beard too, in patches, was more white than anything. He reminded me a little of a badger. It was also clear to me from the very start that Katherine was far more intelligent than her husband. I had heard tales of Brandon's past while I was in Calais, how he was the King's great friend, had been brought up with him, and was the son of the last King's standard bearer. His father had fallen in battle, and the son had been taken on out of gratitude for this sacrifice as a ward by the King's father. When Brandon was young, he had many a mistress and a rather florid marital history, having been wed to one lady then annulled the match, then had wed the King's sister, Mary Tudor, when she was supposed to still be mourning the death of her first husband, Louis of France. The pair had encountered a lot of trouble from their clandestine match, since it had happened without the knowledge or approval of the King, but it was said he loved both of them so well that he had forgiven them in the end. I did hear, however, from Lady Lisle that they had also paid to the King a great deal of money, which no doubt had aided his forgiveness for their radical match.

Mary Tudor had died some years ago, and Brandon had gone on to wed Katherine Willoughby, who had been, in fact, engaged to his son by Mary at the time. Katherine had been Brandon's ward, her mother being Maria de Salinas who had been one of Queen Katherine of Aragon's most trusted women and the only one from that Queen's entourage who had stayed in England when the rest had gone home. Maria had secured herself a husband and a permanent position at court. This tale I knew from Cleves and many had said Maria had only wed her lord in order to stay with her great friend. This Katherine was their daughter, named for Katherine of Aragon, and a mighty heiress she had been. Katherine and Brandon both claimed to me, later in our relationship, that theirs was a love match, and perhaps it was, but once again and like his friend the King's decision to forgive, I would think that her inheritance, all that money, had a great deal to do with Brandon's decision to marry her.

"We are supposed to be headed to Canterbury in the morn," said the Duchess when we had re-joined the party entire by the fire in the hall, "but with the weather the way it is..."

"A little rain will not harm me," I said when this had been translated to me. "Far I have come, and now that I am here, I would see all of England, this place that is now my home."

The Duke looked astounded, but smiled quickly, noting to my translator that it was good I was not easily cowed by the English weather. The Duchess looked pleased too. "Archbishop Cranmer is to meet you there, Majesty," she said. "And he is most anxious to meet you, it will be good to not have to delay and cause him more pain."

"I would not have pain brought to any of my new people, by me," I said.

As I was taken to my rooms that night Olisleger told me he had overheard the Duke say to his Duchess that I had the manners of a princess, and the gentle bearing of a lamb. "All reports of you are favourable, my lady," he said. "You are doing well."

I smiled, although I knew full well that only one opinion mattered; that of the King I had yet to meet.

# Chapter Seven

### Canterbury and London

### December 1539

"In anticipation of your imminent arrival the royal household has fair roared into life," Katherine of Suffolk told me, leaning over to adjust a strap on her reins. "Everything is being checked, everything is to be perfect, and your new ladies are most busy ensuring that everything is in order for you, Majesty."

We were riding side by side, something I had insisted on. Olisleger was there too, translating the conversation between us as quickly as he could, for in the brief time we had known each other I felt the Duchess had warmed to me, and I certainly had affection for her. This had led to a certain kind of animated conversation, common to women when we find love for one another. Lady Lisle had been kind, motherly in a way, but Katherine was different. Something in my soul touched her spirit and immediately found a home in it. I have felt this way with few people in my life, but every one of them became to me as a welcome moment of feeling in company, in a world most lonesome. I had hope that we might become close, friends even. She was of high status enough that this would not be thought unusual or a disgrace, and she reminded me so of Sybylla. Meeting Katherine of Suffolk was like coming home. She was a healing balm upon my ruptured spirits.

"Would you prefer to be in a litter, Majesty?" Katherine asked as it once more began to rain.

"I would not," I said. "For months, years so it seemed at the time, I was in a litter or a wagon as we all crawled to England, so it now is a great pleasure to be free, the wind upon my skin, and even the rain is welcome."

She laughed as Olisleger translated. "You will do well here, Majesty. If rain and wind are your friends, you will like England."

I chuckled. "But in the summer, the spring, it is different?"

"There is still rain, but it is warmer, certainly, and the flowers and forests of England have no equal anywhere in the world, in my opinion."

"You have travelled, Your Grace?" I asked.

"I have not, Majesty," she replied with an impish grin. "And yet I am entirely sure, is not that strange?"

I smiled. "You love your homeland, and this makes me warm to it all the more, for you are obviously a woman of good taste."

Over the past few days, we had been making our way through England. From Dover Castle we had ridden to Canterbury, and I remained unperturbed when ill weather resumed, much to the amused affection of those I rode with. I refused to be sorrowed by the rain, exclaimed much about the little countryside I could actually observe through the mist, and had kept up a merry refrain with the Duchess all the way along the road, and every evening when we rested, announcing myself enchanted with everyone and everything I saw. Brandon could not be more delighted with me, or so it seemed, for everywhere we went he was praising me and my impeccable manners, my courage, resilience, and strength, to the heavens above, and every saint in them.

In truth, about some of the countryside I did not have to exaggerate in order to please my companions. England was wrapped much in rain and fog at that time, and it was cold and damp, but even through this I could see how green the land was, how healthy the trees and earth. The air was clean and had a fresh tang to it. I was a little surprised there were not as many forests as I might have thought. Cleves was a mass of woodland compared to this kingdom, and I was told there had been more, but the King had cut down many for his ships.

But I was impressed with the roads, many of them good and well maintained, with the neat villages we rode through, many with people who came out even in the rain to cheer me. I had been advised before coming here that the food of England was not as refined as the French or as our own, but I saw nothing to complain about. The dishes were a touch different, but the fish was fresh and tasty, the herbs excellent and there were no shortages of spices. I came to think that the tales one hears of other lands are frequently not true and are, in fact, simply created to make one's own nation seem superior to others. To my eyes and tastes there were good and bad things about England, as there was about any nation and I could now speak with experience, being a woman most travelled.

Archbishop Cranmer had greeted me at Canterbury, along with three hundred gentlemen and the Bishop of Ely, and in their company I had gone to the monastery of St Augustine, past crowds who had gathered in an ill tempest to cheer me. I had rested in the gatehouse, but although the weather was terrible, pouring rain and driving wind, I urged them to allow me to continue on to London, "I am greatly desirous of meeting the King." I told them.

This gained me much approval, and Cranmer, a gentle man, spoke of my courage and fortitude for the grounds outside the gatehouse were dim shadows obscured by hammering rain. The skies seemed low, ominous, even malicious in a way. In the far distance roaming shadows told us deer were seeking somewhere dry to sit. They would search in vain. Even birds were sparse in the skies, though I could hear many chirruping in the bushes.

"We will ride on after a night or so here," I was told.

Cranmer was a sweet man. I had expected some beast of fire and brimstone given his reputation, and yet he was soft-spoken, humble, gentle, rather endearing in many ways. "We are delighted to have you here, finally, Majesty," he told me.

"No more delighted than I am to be here, Eminence," I said.

"I understand your late father was a great advocate of Erasmus and was in communication with him often," said the Archbishop.

"There was not any man in the wide world my father respected more, Eminence, than this one. We children of Cleves were brought up on the teachings of Erasmus."

"I should dearly like to hear of some of their discussions, should we ever get a chance, Majesty."

"My door may be guarded, Eminence, but will always be open to you."

He threw me a look then I can barely explain. It contained happiness, for certain, but there was a hint of sorrow and of yearning for something lost long ago. I could not explain how I knew this, but it came to me that in the past, with my namesake, with another Queen, he had possessed that same kind of easy relationship, and he missed it. *He came to Queen Anne, and they talked, and he misses her,* I thought.

*He was my friend.* That voice I had heard before and could not place, sounded in my head again. I knew that voice now. It was the one of my dreams. It was the voice of the eyes of blackness which had come to me when I dreamed in fear, in troubled times, the eyes that held me steady when I was ill. It was her, another Anne.

I should have been afraid, the words of a dead woman in my mind, perhaps I should have thought I was losing that mind, but I was comforted, if anything. She was guiding me.

*Good*, I thought. I was in need of guidance and if it came from heaven, so much the better.

# Chapter Eight

**St Augustine's Abbey
Canterbury**

**December 1539**

I looked back, over my shoulder, for perhaps the tenth time that day. All I was doing was taking a stroll about the buildings of this former monastery, now a possession of the King, yet I felt watched, haunted. This place echoed with a strange silence, as if it was not in truth empty, as if there were many here, hidden, watching from the shadows.

My ladies, new women I had met, women of the English court, trailed behind me in twos, processing with me down echoing passageways about the cloister, through the gardens, their skirts whispering on cobbled paths, their voices murmuring in the stillness. St Augustine had been one of the leading lights of England's monasteries, I had been told. For perhaps one thousand years it had stood and was a place where many ancient kings had been buried, but in 1538, the year before I came to England, it had surrendered to the King and been disbanded and dissolved. Other monasteries had fought back when the King tried to dissolve their houses, and many of their monks and abbots had died, horribly and brutally, their deaths a public spectacle intended to warn others not to follow suit. St Augustine's had taken the warning to heart and had not fought back. Abbot John Essex and his brothers voluntarily signed a document which surrendered the abbey to the King and the abbot went away with a generous pension. Some of the former brothers became parish priests. I did not ask where the rest had gone, perhaps they had found other employment or perhaps they had joined the legion of beggars on the roads, many of which I had seen on the way here.

That was one sight of England which was not as pleasant as many I had witnessed.

After its surrender, the abbey had been plundered and the famous library went to the King's collection, along with relics and anything of value.

Shrines of the saints of the abbey, such as Saint Augustine himself, had been destroyed. Even the tombs holding the bones of the ancient kings were ravaged. We could see buildings which had already been destroyed, the best stones carried away to make other buildings or walkways in the gardens of rich, local lords, the rest lying as rubble on the ground, and what remained of this vast estate was now a palace for the King, a residence. Its church still stood, an impressive building almost the size of the cathedral at Canterbury. There were, too, glorious gardens here, once tended by men of God, as well as a vineyard and orchard. This was a place which should have been filled with life, but it was not. There was an aching here, as if the stones in the walls and the tiles on the roofs cried out for the souls that once had walked here. The orchards, trees empty of leaves and fruit and men to tend them, felt like walking through a broken heart. This building, a home to men of God for almost a thousand years, it missed them. Without people, the buildings here were as a shell left on the beach, tumbling in the froth of the waves, too light without a soul within to stand against the power of the oceans.

You could say it was all fancy, these thoughts of sorrow, yet I felt it. My heart, sick for the loss of my family, could sense how this place grieved too, sorrowed for the life once within it that now was gone. My loneliness had too become not only a feeling within me, but a creature hunched at my side, my companion. That same creature, formed of the hearts and sorrows of others, was here also. There had been purpose here, a ritual and routine of the everyday, a hum of life, and now it was gone. I kept turning as if there was a ghost at my back but in truth this whole place was a ghost of itself, a pale wraith of something lost, a fleeting shadow on a wall, gone when one turns about. We walked within a life which had been hollowed out, inside a corpse.

I heard a small giggle behind me; one of my new ladies evidently did not feel as I did about this place.

It was as we reached St Augustine that I had encountered these women, ladies of my chambers, dispatched from Greenwich to meet me, including a Mistress Stoner who was to become the Mother of the Maids when Mistress Loew went home, as most of my people from Cleves would, eventually. "But this is not my entire household?" I had asked. There were six women there, all richly dressed. They looked fine, to be sure, and all were strikingly beautiful, but they were not many in number and I had been told my household was of a great size.

Indeed not, I was told, these were the *great* ladies of my chambers, those who would serve in the Bedchamber, the most private, trusted and therefore important space of my rooms. "They are the Frauenzimmer?" I had asked Olisleger.

"Of a kind, I gather, my lady," he said. "It is not the same as Cleves. Your Frauenzimmer will exist, but it is a little different here. The more intimate the chamber, the fewer people are permitted in, so try to think of this in terms of circles. In the outer circle are all your household, including the male officers, and then each circle decreases in size until we reach the Bedchamber, where only your most trusted women serve, and no men are allowed except on the door to guard you."

"Pages?" I asked.

"The men on the door will be guards, but yes, there are pages. I think the ages are a little different here, however, they are allowed to be older than the boys permitted into the Frauenzimmer in Cleves."

"I see," I said. "There is the Public, the Privy and the Bedchamber, then?"

"I believe they call the outer chambers the Presence chambers, Majesty."

The rest of my maids and other servants were waiting at Greenwich to meet me, I was told. "They are quite breathless with anticipation, Your Majesty," said one of the women. I smiled, looking on her beauty, for it was delicate and inviting, and she had bright green eyes which were arresting.

When I asked who she was, I was told her name was Jane Boleyn, Lady Rochford, and it took all I had within me not to react with shock. I had assumed all the Boleyns had died with their Queen or had been cast out. I did not want to ask, and make a faux pas, but for at least a day I thought this might be another sister of the Boleyn Queen's that I had not heard of, and only later worked out that Jane was a Boleyn by marriage alone, once wed to Anne's brother, George.

I also had the impression, from the start, that no one liked Jane Boleyn. Conversations with her were cut short by people. She was not welcomed in as a friend, was not smiled at. People seemed to discard what she said as if it was not worth much. She was at court, certainly, but here she was a ghost to many. Perhaps to some she had died with her husband and sister-in-law, perhaps people wished she had. She was a reminder of past pain at best, a walking, talking memory of a hard and dangerous time. I knew why people tried to avoid her, or I thought I did; she called bad events to mind, simply by being there.

I felt sorry for her, and also wondered at her possessing a high position at court. She was to be a lady of the Bedchamber, one of my most trusted women. No one appeared to trust her, however. It seemed odd that one, even if only by marriage, of this family so infamous and herself so personally disliked would be in a trusted position at court, so close to the King.

She was behind me now, as we walked through the empty cloister. My steps seemed to echo hard along the covered walkway, bouncing out into the square lawn outside. Once every archway here would like as not have had a man in it, some weaving, sewing, tending to projects, the old would have come here to warm their bones in the sunshine. The inner parts of the abbey were cool, their heavy, deep stone walls keeping the sunlight and its warmth away. It could be hard on the older monks at times, that coldness. When I looked up I could almost see them, faces hazy in the sunlight, a silence upon them as they carried out their work. In truth I had no idea if this had been a silent order, but I felt it might have. Yet though now there were voices here, giggles even, when my ladies shared a piece of gossip or a jest, there was a deeper silence now in the background than when the quiet monks had lived here.

This place, I did not like it. The King had cut out its heart and rent its soul and now it stood here still, a ghastly mockery of what it had once been.

Perhaps that was the point.

*

We rode on from Canterbury on the 30th of December to Sittingbourne, and stayed there a night. On New Year's Day, our party made it to

Rochester where I was met by Norfolk, another Duke and yet another person no one seemed to like, though they disguised their aversion better, along with a hundred horsemen dressed in velvet coats and golden chains.

"Is the Duke ill?" I asked Katherine of Suffolk after I had spoken with him a while. Norfolk looked like some kind of emaciated hawk, and he kept rubbing his belly and then his back as if in pain. He let out a great deal of odd little noises too, as if troubled by an affliction of the bowels. I was made rather uncomfortable meeting him. I kept expecting him to excuse himself and flee to the privy.

She tried to smother a laugh and managed to cough instead. "Norfolk suffers many bodily afflictions, Majesty," she said. "They are all permanent."

"He is like this all the time?" I asked, unable to keep the horror from my voice.

"Oh no," said Katherine, her eyes wide. "Sometimes he is far worse."

I glanced at her and chuckled a little. "Will he be able to stay on his horse?"

"Of a surety. Norfolk is terrible at many things, but he is most talented at two skills; riding a horse and commanding an army."

"There are enough men here to make a small army, indeed."

"Then you will be safe as they escort you now to the Bishop's Palace in the city."

The Bishop's Palace was another place taken from the clergy, from none other than John Fisher, the Bishop of Rochester, who had been beheaded in the same year as Thomas More, this man my father had much admired. Norfolk told me this as if I should be happy about it, and I realised that as the King had seized this place and I was supposed to be his adoring wife who approved of all he did, I would have to smile and admit myself pleased. I did so, but it was a lie.

"Yet another place with too many ghosts," I muttered to myself in High German as we rode to the gates.

"What was that our good lady said?" Norfolk asked Olisleger.

"Her Majesty was remarking on how beautiful the houses of England and her palaces are," my translator smoothly lied to the Duke. "And she thinks it a reflection of the greatness of England's King."

I smiled at Olisleger gratefully as we clattered through the gates, into the Bishop's Palace.

And it was here that an incident most unfortunate, or fortunate, depending on how one takes an accident of fate, occurred.

In truth, in order to decide whether something is of poor hap or not, one has to look at the long game of life, how it turned out in the end. At the time, I thought this day a disaster, but from every great disaster there springs new life. A building may fall, a life may be destroyed and all can seem lost, hopeless, but it is not. It simply takes some time for new buds of fresh shoots to be seen, peeking through the rubble.

## Chapter Nine

### The Bishop's Palace
### Rochester
### England

### New Year's Day 1540

After, when I thought on it, I wondered why no one warned me that the King was to do what he did. I had made friends, even in that short time, with the Duchess of Suffolk. Brandon and Cranmer seemed to like me, even Norfolk had not been entirely unwelcoming, though he seemed more comfortable talking to the men in my party rather than to me. I was, too, surrounded by the highest of my new women, noble ladies of England. It seemed odd to me later that none of them had warned me their King might do something as lunatic as he did, and for a goodly time I was puzzled by it, even thinking, unfairly, that some of them wanted me to fail the moment I got to England, but although I have no doubt there were some who wanted me not on the throne, I came to believe they did not warn me for a simple reason.

They thought I would know what he was up to.

It is this way for many of us, we think our ways are the ways of all people, our traditions, games, compliments are the way all people operate. We suppose that people possess the same morals and values we do, that they are like us, yet it is not so. These people I had met thus far were so accustomed to the ways of their own world that they thought those ways were, too, the ways of my people, and they were so used to the figure and face of their King that they could not imagine anyone not knowing what he looked like.

But of course, I did not.

I was at a window when it happened, watching a feat of bull-baiting arranged to entertain me, which was going on in a courtyard below. In all honesty, I hated the spectacle, feeling sorry for the hounds set upon this bull and pity for the bull, who was tormented by them. Blood sprayed up the white walls when a dog was gored through the throat by the horns of the bull, and the bull had a flap of skin hanging from his thigh, so I could almost see the bone. I was feeling a touch nauseous yet was attempting to maintain an expression of pleasure and lively interest upon my face all the same. Perhaps, had I not been already distracted, I might have realized what was going on sooner.

There were others in the room, my ladies, various gentlemen, chatting away, drinking wine and betting on the baiting, and I noticed a little commotion as what looked like a gang of vagabonds entered the room. Although I thought this odd, no one moved to send them away. They were most curiously dressed in hooded cloaks of many colours, and I thought perhaps they were jesters, fools brought in to entertain the company.

One of them, an old man with a limp and a head I could see was balding even under his cap, made straight for me. He came before me and bowed. My translator was not at my side, so I did not understand the words this man said, and therefore knew not how to respond. He stared at me as if I should respond and my eyes were caught by the red, spidery veins upon his cheeks and his nose which had thick, almost purple skin upon it. Perhaps he was a drunkard, I thought, brought to me for that custom the English still kept where royalty put their hands on sick people and cured them, but I did not know for sure.

I inclined my head to him, thinking this was simply a custom I did not understand, a poor man brought to view the Queen perhaps, then I turned back to the baiting. I had not been brought up to converse with the poor, certainly not beggars, and it would have been beneath my new royal dignity to do so, and might displease the King, but as I turned my back on this aged, limping man, a strange, tense silence fell upon the room. I felt cold, though I knew not why.

The man made another noise, and I turned back only to find him embracing me. I went stiff as a corpse in his arms and stiffer still when I caught a whiff of foul breath not quite disguised by a mint lozenge, as well as a scent of something else, like rotten flesh.

Feeling my shock and reserve, he released me, opening his hand to show me a little gold coin. My translator, who had appeared at my side, said the man was telling me the coin was a token of love, from my husband. "But why has this pauper – or is he a fool? – been sent to give me something from the King?" I asked.

Olisleger was clearly as baffled as I was, and everyone in the room was staring at me with ill-disguised horror writ plain on their faces. Whatever this custom was, I clearly was not doing well at it.

The beggar stared at me, which I found remarkable in itself, that he would dare to lock eyes with me, and I watched the wrinkles about his eyes and on his brow furrow with what looked like rage. I took a step back but thanked him for this token sent by my husband. "It pleases us that our husband would send more gifts to us," I said. "And yet the gift we most wish to see, is our husband."

He looked as though he might strike me.

The silence in the room deepened.

The man left abruptly, barely even bowing to me. In the next room there was shouting. "What is going on?" I asked my man.

His face had turned a little pale. "My lady," he said, listening to the shouting. "I think that man was the King, your husband."

I laughed, half with nerves and half because I truly thought he was jesting. "That cannot be the King," I said. Although I had never believed he was as young and fine looking as the portraits I had been sent depicted him as, I had not though him so aged, and why, if he was the King, was he dressed in such clothes? But my laughter stalled as I thought of the limp. His injury, to his leg. I cursed myself inwardly. I had known of that! But how was I to know the King would come to me dressed as a jester at our first meeting?

He changed his clothes and came back, this time presented as the King. Then, of course, I understood my mistake. My cheeks flamed into life, and I was mortified, but baffled. I was informed it was a game, apparently even without meeting him I was supposed to know it was the King. I told my man to apologise for my not having understood. It seemed this was accepted, and we talked for a while, through my translator. The King was polite, and I was humble, but our conversation was awkward from the first, for it was clear I was embarrassed, and he was utterly humiliated. He thought I, his perfect love, would know him in any garb, but I did not.

I ran my eyes over him, now that I knew this was the man I had been promised to. He was enormous, now that he was not stooping. I had never seen a man so big, so broad of shoulder and of waist. He seemed to take up half the room. Now he was richly dressed, he was an assault on the eyes. Gems glittered from every fold and crease of his purple and crimson robes. His shoulders were naturally large, made extraordinarily so by puffed, padded sleeves. A flared doublet exposed his legs, bound in white hose glimmering like fresh ice, and his jewelled codpiece was absurdly large. It was common for men to wear them here, that I had noted, but I, who had never seen a man naked, had trouble keeping my cheeks from blazing crimson at the sight of this obvious, threatening, display of manhood. Had he appeared before me for the first time dressed as he normally did, I would have known he was the King without question.

Gold cloth glimmered, catching the light of guttering candles and the afternoon sun streaming in through diamond windowpanes. My eyes were set to water from the shimmering light cascading from rings on his fingers, gold about his neck, his clothes and his black hat, sitting atop a head with thin hair, which nevertheless shone gold and red, like the rest of him. To look upon him was to stare into the sun. He was blinding.

The King was forty-eight when first I met him; not a remarkable age, but most people beyond forty were thought old. I was only twenty-four, so to me he seemed ancient, and time had not been kind to him. The hair on his head was thin, and since his cap was set back a little, I could see his scalp, pale and laced with flaky skin. The King's head seemed stuck to his shoulders, for I could see no proof of a neck. His body was enormously corpulent. Three men could have climbed inside his doublet and camped there a week. His wide, sagging cheeks were flushed with those broken veins I had noted, spindly and bright. The same was true of his nose, which was tough, like leather. He was built like an ox, with those broad shoulders and a wide waist, and I could tell he had once been more powerful than corpulent. And he was certainly tall. I was a tall woman, and he was a head higher than I.

His mouth was small, a little petulant rosebud. His auburn beard was flecked with white which made him look as if he had spilled his soup in it, and his hooded eyes were an arresting shade of blue, but were almost lost in his face, rolls of skin swallowing them from underneath and to the sides. When he shifted, I could hear the creaking of a corset, worn to keep his belly in check.

His fingers looked like sausages. From his collar of gold there hung a diamond the size of a large walnut. His skin wafted scents of musk and ambergris, myrrh and rose water, and his sagging jowls wobbled as he talked. There was a constant ill scent which came from him, not quite hidden by the generous amounts of perfume he wore. It reminded me of death.

Ours was not a long conversation, and he did not look pleased for even one moment of it. He kept looking me up and down, as if I was a horse he was buying, and I do not think he would have paid much for me. Though I knew little English, I understood some words, and as he left the room the second time I heard him say there was "nothing fair" about me. I turned back to the baiting, trying to conceal how red my cheeks had gone as I had heard his insult. *What manner of man is this, to behave in such an odd way, then in such a rude way?* I wondered. Even if I had known no English, as clearly he thought I did not, he should not be saying such things about me, a stranger to his lands, a guest, the daughter and sister of a Duke, and his new wife, to anyone, let alone where others could hear him.

This man might be a King, but he was no knight.

This marriage was not off to a good start. That first meeting, you see, as I understood later, was not only a game to the King. It was a test. I, his perfect love, should have known the missing shard of her heart in any garb, and I had failed.

And I knew what happened to women who failed this man.

# Chapter Ten

### Rochester
### England

### January 1540

"You are doing well, my lady."

Olisleger's words of reassurance had a hollow ring to them as we prepared to leave Rochester for Greenwich Palace, where I would meet my household. In the small time we had been here the King and I had met rarely and spoken little, though this was not the tale apparently being told in the streets.

"The people hear how you and the King met and conversed with gentle ease, Majesty," the kind Duchess had said the day before. "Some say you love each other already."

"The King is gentle, and wise," I said to her, trying to insert warmth into my voice. "I am fortunate to have such a man as my husband."

If the King knew not how to behave, I did. If the King thought to insult me before others, I would compliment him. Perhaps by shame he could be ushered into gentlemanly behaviour.

Katherine was seeking to reassure me all was well, much as my translator was, but my ladies had been a little more candid. They too were entirely baffled by the odd behaviour of the King, and many thought him strange of mind, "as old men sometimes are," Mistress Loew said. When I pointed out that the King was only forty-eight years, she was amazed, having believed him much older.

"But... his face, his hair, the way he limps," she said.

"He had an accident in the joust some years ago," I told her.

"Oh," she said. "I thought it gout." She paused a moment. "Perhaps the strangeness of age has come upon him early. It happens to some men, I have heard, their minds wander and they become as children once again. Why else would he act in such an odd way? It *was* childlike, the trick he played upon you, and I do not understand what the purpose of it was. Were we all supposed to laugh?"

"I think we were supposed to secretly know that it was the King, because in any garb he would be majestic," I said.

"There is a reason kings wear crowns," she said, shaking her head. "And that is because most of them are quite ordinary looking men. The crown, the clothes, they define a king *as* a king. He cannot be upset with you because his disguise worked so well that you were fooled."

"And yet I would say he is upset with me, even if it is not fair."

The Duchess, who was trying constantly to be kind and bolster my spirits, must have heard some of the words my ladies and other servants had, words of rage coming from the King, and all about me. He had said I was not fair, that he had been lied to, and that Cromwell would pay for sending me to him. He liked me not, he had said, and more than once had he repeated this.

He was not alone in his disappointment.

As far as I was concerned, I thought my new husband foul to smell, unpleasing in character and distasteful to look upon. His physical defects I could brush off with ease. I had been aware that he would not be all the ambassadors had told me he would before coming here, and I had been prepared for an older man, with troubles with his health. What led to me feeling actual revulsion for him, contempt even, was the way he comported himself.

His manners when standing right before me were fine, but I had heard what he had said about me in private, although not *that* private, to his men. He had insulted me, talked ill of me and done so in front of many people. I was a stranger to these lands and a lady who was under his protection, and on all those counts or just simply for the fact that I was another soul, he should have shown more tact, manners, and kindness than he had.

And the fool's game he had played with me was ludicrous, beneath his dignity and far, far beneath his years.

I thought of my father and could not imagine him gallivanting about, pretending to be another man, just to test his wife. I had acted with decorum and dignity, and if the King had been made to look a fool it was only his own fault. He had dressed as a fool, acted as one and I had thought him one. All this indignation about my looks seemed to me to be a front to cover the fact that he was shamed I had not understood he was the King of England. He had brought this upon himself.

Yet I knew I would be blamed for this event.

My marriage had not even taken place, and already it was in danger.

# Chapter Eleven

**Shooter's Hill
Greenwich Palace
London**

**January 1540**

On the third day of January, we mounted horse to ride to a place called Shooter's Hill, a name which to me seemed ominous, at Greenwich Palace, "and there your servants and entire household as well as much of the court have gathered to welcome you, Majesty," the Duchess told me, that now familiar false brightness of tone riding high in her voice. I had heard it in many a voice since my first, disastrous, meeting with my new husband.

Katherine looked strained, as did everyone else. Up until the moment I had met my obviously deranged – as I, as well as most of my household had now decided he was – husband I had been doing well, but now I was most assuredly not. I had some ground to catch up if I was to make a success of this marriage, which had not even taken place yet.

Would he refuse to go through with it? Refuse me and the ceremony? It was possible, since anything was possible with those who are unhinged of mind. Would he send me home? The thought made my cheeks flame with chagrin. It not because of a true desire to not go home, at moments home was all I wanted, but to be sent back in disgrace for not being the wife he wanted, for not being thought suitable enough, pretty enough, queenly enough, I would never have another offer after such a public defamation and my country would be humiliated. Amalia might suffer for it too.

Would he dare do this? Set me aside before he had even taken me as his wife? I knew not. The alliance with Cleves was something England needed more than anything I had been told, yet this was not a man to keep women near him who disappointed him. There were other ways to be rid of me that might not cause trouble with my brother, or war with another country. He had killed, perhaps more than once if the rumours of Katherine of Spain and poison were to be believed, to ensure he had not a woman unwanted at his side.

And yet, with all these questions in my mind and fears in my heart, I had to go on trying to win the hearts of this country, as well as the heart already turned against me, that of the King.

That day was a buzzing whirl of activity. In truth I was glad of it, for people were busy and not watching me to see if I was doing well or badly, if I was showing signs that I knew of the King's intense and obvious disappointment in me and my face and form. We were readying to leave again, more time on the road before a long rest, so I was told, at Greenwich, one of England's most gracious and stunning palaces. The women with me told me of the gardens, of my chambers, of my household, and all of them had that bright tone of false sunlight in their mouths, trying to ignore the ill events of the last days. For two days, I had been told, men had been constructing a sea of tents in the grounds of Greenwich, so I would be dazzled before I even reached the palace.

The ride there was pleasant, and I felt more at ease, for the King was not there. This made me relieved and anxious in equal measures, truth be told, for I was glad he was not there so we could embark on yet another strained conversation, and yet if we were to be married it would be a good thing to know him better.

Seeking to make up for the absence of a King, the Duchess struck up a lively conversation all the way, filling any gap with tales of court, scandals, gossip, which I appreciated since it gave me something to think on other than my glaring failure to recognise the King in a jester's costume.

Yet I could not help but feel that this was not my fault, this disaster. If the King had simply presented himself as himself, and not played this fool's game trying to test me, we could have met, conversed as our own selves and begun to get to know one another. This lunatic way he had decided to 'greet' me had not turned out well, but I did not see that was my fault.

He, however, did believe it was my fault.

Clearly this man lived in fantasy, and that made me fear him only more. Was that why he had rid himself of three wives – for they said Jane Seymour might have lived had she been taken care of better – who did not live up to what he wanted? Could any woman become what he wanted, or had he tested all of those who had come before me and found them wanting?

*The greatest test is a male child*, said the voice within me. *Jane might have survived, but once the boy was here, she mattered less to him.*

The ghost was wise.

As we reached the park of Greenwich Palace, a forest of green, white, red and purple canvas came into sight, as though the King's court were on a hunting trip or going to war. At the centre of this ocean of colour was a tent of cloth of gold, shimmering in the dun sunlight. For a moment I thought it magnificent then swiftly I thought how foolish it was to make a tent, which had to protect one against the ravages of the weather, out of so precious a material. This tent was not the only light shining on this grey day. Hundreds of fires had been lit along the path leading to and from the palace, with braziers burning sweet incense beside them. Smoke plumed into the air, dancing blue and grey in the wind, twisting white. The air was musky, rich with incense, which did not quite block out ranker smells coming from the river, and London itself. Thankfully, it was not raining, but the skies were grim. Clouds dark and promising hung heavy in the skies. There were gusts of wind, which blew hard behind us, threatening riding cap and cowl. A storm, yet another one, was on its way that night.

"The grounds and route to the palace have been cleared of old branches and debris," Katherine told me.

"Hard toil after all the storms of late," I replied, one hand on my headdress which, despite a thousand pins or thereabouts I thought struck into it that morning, was trying to fly away from my head.

"Oh, indeed, Majesty, for trees uprooted from the earth in the late storms had to be chopped into bits and dragged away by men and oxen, through rivers of mud. Carts carrying smaller branches, twigs, and heaps of rotten, sodden leaves have struggled on the wet ground. But they were determined that you should ride unhindered to your palace." She smiled at me.

The procession way was magnificent, that trail of bonfires burning valiantly against cold air, incense holders pouring wonderful scents into the wind, and the ocean of brightly coloured tents, with the hundreds of people milling about, drinking steaming cups of spiced wine.

I could see crowds of people ahead, and they were all waiting to see me.

Merchants, aldermen, councillors, officers, esquires, knights and palace servants were all in place, dressed in their finest, to cheer me along to the palace. I could see only glimpses of the palace itself. Everything far away was grey. Despite the wind, a low mist was attempting to creep from the trees. As it slunk from the bushes, a creature of shadow and greyness, it was caught by gusting wind and swept into the air to join the smoke and incense.

Some ladies of my train had been sent ahead to ensure all was taken care of, and Jane Rochford, along with the ladies Douglas and Howard, was amongst them. When first we arrived we were asked to delay a little, to allow the last of the preparations to take place, so we sat on horseback drinking wine, heated and rich with spices. By noon, I was told all my people were outside in the wind, waiting to be presented to me, and found myself helped into a chariot, which seemed faintly ridiculous, that I would ride in towards them.

*Another show of pageantry*, I thought. In all honesty I had thought such spectacles as these had died out with the Burgundians, and yet still they were adhered to in England. The foolish fantasies of the King took form and became real here, where he had power, I realised. Perhaps I could have looked on these customs of the English, all this playacting, with a little more acceptance had I not just been on the ill end of one of them going wrong.

Doctor Daye, apparently my new almoner, was preaching a sermon in Latin to my household as we rode up to the party. I watched with some amusement as all present checked their clothes, touching hoods and hats, smoothing gown and tunic, so they were ready to meet me. I thought of the days when Sybylla was the only one everyone looked at, or when my mother and father would have been the ones for whom people ensured their dress was perfect or tunic in place, and I missed those days. I would rather have met people with ease between us, rather than them all trying to impress me, and the trouble was I was fairly sure now that I was the one who had to impress. This show of my people making themselves perfect to greet me hid a truth lurking beneath, that I was the one to be assessed, and I had already been found wanting.

Margaret Douglas, Mary Howard and the Marchioness of Dorset were the first in line to greet me when I stepped from my chariot. I saw the maids of honour were at the end of the row, with a girl I supposed must be Lady Lisle's daughter, Anne, at the head of their line, as well as a girl who looked entirely too young to be at court next to her. She caught my eye, the young girl, partly because she looked so very young, and she was pretty too. All my women were striking of looks, but there was something about that girl, some lightness to her I welcomed. It is hard to judge a character before meeting a person, but she exuded friendliness, openness. Some are unable to hide their feelings, and that girl looked so pleased to be standing just where she was, not caring she was not higher up the line, or glad she was not further down it. That acceptance of her place and position, without rancour against others, was something to be admired.

I made my way down the line, women dropping to curtsey before me, then rising to be introduced. God Above, I tried to remember all their names, but there were so many. As I moved along, finally I came to the end where Anne Bassett and the young child at her side dropped into curtseys and rose when I bade them to.

"Mistress Anne Bassett and Mistress Catherine Howard, Majesty," I was told. "The heads of your maids of honour."

"I am pleased to meet you," I said slowly in English.

"We are only more pleased to meet you, Your Majesty," said Anne.

"I am honoured to serve you, Your Majesty," the pretty child said, curtseying again.

I looked upon this little flower. Although I was aware girls had to be a certain age to be deemed suitable for court, she looked no more than ten years. Yet her bosom was more developed than I would have thought for a girl that young, so I surmised she must simply be one of those who looked younger than their age. She had an appearance of such joy and innocence, so bright and eager, so pleased to be there. Anne Bassett too was a handsome girl. I wondered if these women had, in fact, been chosen for court because they were pretty, or if all the women of England were as lovely as these few I had seen, chosen for my household. I smiled at my translator. "Please tell them I am quite overwhelmed by the beauty of my women," I said. "I am delighted so many flowers of England have been sent to adorn my royal garden."

He repeated my compliment, and they all smiled, the Howard child especially blushing like a pink rose.

I kissed the chief ladies of my household, and my translator thanked them all heartily on my behalf. Being told it was the thing to do, I then also kissed my councillors and officers. I blushed a little to kiss men who were not my father or brother, but in England, as I had been told and observed, everyone was kissed by the women. Not to my surprise, I had been informed it was a custom which Englishmen and men visiting from other countries much admired.

"We are to wait for the King to arrive now, Majesty," said Jane Rochford. "There is a tent prepared for you, here, out of the wind."

As we turned to head into one of the tents, so I could warm myself at the fire before the ride through the long parks of Greenwich, Anne turned to Catherine Howard. I did not catch all they said, but I did hear something about my clothes. I surmised they, like many I had met here, were not enamoured of my dress. I looked down at my gown of crimson and gold for a moment as we walked into the slightly damp interior of the tent. I had sewn much of the cloth myself, embroidered the clovers of Cleves, the swans on the hem of the skirt. I was dressed differently to all of these women, and even with eyes that were accustomed to the clothes of my country I could see the clothing of the English women was more flattering to their figures than mine was. Theirs displayed more *of* their figures, for one thing. Mine, although tight at the waist, covered a great deal of me, but that was, of course, the idea. In Cleves it had not been thought modest to display so much of oneself. Here, it seemed, it was perfectly acceptable.

Once in the tent, I asked that my ladies and maids come close to the fire, a brazier set in the centre, with me, for at first they hovered about the edges of the tent where it was much colder. "Tell them I do not want my wonderful flowers to wilt," I said to Olisleger, and they smiled and came a little closer. But still they maintained a distance. It hurt my heart a little to see it, to know it would always be that way now. These women did not see the Anna who had grown up in the shade of her elder sister, the child who had always been more comfortable in the shadow than light. I was their Queen now, and that was how they treated me. I would ever be apart from all of them, set in their centre, all the light of the world trained upon me.

They warmed wine, and Margaret Douglas brought it to me. I thanked her by name, hoping that if I kept repeating their names in such a way, I would learn them quicker.

I cupped the golden goblet in my hands, the warmth soothing, the spices heating my tongue and my blood. Outside, the wind was rising, and the sides of the tent snapped and cracked. I kept up a little stream of conversation with my great ladies of the Bedchamber, my translator working hard, but where I could I answered in English before he could speak. I was already better at understanding the language than I thought I might be, and they all smiled as if I were an obedient lapdog when I managed a word here and there, even if it was only yes or no.

After a while of this, they seemed more relaxed. I supposed they were grateful I had not turned out to be some demanding harpy sent to torture them.

As wind slapped the tent again, and Mary Howard apologised for the weather, I smiled. "England is made fair and green by the rain that comes to her skies," I said, and Olisleger translated. "Therefore, I sorrow not, for I see what beauty trials may bring. A lesson from God, I think, that what is worthwhile comes with trial and suffering."

They seemed to welcome this compliment to their country and they beamed at me. *Courage, Anna*, I said to myself as I sipped my wine, feeling their eyes heavy on me.

Once I was warmed, ladies-in-waiting helped me to change into a gown of cloth of gold with a pearl-encrusted bonnet on my head, the twin of one made for Sybylla for her wedding. My gowns lacked trains, whereas all the ladies of court wore them here, some quite long. They were elegant. But I did have a stunning necklace of stones glimmering like snow in the light of the fire to set off the costume, and my ladies much admired it.

They tried to encourage me to wash a little in hot water brought in a bowl. "They are bent on making me ill," I said to my man, and he smiled. I had ever been taught that to wash all over in winter was certain to make a person sicken. During the journey here I had changed my underclothes each day and washed my hands, neck and face, but a full wash, especially in a tent in the middle of a park, was surely not advisable. "It will bring death," I said to them in English as they tried to get me to wash more. They fell back, looking mildly annoyed and I knew not why. Plenty of nobles did not wash in winter, some only had two baths a year.

They came at me with perfume, and although I allowed a little, they attempted to almost drown me in pungent liquid. I shied away, shaking my head, and my translator told them that only high-class women of the night wore scent so pungent in Cleves. This perfume was, of course, of a higher standard than such women could afford, but still, I was almost set to choke on the scent as they tried to soak me in it.

I began to wonder if they thought I smelt.

I had noted nothing, and my ladies had said nothing either. They had washed as I had, changed undergarments as I had. It was to be expected that after a long journey people might not be as fresh as they were on a summer's day, but for the good of my health I could not soak myself to the skin, or indeed soak my skin, in an open space in winter!

The King arrived not long after, and as trumpets blared to announce his arrival my women took me outside, guiding me and my ladies of Cleves to the front of the tent. Each of my women wore an abundance of gold chains, which were rattling in the light, chilly wind. The women of England kept glancing at them, some of the maids trying to hide snickering smiles, and I gathered they found the clothing and chains of my women outlandish.

Surrounded by councillors, gentlemen attendants, bishops, nobles and a new division of the King's bodyguard, the Gentlemen Pensioners, a special contingent gathered from the sons of the nobility, the King rode up, magnificent in purple and cloth of gold with buttons of diamonds, pearls and rubies. The handle of his sword was rich with emeralds as green as Jane Boleyn's eyes, and a collar about his throat was weighted down with pearls and gems. Ten footmen dressed in gold tunics stood about the King, and near them ten pages in crimson.

I looked up at my husband and wondered at the English, for they all looked upon him as if he was indeed this man the ambassadors had spoken of, virile and young, handsome and wise. But to my eyes, though his clothes were fine, he was aged and not by the years he carried. There was suspicion in his eyes and covetousness in the lines about his mouth. He pouted often, like a spoilt child told they can have no more honey cake, and his features were fast vanishing into the folds of his face, a condition brought about, as I had seen when at dinner with him, by him eating more than any man needed. He was hungry for something, but it was not food. I suspected what was missing from his life was love, in the form of romantic or friendly affection, and that whilst he might have excused to himself the killing of Anne Boleyn and the men who were once his close friends, those deaths had left a hole in him, one that could not be filled. He felt that hunger in his body, but refused to see it was a hollow aching left not by lack of food, but lack of love. And he had brought this relentless hunger upon himself, had hollowed out his own life, had made himself lonely, had condemned himself to be always seeking what once he had possessed, yet had destroyed.

He had done the same with Katherine and his daughter Mary. Once they had meant much to him, this I had been told in reports from England. Once he had rejoiced in his daughter Mary, complimenting her about court and showing her off with pride, but he had cast her and her mother, more people who might truly have loved him, aside.

His clothes were magnificent for certain, and if one only looked at them then he was all the ambassadors had told me he was, but I looked past the clothes and saw a frightened, empty, lonely and fearful man. I wondered why the English did not see this, and suspected they did not dare look so close at their King. He was the one in ultimate control of them. Perhaps they did not wish to see him, truly. It was too frightening to know what kind of hungry ghost was their master.

And if my women thought I smelt, I wondered that they could not smell the King, for I could. There was a waft, every now and then, that putrid smell of death. It was his leg, that I had worked out by then.

But I was a polite woman and had been raised to be dignified. Even if the King, this man who had sworn to keep me safe and honour me, had no manners, or very few, I would not behave as he did.

My women flanking me as soldiers, I was helped into a saddle decorated with the heraldic devices of my family, and I rode to the King. Surrounded by footmen wearing the Black Lion of Julich – although again, just like in Calais, everyone here kept saying it was a symbol of Cleves, evidently knowing nothing of my country – on their livery, I handled my slightly excitable horse well and as I came to the King he doffed his cap, saluted, then embraced and kissed me. His mouth smelt too, stale wine and rotten teeth. The King's manners before others were impeccable, but I could feel stiffness in him, reserve, as he embraced me. He tensed when I came near. I knew not much of men, but I did not think this a good sign.

But I persevered, I had to, did I not? I had learnt some longer words, phrases, and I used them with the King, telling him how beautiful his court was, and how gracious were his people. "They emulate their King," I said, and received what looked like a genuine smile. Flattery was the way to this man's heart, evidently, no matter how false.

The people about us cheered, shouting, "God save the King!" and "God save the King and Queen!"

I rode at the King's side to the palace, speaking only when he spoke to me and smiling all the time. My face began to ache with the strain.

With my new Master of Horse, John Dudley, at my side, I tried to appear entirely composed as we took our horses along the gathered ranks of lords, Council members, ambassadors, bishops, archbishops and foreign dignitaries, including Phillip of Bavaria, pointed out to me by the King, who was evidently still waiting for Lady Mary to agree to wed him. The line stretched from the tents back to the gates of Greenwich Park, and the men had all been standing in the cold waiting for this moment. I pitied them, but they all managed to get through the ceremony without shivering too hard.

For the procession back to the palace, the King rode, but I dismounted and was set into a carriage gilded with the arms of Cleves along with two ladies of my country, one of them Mistress Loew, and two of my new household. After us came a carriage full of my younger ladies of Cleves. Then came one carrying lesser servants and another, an empty litter made of cloth of gold, which was a gift from the King for me.

"What of my English ladies and maids?" I asked, for I did not want them out in the cold. They were put into open carriages, I was told, unwieldy contraptions that were vastly uncomfortable, and they too trundled behind my carriage. As we set off, Mistress Loew pointed a finger to the river. "Look," she said. I did, spotting boats rowing up and down the Thames, banners and flags streaming from their masts and sails. Despite cold air, and skies threatening snow any moment, there were thousands upon that river.

"They sail in honour of you, Majesty," said Jane Rochford, and I smiled, looking on them in wonder. *At least,* I thought to myself, *the people of England are happy I am here.*

*Even if the King is not?* whispered that voice, completing my sentence.

*I am not a child to be frightened by my own imaginings,* I told myself.

*You are not a child,* said the voice. *And the danger is real.*

# Chapter Twelve

### Greenwich Palace
### London

### January 1540

They took me to my rooms, so I could prepare myself and dress for the evening's entertainment. To dress was one thing – I was certain I could accomplish that feat – but to prepare for another night of the King acting as if I was the last person he wanted near him, whilst everyone else pretended all was well and their King was not impolite, infantile and sullen, was another matter.

Through the corridors of court we came, and passed crowds of people loitering, all trying to catch a glimpse of me. They bowed or curtseyed as I walked by, greeting me as the Queen, but I was starting to feel as if I were a bear of the frozen north, brought out as a novelty to amaze and entertain these people. Many of the loiterers seemed to be young men, and I ascertained that they outnumbered the women greatly.

"Who are all these men?" I asked and was told I was to pay them small heed. There were always young men hanging about, trying to catch a glimpse of the Queen's ladies and maids.

"And they are allowed to pester my women?" I asked, somewhat aghast. In Cleves they would never have been permitted to loll about so, without purpose and clearly with predatory notions in mind, if one went by the bold, somewhat lewd glances they threw at my women.

"They are, apparently, moved on from time to time but always come back," Olisleger told me, after listening to Mary Howard, to whom he had posed the question. "There is not much discipline at the English court, apparently, my lady." He tried very hard not to look disapproving and failed.

"We must be careful not to judge too swift and harsh, friend," I said, setting a hand to his arm as we walked, although I admit I had had the same thought leaping to my mind. "The ways of the English are different to ours, but we are the strangers here, so we are the ones who must adapt. This is their house, and we are the guests, so it is their rules we must follow."

"As you say, my lady," he said. "Although, I understand the maids of honour in particular make sure to travel in twos or threes, for protection."

"For protection? They must protect each other?"

"Apparently so. They are, I am told, the lowest of the high and so do not have the protection of rank which the greater ladies of your chambers enjoy. Your maids are noticed by all, but not so guarded as the higher ladies, which sets them at risk. The chamberers, below them, are also ever on guard. This court may look refined, but for some it is a dangerous place."

I was astounded that any women could be at risk at court but reminded myself again to be careful not to cast judgement until I fully understood. It seemed sad to me, though. I had been admiring the freedom, at least relatively, which English women seemed to enjoy, but this freedom of clothes and choice, it came with risk, apparently. I wondered which was worse, to live as I had, quite shut away from the world and its men, or to walk amongst them but endure the possibility of nuisance at least – and at worst? I was not sure what the women here might be risking at worst. Would any of these lewd-eyed loiterers dare attack my women? Would it not be a fine thing to be free, as the women here were, but not have men try to take advantage of them? I wondered if such a thing was possible. The notion this was not possible was why, after all, we had been separated from the court of men in Cleves.

"You mean, they are at risk?"

"There are dangers at court, for everyone," he said, glancing at a fine tapestry as we passed it in an outer corridor. "Men can become too familiar with maids of honour, this happens in many courts, and if found in a compromising position, even if not their fault, the woman will be blamed. That is why your ladies stick together, travelling in packs. If shame falls on one of them, it falls on them all, so they look after each other."

"And their fathers know this, when sending them to court?"

It was, I was told, worth the risk to the fathers or brothers of these women. There were few places at court for women, and it was a prestigious place to be, positions here leading to higher marriages and greater favour, so some thought the risks worth it. "It is a gamble," I said, understanding. "They wager on their daughters' safety, hoping for higher wins by the end of the game."

The same had been done with me, I supposed.

I looked to my maids, feeling sorry for them. There was Anne Bassett and Catherine Howard, of course, and another called Katherine Carey I recognised by name and face now too. In time, I found this girl was the daughter of Mary Boleyn, and also, possibly, the daughter of the King.

Katherine was an exquisite girl, blessed with fair hair that had a touch of red fire in it. Her skin was pale, almost translucent, and her features pleasing. With her wide-set eyes and pretty, rosebud mouth, she was a beauty. She had been serving in the household of the Lady Elizabeth, her cousin, or possibly half-sister, – who was now, I reminded myself, my step-daughter – but now old enough for court, Katherine had been brought to Greenwich.

Another was Mary Norris, who was not as pretty as Katherine, but by no means ill-favoured. One of the requisites of being a maid of honour or lady of court, as I had by that time worked out, was that you were pleasing to look upon. Later, I found out all the maids and ladies were chosen by the King himself, so they were, in truth, all women he thought attractive, therefore it was no wonder he had found two wives from amongst his Queens' households. Mary was engaging, with sharp features, high cheekbones and large, grey eyes that reflected all the colours she looked upon, so at one moment her eyes were blue, another green, or even gold.

Some days later, I learned that Mary's father had been Henry Norris, one of the men executed with Anne Boleyn. Mary's brother had recently regained some of their father's lands and estates, and Mary had been brought to court to demonstrate her family were in favour again. She had been the ward of the Duke of Norfolk since the death of her father.

It seemed many relatives of people who had died as traitors were at court, no matter what their kin had been up to in the past. I found this curious. Was it a sign of the King's generosity, that he would not hold all of a family accountable for the crimes of one member, or was it because he wanted to keep an eye on people who sprang from a traitorous graft of a family tree?

I glanced back at some of my women walking behind me with dignity, meaning to have a word with Mistress Stoner, the Mother of the Maids. She was a gentle lady who nonetheless had some strength in her soul, I could see that. I hoped she would take care of these young girls. It seemed few others did.

The household was explained to me as we went along by Jane Rochford, through Olisleger. The maids of honour were the lowest rank of the 'above stairs' women of my household aside from chamberers, whose task it was to clean and tidy.

"What is, 'above stairs'?" I asked, baffled.

Jane Rochford smiled. 'Above stairs', she explained, was the area surrounding the Privy Chamber. "Maids are to be up early with the light of dawn, to oversee chamberers as they light fires and clean away pallet beds where your women will sleep when in your chamber, Majesty. They are overseen by Mistress Stoner and by ladies-in-waiting, such as myself. The Lord Chamberlain and Vice-Chamberlain are officially at the head of our branch of this tree of court, but the maids will get their day-to-day orders from the great women of your chambers." Jane grinned. "The men are, of course, too important to concern themselves with your girls… unless the maids do something wrong."

She went on to explain that the Chamberlain and Vice-Chamberlain ensured the household ran smoothly, in keeping with the sacred, royal dignity of the King and Queen. Below stairs, another phrase I needed explained – what was so important to the English about stairs? – the Lord Steward ruled, and he was responsible for domestic staff and their tasks.

He kept the four masters of the household in check, as well as the controller, the master of jewels, the King's fools, the cooks, the groom of the stool and children who toiled in the squillery.

"What is this word?" I asked, thinking it had quite a charming sound to it.

"The squillery is where all the plates, dishes and goblets are stored and cleansed, Majesty," said Jane.

To my amusement I learned that technically the Duke of Norfolk, as Lord Treasurer, came under the mastery of the Lord Steward, but since he was a duke, and one of the men of the King's Privy Chamber, he was also *above* the Lord Steward. It sounded quite confounding.

"I am sure it will become clear to me in time," I said.

"The Lord Steward caters for the needs of court," Olisleger translated as we walked. "He decides when everyone eats, what they eat, and sees to charitable giving. It is custom here to always leave something in the dishes granted to you at each meal, for it is given to the poor, so it is thought if you eat all of it, it is not only greedy, but uncharitable. You must lead this custom here, so your women ape you in it, Majesty."

"I understand."

"Your ladies will each day help you to wash and dress," he went on, listening to Jane as she explained. "And the maids help them. Sometimes maids will serve when you eat, my lady, but mostly they will fetch napkins and pots of ale, bring them to your ladies, and your ladies will serve you. The ladies and maids are here to look after you all day and night, Majesty, so if you wish they will sing or dance for you or read from the Bible." He smiled as Jane Rochford said something evidently amusing.

"What makes you smile?" I asked.

"The Boleyn Viscountess tells me they have all learned *Cent*, Majesty, making sure all in the house know the rules, as they heard you enjoyed the game in Calais. They have also gathered small purses to aid their playing, or perhaps their losing at the game, since they have heard you are quite the master of the cards."

I smiled. That was a sweet touch indeed.

"There is another game, called Primero, which is popular here."

"Tell my women they will teach it to me," I said.

We came through the outer chamber, and I watched all of my women curtseying in turn to the empty throne on the dais, a custom they had apparently been observing in my absence. *My throne*, I thought, and a shudder went through my heart. Suddenly, I had no wish to be a Queen, no matter the honour.

"If the King and his men come," Olisleger said, as Jane Rochford and Margaret Douglas took us along a gallery from the Queen's Presence Chamber to the Privy Chamber, "your women are to do whatever is asked of them to amuse him. When His Majesty is here, it is his desire the court follows, so if the King calls for music, they play, if for dancing, they dance. Your women will make polite conversation with his men, they are trained to be engaging."

*I suppose it is also what I have come here to do,* I thought. *If this King wishes for this, I will do it, if for that, I perform it.* The trouble was, I could not wish myself, nor with any training could make myself, more pleasing to his eyes. *You can do much else,* I told myself. *There is more worth to a woman than merely beauty, and you are not ugly.*

I wondered why the King thought me so, why he had also, as I had heard, remarked to his men that I did not smell pleasing. It was odd in a way, for he was not pleasing to the eyes, was in truth far more displeasing than I could ever be, and he smelt worse, to my nose at least, than any smell coming from me.

*You are a mirror to him,* said the voice. *When you failed to recognise him, you became a mirror in which he sees all his faults, all the base flattery of the fools about him. He looked into your eyes and saw himself, finally, after so many years of fooling himself. He did not like what he saw.*

Perhaps the voice was right, and if I was a mirror to the King then all these faults he plucked out about me, all these things he had criticised which no one else had mentioned, were in truth not my faults. They were his. I was a reflection, a projection, of all he feared about himself.

This did not make me feel any better about my situation, but it did explain a few things.

There was much to see, walking from one magnificent room to another. The perfume of rosemary, lavender and mint rose from rush mats on the floor, and from the walls wafted a mild scent of vinegar, so I ascertained they had been washed fresh for my arrival. The rooms were explained to me. The Presence Chamber was where I would sit each day when petitioners came begging for my aid, but only my household were allowed into my private rooms, the Privy and Bedchamber. Not many were permitted into these intimate chambers, I was told and was glad of it. Perhaps it was not exactly like the Frauenzimmer, but this restriction allowed some semblance of privacy. There were differences, for there were men in here. Men guarded the doorways, restricting access to each inner chamber. The palaces, Jane explained, had been built and arranged to offer privacy to the royal family. Public rooms were separated from private ones by galleries, keeping prying eyes and ears at bay.

"Here is where your food will be brought up, Majesty," Jane said as we stood in one of the galleries. "Men will bring it from the kitchens, and give it to your maids here, at the doors to the Privy Chamber. The same will happen with clothes ordered from Your Majesty's wardrobe. Your maids will clean them each week, ridding furs of moths and other insects, but they always check them carefully when they come into their hands here."

"I am well taken care of, I see," I said.

As we walked along the gallery, Margaret Douglas indicated to a chamber. "In here, is the little chapel; a private room with an altar and a *prie-dieu* for Your Majesty to pray in each morning. Your ladies will hear Mass here with you, Majesty, during the day. Only in the morning and evening will you need to go to chapel, unless you decide otherwise."

"How many times is it customary to hear Mass each day?" I asked. Twice had been the norm in Cleves.

"It depends how many times you wish to hear it, Majesty," said Jane. "Some Queens have heard it twice, or three times. Katherine of Aragon sometimes heard Mass ten times in a day."

I smiled. "I think we will not need to hear it so many times," I said. "I have trust in the goodness of my women, and I do not think they will need to be so often in church to keep them virtuous."

"The Queen's priests and chaplain are not supposed to come into the inner chambers," said Margaret Douglas, looking relieved about what I had said about Mass, "for they are not part of the Privy Chamber staff. There is a separate space for them in the gallery, here, where they may talk to you. On saints' days there will be a grand procession from your rooms to the chapel, where you will meet the King and hear Mass in public. All other days, it will be more intimate, with less ceremony."

Olisleger translated this for me, and I nodded. "This is acceptable," I said.

"Your lady Margaret Douglas says that it is your women's task to make sure no one is in here that should not be. They are all signed in and out, so there are always the correct number of ladies and maids waiting upon you, Majesty. The same is done in the King's chambers."

"And my women are paid?" I asked.

"The ladies and maids of honour have a generous sum per annum, but other gifts come as well, from you, Majesty, and it is expected that you will offer them from time to time; combs, fans, handkerchiefs and even cast-off gowns from your wardrobe. Most go to ladies of the Bed and Privy Chambers, but even maids or chamberers sometimes get something, if they please you."

I nodded, trying to keep all this straight in my mind. There was much to remember here.

"The King is apparently most fastidious, so your chamberers are instructed to clear and tidy often, so no plates are left. The ladies..." – here Olisleger wrinkled his nose a little – "... some of them have lapdogs, which might try to make a mess on the floor. The maids and chamberers are to ensure this does not happen."

Into another set of rooms we wandered. Greenwich Palace was vast, a long and winding maze of corridors and rooms. I felt a little dizzy trying to remember all the turns we had taken to get here and was sure I would be entirely lost on my own. The palace was also dazzling, painted in many bright colours, with glaring gilt shimmering from the ceilings and walls and even around windows. Tapestry covered almost every wall in the royal apartments, and in my new chambers was a set depicting scenes from the life of King David.

"Most of this particular set hang in the King's chambers," Olisleger told me as I stood dumbfounded before this work of glory, with threads of gold, silver, azure and crimson running through it. "But the King ordered these moved here, to please you, Majesty."

This set depicted King David spying on the maiden Bathsheba as she bathed, the event which had sparked his quest to take her as his wife. It was stunning, but was, I thought, an unusual choice for the chambers of a woman. I wondered if the King thought himself David and me Bathsheba, or if this was supposed to titillate me. In all honesty, it left me a little cold. I never had liked that particular story of David. In many other ways I thought him an upstanding man, a wise King, so to hear of him spying on a naked woman when she was unaware of it tarnished my good notions of him. *It is like the King,* a whisper said in my mind. *So many have a good opinion of him, because they do not care to see the worst in him.*

*If only that was the worst*, I thought. From all the stories I had heard, there was much worse in the King than being like the Tom who peeped upon Lady Godiva in the tales Sybylla had told me.

Sybylla... with one thought of her I was homesick again, and it was an odd thing for she was no more at home. Perhaps I was sickening for the company of those I knew and loved, rather than a place.

As we walked, my eyes darted from wonder to wonder: ornamented ceilings, with balls and ribs flanked by octagons and lozenge shapes enclosing escutcheons shimmering with gilt paint and shockingly bright reds, blues and greens; heraldic beasts, glimmering gold and entwined with lovers' knots; entire suites decked out in livid green and stark white, or royal purple and sense-shocking crimson. There were halls upon halls lined with cupboards the size of oxen which held plate in gold, pewter, silver and gilt, hangings about beds dripping with pearls so thick they rattled when we passed by, and chairs upholstered in velvet, in hues of gold, ruby, cerulean, jade and shimmering silver.

It was enough to make the eyes water. My father's palaces had been, I thought, opulent, but this palace was so sumptuous it was almost garish. My ladies from Cleves were staring in open-mouthed wonder at the richness surrounding us.

In my chambers, chairs were scarce, but there were more there, Jane Rochford told us, than in the King's rooms. Chairs were generally for women, for they were weaker and needed to sit down more, we were told, but there were many bright, plump cushions by the fire, which pleased me. That touch reminded me of home.

There were a few tables, but not many, for most were used only for eating, or playing cards, and were not set in pride of place, since they were functional items, but were packed up and stowed away at the edge of the room, taken out only when needed. I was shown a beautiful writing desk and was told it was to be mine, for writing to the King when he was away, or to my family. A swan-feather quill sat waiting for me, and I stroked a finger to it, feeling a wash of homesickness so strong I could have drowned.

I started to feel tired. All I wanted was to close my eyes just to be surrounded by blissful darkness. It was all a little much, a little trying on the eyes, a little too much for the nose, a touch too much for the senses.

Even my closed stool, a privy just for the Queen, was ridiculously magnificent. I had never seen the like before. It was a privy covered in black velvet, the seat and sides stuffed with down. Large gilt nails held material to the seat, and from it there wafted a rather pleasing smell. Clearly herbs were being crushed and thrown into it each day. It looked like a throne, and I felt almost nervous to think of sitting on it.

I was quite stupefied by the riches I saw, and if this was true of rooms and furnishings, it was equally true of the courtiers. I could see them walking below from a gallery leading out from my rooms, from windows which looked out onto the great park. Ladies' gowns, resplendent in white, scarlet, azure and emerald whispered on fresh rush matting as they walked by me in my rooms. Noblemen in silks, velvets, cambric and damask, with swords and daggers at their sides, were like a flock of peacocks strutting about the gardens and halls, their tapered waists, padded chests and huge, almost embarrassing, codpieces jutting out before them, glittering with gemstones to draw the eye. Perfume rode the air along with the scent of rushes and herbs crushed underfoot, yet under those sweet smells crept the rank stench of sweat, piss and dog shit. *It is like the King*, I thought, he was covered in gems and gold and sumptuous cloth, in perfume and scent, to disguise all he was trying to hide underneath.

"They are all so rich," I said to Olisleger.

"They say a man may wear an estate on his back when he comes to court," he said as we watched one man go past in the gardens below, and I marvelled at the opulence of jewels winking from his slashed sleeves. "Some lords set themselves into debt just to afford clothes rich enough in which to appear at court."

"What a strange place this court is," I murmured.

Walls blazed, plate shimmered, gilt glimmered and bright colours sang from every part of the palace and her people. It was a constant assault on the eyes. My head began to throb, looking on this gaudy show.

"Your Majesty is pleased?" asked another of my ladies, Isabella, Lady Baynton. Her husband was Sir Edward, my Vice-Chamberlain.

"I could not be more pleased," I said slowly in English.

*Or more scared,* I thought as all my women and maids smiled at me.

# Chapter Thirteen

**Greenwich Palace
London**

**January 1540**

That night there was a sumptuous feast in the great hall. I arrived dressed in one of my most becoming gowns, one of taffeta with long, flowing sleeves. On my head was a cap of lawn, adorned with pearls and jewels, and to please the King I was wearing jewelled sables he had brought to Rochester and apparently had forgotten to give me. The Duchess of Suffolk had brought them to me, explaining they were from the King.

We feasted on venison accompanied by frumenty and peacock, roasted whole and re-dressed in its own plumage. There was pottage of leeks, chicken and greens, as well as a thick cream, crab and fish stew, *mortis* of capon and almonds, thin slices of beef rolled and stuffed to resemble larks or *aloes*, as it was in French, as Olisleger explained to me, and what the English called smothered rabbits. I thought initially the creatures had been smothered to death, but was told it was so named for the wealth of sauce served upon them. There were legs of mutton laced with currants and pepper, along with salty, buttered cabbage, rice of Genoa, and fritters of leek and onion.

There were custards of all descriptions to finish, along with sugary tarts of apple, pear and damson. Roasted oranges and cream were brought out to great cheers, along with prunes in syrup, conserves of cherries, marchpane knots and white gingerbread. The English had a penchant for the sweet.

The conversation was merry, but that was because all conversation was held with my ladies, who served me. The King was hard to engage. I kept trying, however, and eventually he surrendered and talked a little to me. "Your table is fine, so many good foods, Majesty," I said. "Your people tell me you are fond of lamprey, so I must try dishes of them here."

"They are good to eat," he said.

"I hear too that you have been known to fill an entire feast fit for all at court with the skill of your arrows and sword in the hunt," I said.

"I have hunted little, of late," he said and then seemed to try to pull himself into the conversation. "But I do enjoy the hunt. 'Tis a noble pursuit."

"I do too. Although in Cleves we ladies often went along on the hunt and merely watched as the men made the kill, Majesty, it is a diversion I greatly enjoy."

For a while we managed well enough as the King launched into a tale of one of his hunts, from however many years ago I know not, and I pretended to be amazed and enthralled by his conversation. In truth, there was a great deal of hot air and boasting, and little to be amazed at. *What a bore this man is,* was a thought which floated through my mind, and I tried to eject it swiftly. What if my expression should slip and I should display such an emotion to this man? I would be thrown from court.

Yet it was true enough, for he was dull, boastful, and entirely preoccupied with himself. His conversation was all about himself, he asked no questions about me or my experiences. He seemed blithely unaware of this, however, and simply continued to rattle on, as I fought to keep my mind from wandering away. He reminded me of the old men at my father's court, telling the same old, tired stories of their glory days over and over again as the young about them rolled their eyes.

There was dancing after the feast, and although I did not dance, mainly because I knew not the steps of these dances the English performed, I watched with glee. The young women had such abandon and the men such prowess. It was a pleasing spectacle. The music was also delightful.

When I looked to the King, he too seemed intent on the dancers, and I mentioned how elegant his court was, and how it obviously took after his example. He smiled and went back to eating a dish of comfits, stuffing one after another into his mouth, not waiting until the first was chewed and swallowed before inserting another. I tried not to curl my lip in disgust. His manners at the table were well enough, but his manner of eating continuously was quite revolting to observe. There was something of the cow about him, rhythmic jaws crushing and chewing all the time. The Duchess of Suffolk, seated to one side of me, decided to take it upon herself to aid me, and pointed out some of the people there gathered.

"Lady Mary Howard…" she said, her chin jutting out almost imperceptibly towards a handsome young woman surrounded by men. The Duchess spoke softly, and I gathered the King was perhaps a little hard of hearing, for he seemed to note nothing of what she said, "… is the widow of the Duke of Richmond, the King's bastard son, and she is daughter of the Duke of Norfolk."

"I met her at Rochester?" I asked. I had met so many people, it was hard to keep them in my mind. "And she was here today?"

"Indeed, Majesty."

"She has not remarried? She looks young and popular."

"No, Majesty. She is one of the elites of your chambers and it is true she is a star of court, but she has not remarried. Since her marriage, she has been at court, and since widowhood the King has been ever more attentive, sharing her sorrow. When her husband died, their union had remained unconsummated as the King had feared to exhaust his young natural son with rigours of the bedchamber. That is frequently the case in England. Young men are often held back from engaging in sex too early as it can be damaging for their health."

"And for girls it is the same?"

"It is not, Majesty, for girls can be married at twelve and bearing children soon after, where boys must be fourteen or thereabouts. But maids suffer greensickness and men do not."

"Greensickness?"

"It is thought, if a girl does not satisfy her maiden's lot and become a wife, she will become ill, longing for the seed of a man."

I almost laughed, then realised the Duchess was in earnest, although she too looked as if this was not something she truly believed. It sounded rather like something made-up, to me, to entice credulous young women into risky behaviour.

I gazed at Mary Howard. She was a striking woman; pale cheeks and a high forehead set against a slightly flat nose. Her eyes were brown, and her hair too, but bearing a hint of red flame. She had a little mouth, perfectly shaped, like a heart. She would have had no trouble finding another husband, even had she not been the daughter of a duke.

The young bastard of the King had died in the same year as Anne Boleyn, that I knew. "Mary Howard has experienced problems in gaining her jointure." The drop in volume of the Duchess's voice to a whisper told me this was an even more sensitive subject to speak of in front of the King. "Since the match had not been consummated there was a question over its legality. The King did not want to sign over her lands and money, but her father, Norfolk, is attempting to press for her rights."

"Because they will benefit her, or him?" I asked and the Duchess laughed when this was translated to her.

"You understand Norfolk well already, it would seem, Majesty," she said. "She has many suitors," Katherine went on. "They say Cromwell wants to marry her, and Thomas Seymour, brother to our late mistress, Queen Jane, certainly has his eye on her, but Mary Howard's brother is *utterly* opposed."

"To which match?"

"Both. He thinks Cromwell too low for his sister and calls the Seymours upstarts too. He once said they were saucy fellows who crept into court under their sister's petticoats, which did not win him friends with Thomas or Edward, the elder Seymour brother."

I followed her eyes to two men, one fair and one dark. I had met them in Calais, I remembered. Count von Overstein had liked the elder but not the younger. Regarding them now, I saw they did not look as though they wanted to stand near each other, yet they made no move to escape. The younger had a high flush on his cheeks as his lips gabbled excitedly about something. The elder looked on, his eyes on the company before him. He appeared grave and calm, ignoring his brother as he sipped from a goblet of wine.

"They do not seem… as friends to each other," I said.

"They hate each other," Katherine said.

"But they are brothers."

"Brothers often resent each other, Majesty. Thomas hates Edward for being older, taking all the spoils. He thinks Edward is rewarded for his age, but our serious Seymour is cleverer than naughty Seymour. Edward is cautious about Thomas. He feels him nipping at his heels, panting for him to fall so he might slip into his position at court. He knows Thomas is reckless. That kind of fear leaves no man feeling secure, and insecurity is dangerous. It makes people vicious."

"The younger is pleasing to look upon," I said.

"And knows it well," Katherine said, scorn in her voice. "Thomas Seymour is trouble for women, Majesty, especially if they are lower than he in status. The chamberers and kitchen girls *all* have stories about his wandering hands and forceful ways."

"But he remains at court?"

"The King finds him amusing, at times."

I looked back to Mary Howard. She was twenty or thereabouts I thought, a woman of great learning, and a poet in her own right, the Duchess told me. Perhaps not as talented as her brother, the Earl of Surrey, who was also a poet, Katherine informed me, but Mary's verse was nonetheless respected at court. I thought of Amalia, having to hide her efforts at poetry, and was sad for my sister suddenly. Here a woman could write, and although I supposed she would still have to take care what she wrote, there was a little more freedom. I cast my eyes to the Earl, her brother, who was not far away, also making people laugh. A witty family, it seemed. "You will not see his wife," said the Duchess. "For she is in the country, preparing to birth their fourth child."

"A blessed union," I said.

"To her side, in the green and white, is Lady Margaret Douglas, who you have of course met," said Katherine.

I had, but she was worth another look, and besides I still did not have all names straight in my mind. There were a great deal of women who all owned the same name in England, *so* many Katherines, for instance, and others whose names were most similar to one another, so it was good to fix their faces in my memory. Margaret Douglas, evidently a great friend of Mary Howard's if one were to judge by their closeness, was another arresting looking woman. She had a long, sharp nose, slightly hooked at the end, a common Tudor trait I had noted from the King and portraits of his family, and sparkling eyes. Her mouth was large and wide, seductive and sweet, and her face was pale, long and elegant. The Duchess said she resembled her mother, Princess Margaret Tudor, sister of the King and once Queen of Scotland, who was a beauty, or had been in youth. "At court, you are to address her as 'Your Highness', or 'Your Grace'," said Katherine, "for in England she is considered a princess."

"You say, 'in England'," I noted. "How can she be a princess here and not elsewhere?"

"Her mother was Princess Margaret of England, Queen of Scotland," she said. "But the Princess was born to her mother's second marriage, after her mother's first husband the King of Scots died. Margaret's father was Archibald Douglas, Earl of Angus. In Scotland, Margaret is not considered a princess because of her father's blood, but as she is the daughter of an English princess, here she is royalty, and therefore one of the six most important women in Your Majesty's household."

I nodded for I knew a little of this princess. Her mother had fled to England when her father had faced trouble in Scotland. Threatened by the King of Scotland, Angus had sent his wife to England to seek sanctuary. As an infant, Margaret had lived in the house of Cardinal Wolsey, and later with her cousin, the then Princess Mary, who since her father had abandoned her mother had become the Lady Mary, daughter of the King. Margaret had spent time in France after her father snatched her from her mother but had returned to England in adulthood. She had been recently offered to the Emperor as a potential bride in an attempt to stop him from forming a permanent alliance with France. The Emperor had not been enthused, so we had heard in Cleves. Margaret was not high enough for him to consider as his Empress.

She was close to the English throne, however, therefore a valuable prize in marriage, and had served as a lady-in-waiting before. I remembered her as waiting on Queen Anne. "She has recently been imprisoned, house arrest, but was released and returned to court," said the Duchess.

"Imprisoned? For what was she imprisoned?"

Margaret, I was told, had got into trouble by falling in love with one of the Howard family, a cousin of Queen Anne Boleyn. They had been detained for this. He had died in the Tower, and she had been released upon promising better behaviour, presumably meaning she would no more dare to fall in love, and had been brought to court to demonstrate her restoration to the affections of the King.

"What of Lady Baynton?" I asked, looking to another woman of my household, another of the greater ladies.

"Isabella is a good woman; her husband is strict with the household, though, perhaps a little too much so. She is half-sister to one of your maids, too…" the Duchess looked about the throng and inclined her head towards the Howard child I had noted before. She was standing with friends, giggling. I almost smiled; they looked so innocent. "Catherine Howard."

"She seems too young for court," I said. "Though a merry little soul."

"She is of age, Majesty, fourteen or fifteen, I believe. Catherine was raised in the household of her grandmother, the dowager of Norfolk."

"So, she too is kin to the Duke of Norfolk? He has many relatives here."

"The Howards are a large family, it is true."

"And what of the King's children?"

"There, in the crimson gown with the high neck is the Lady Mary Tudor, daughter of the King and Katherine of Aragon," said Katherine, indicating to a lady standing within a group of women. They looked as if they were guarding her. "She has been hiding from court, it was said she was ill, but she often seems to become ill when a suitor is suggested for her. I would expect her to vanish again soon enough, for there is talk of a marriage between her and your brother of Cleves, Majesty, another way to secure peace between our countries."

That was something I had heard nothing of. As far as I had been informed my brother was to wed the niece of the King of France.

Lady Mary had the look of a tired warrior, one who has seen too much death. I could see why people had called her pretty, but her prettiness had been stolen away by stress and care. She wore crimson velvet and silk, the edge of her gown trimmed with pearls. French sleeves of silver graced her arms and brushed fingers bearing gold rings, with gems of agate and diamond glittering from them, catching the lamplight. A large, obvious cross hung at her neck, set with emeralds, matching a brooch of the same stone on her breast. She looked magnificent in her dress, but her eyes were shadowed underneath, deep and dark, making her face look hollow, haunted almost. There were lines about her eyes and mouth more at home on a woman twice her age. She was only twenty-three or four, almost the same age as me, but Mary seemed aged. She stood awkwardly, uncomfortable in the company, keeping close to her group of women as though afraid of men, something I could understand. Her hair was a dark russet, and her body small and slim. There was much to recommend her, but those eyes betrayed great pain. Lady Mary looked as though the cares of the world and his wife rested on her slim shoulders.

"She submitted to the will of her father, admitted her mother's marriage to the King was false, and has dutifully accepted him as Head of the Church," said the Duchess. "It cost her dear, for she adored her mother, but her father is the King, and what he wants he will have."

I had heard Mary loved her mother more than anyone and I knew too that for a long time the princess had defied the King along with her mother. Having to surrender and betray her mother like that, the Duchess was right to say it had cost her. Some acts in life strip soul from us, just a little, but enough to sting, always.

I looked to the King, who had wandered off to talk to Katherine's husband, Brandon. "Your husband is older than you," I mentioned.

"More than twenty years," she said and smiled. "You will hear from others, so I may as well be the first to tell you, my Charles had a rather complicated marital life, truth be told. Engaged to this woman, then that, and then he married Princess Mary, younger sister of the King. There was a great scandal. She was the Dowager of France at the time. The French King had died, some said for her dancing and bedding the old man to death. Charles went to France to send our King's sorrows and escort her home, and there they were secretly married. Mary Tudor had loved him all her life, you see, and there was a secret promise between her and her brother that if she married once as he wanted, she would be able to choose her second husband. They say the Princess knew her brother would go back on his word and marry her to another foreign prince, and thinking she had done her duty by marrying where he chose the first time, she followed her heart the second and wed Charles."

"I wonder the Duke dared," I said. "He must have known the risks."

Katherine chuckled as Olisleger translated. "Charles was talked into the match so fast he did not stop to consider that the King would be enraged when he found out. The Princess was a clever woman, and she knew him well, so she knew how to convince him. Charles was talked into marriage, some even say he was tricked, but he loved her too, that I know. The King was his great friend, they were raised together, love each other well, but all the same, you are right it was a grand risk. But with time, and a great deal of money paid to the King, they were forgiven. The Princess died some years ago. They had two sons, but they are gone now too, sadly. Charles married me, a love match, and we have children, none destined for the succession of course, but my husband had daughters with the Princess. They are likely to be included, especially if they bear sons, after the King's children." She dropped a little dainty to her pet dog, which, as she had informed me with an impish cast to her eyes, was named Gardiner, after one of the King's highest men, a bishop no less. It was not meant to honour the Bishop, but to playfully insult him.

One might wonder how she dared. Katherine also had a salon of women who talked on faith and politics, and who sponsored promising scholars in the great universities of England. I had learned Mary Howard was prominent amongst the women of the Duchess's salon, but there was also Anne Herbert, Elizabeth Tyrwhitt and Lady Jane Dudley, wife of my Master of Horse. Katherine was a reformer, some whispered a Lutheran, and despite the King's aversion to such people she was in high favour. It would seem an impossible mix, but seeing how the King looked at her, I knew how she dared. He had great affection for her, lust perhaps too, and if one had the eye of the King resting on them in a favourable way, it seemed one could do anything in England.

"And that, of course, is Jane Boleyn, Lady Rochford," said the Duchess, an edge of something – dislike? – creeping into her tone.

"Am I wrong in thinking she is unpopular at court?" I asked.

"She is the Dowager Viscountess of Rochford, once married to George Boleyn." The Duchess's voice dropped even lower, and I ascertained the names of the dead Boleyns were not to be mentioned at court.

"Lady Rochford is Cromwell's pet," Katherine whispered. "Some say, when her husband and sister-in-law fell, she offered him evidence to use against them, and some say she did nothing of the kind, but tried to protect them, but since she was sent money by Cromwell soon after, and he helped her to retain her estates and got her a position at court in the household of Queen Jane, I think those who suspect the former are more likely to be correct. No one likes her."

"Because she betrayed family?" I asked.

"That is one reason, although plenty at court have done the same or worse. The true reason is everyone knows she works for Cromwell. She is his creature, but she does not seem to like him. It is hard, therefore, to know which side she is on, but even those who want Cromwell reduced in power would not work with her. She is slippery. An eel about court. Be wary of what you say to her, Majesty."

"Cromwell supported my marriage," I pointed out.

"Cromwell supports Cromwell, all others are as dust to him."

Jane Boleyn moved gracefully. She was beautiful, with those wide-set green eyes, a pretty mouth and pale skin. A large cross of diamonds with three large pearls suspended from it hung at her throat. Her nose was small, her figure glorious. Her gown was intricate, in various hues of green, making her eyes even brighter, but as I watched, I saw she was allowed to the edge of circles of courtiers, but not within. There was no move to exclude her, but people made no effort to talk to her. She was always just outside the company, always a stranger. I felt a spike of pity break in my heart.

Her father was Henry Parker, Lord Morely, a famous scholar and translator, Katherine told me. Jane had joined the court in her youth, and like many present that night had not left. In youth she had been favoured by the King and Katherine of Aragon, chosen for pageants and dances, for she danced gracefully and was a beautiful creature. When she was married to George Boleyn some thirteen years ago or so, the couple had been in high favour, granted income by the King and stewardship over a range of royal houses. George Boleyn had become Lord Rochford, and Jane a lady-in-waiting to Queen Anne with a husband set to inherit the earldoms of Ormonde and Wiltshire. That inheritance had come to an end when George had been arrested and executed, but Jane had served Queen Jane later, and now served me.

"But you say some think she tried to save her husband?" I asked.

"Some say she went begging to Cromwell and the King, but no one knows the truth. She might have given evidence under duress, many did, or she might have volunteered it as a means to save her own skin."

"There," she said, evidently trying to change the subject, "Is the poet, Sir Thomas Wyatt."

He was a tall, handsome man with a thick beard and bright, dark eyes. He alone talked to Jane Boleyn. "*He* speaks to her," I said.

"He is Cromwell's pet, too, another in our Chancellor's debt. Wyatt was imprisoned with the Boleyns, and some said was to lose his head for it, but Cromwell spoke for him and he was released. Now, he is sent to other courts to spy on princes for Cromwell. But he is a poet, too." Her voice dropped so low I barely heard her next whisper. "He was once in love with… another Anne," she murmured. "And it was said she loved him, too. They were friends as children, and when she came to court he tried to make her his mistress. He even challenged the King for her once, over a game of bowls."

"And that is Cromwell?" I asked, changing the subject, looking at a man in a dark doublet of russet with a black cloak pinned to his shoulders. I had met him but briefly, this advocate of my marriage and the downfall of that of the first Queen Anne.

"It is," said Katherine. "He is far off; how did you know that was him?"

"He seems important, without making effort to make himself appear so."

We could little see him from where we were, but I had gathered an impression from my brief encounter with him. The man was fleshy, broad of shoulder, and had the look of one who in his youth had been athletic, but any muscle of youth had run to fat in age. His waist bulged with excess of wine and lack of exercise. I would have placed his age somewhere around fifty-five, but the lines on his face made him seem older. When we had met, I had noted that Cromwell's eyes were dark, reddened and a little swollen about the rims, but sharp and intent. His nose was prominent, bulbous at the end, his lips thin, and a delicate shade of pink. Like the King, a second chin rested under his first and his skin was pale, the mark of a man who spends more time inside than in fresh air. Richly dressed he was that night, with a golden chain of office about his neck, a large pearl pinned to his chest which winked in the candlelight, and plenty of gold rings glittering on his hands. He managed to appear subtly dressed and extravagant at the same moment. He affected humility, which did not quite work, for everything about him was ostentatious.

He had an awkward gait, and did not look bright or merry, but that altered as he spoke. It was like watching another man come to life. As he conversed with his servant, a smile spread up his face, lightening those swarthy features. Suddenly, the grim man became pleasant, his smile roguish, charming.

"That is he," she said. "The great Cromwell. No man but the King is richer. Some say he is wealthier than even Norfolk and my husband."

"I hear he was low born."

Katherine chuckled. "His father was an innkeeper, so they say, of Putney, and once a farrier in the King's father's army at Bosworth. Cromwell trained as a lawyer and worked as a hired soldier in France and Italy. He is of common blood, there is no denying it, but the King cannot do without him, even if he does not like him all the time."

I turned my head and lifted an eyebrow.

"He hits Cromwell," she said. "Boxes his ears, slaps him as though he were a dog. When the King loves him, he will listen to no one else, and when he does not, His Majesty treats him like a serf. He is your ally, though, Majesty, at the moment at least. He supported the match with Cleves and rests hope upon it for the future of England. Many cannot trust Cromwell, but within reason you may be able to rely on him."

"I will take no side on religion," I said, and the Duchess looked faintly disappointed, although oddly pleased at the same time.

"Then you should know, Cromwell is part of the reformist faction. He hopes that you, from a land with Lutheran sympathies, will drive forth further reformation in England." She looked to the other side of the hall. "And Bishop Gardiner, who with Norfolk leads the conservative faction, holds the same hope, for your land, we are told, is officially Catholic. They are both waiting to find out what your stance on faith will be. Each hopes you will offer them support. But if you wish to please the King, I advise you to stay out of politics, as Queen Jane did, or did most of the time."

"The Queen tried to interfere?"

"Once, during the Pilgrimage of Grace, Queen Jane sorrowed for the rebels and pleaded for mercy for them. It was her natural place as Queen to do so, but the King told her to desist." She cast her eyes about, and leaned in to whisper. "He told her not to interfere, for the Queen before her had meddled with politics and that had been her downfall."

"That was the reason... a Queen fell?"

Katherine's face became wary. "It is better not to speak of such things. But many say that was the way of it."

I looked at Gardiner, he whom Katherine's dog was named after. The Bishop of Winchester was in dark robes, his face blank of expression. He, like Cromwell, had a fat face, folds of skin hanging loose and baggy about his chin. His eyes were large, like a hare, but set deep into his face, and his eyebrows were high, as though he was always asking a question, although when they furrowed, which was often, they plunged deep. He had a hooked, hawkish nose and wide nostrils. His mouth was small and his hands large. Gardiner was an odd-looking man, and I did not warm to him. I had the impression few did.

"Gardiner and Cromwell served as youths in the household of Cardinal Wolsey," said Katherine, sipping her wine. "But after his fall, they became enemies, on opposing sides of the religious divide."

"More men who are enemies," I said.

"Indeed. They cannot stand each other, either."

"Do most enemies not repulse one another?"

"Between some enemies there may be respect, odd though it might sound. They might hate each other but hold some respect for one another. That is not the case here."

"Oh?"

"Cromwell used to taunt Gardiner openly, but when Gardiner defended the King against the Pope, and did good work in France he was welcomed home and became important. Cromwell did not like that. They are as opposed in character as in policy. Cromwell is cold as a pond in winter, never loses his composure, whereas Gardiner abandons all control continually, spluttering and choking as if in a fit of apoplexy if he thinks a man has insulted him. Near to Cromwell is Cranmer, Archbishop of Canterbury, who you have of course met. He is a good man, gentle and surprisingly naïve, but with great skill in writing. The King trusts him completely. Many say His Majesty loves him as no other man."

"I liked him when we met."

Cranmer looked young. I could have taken a guess he was twenty-nine or thirty, although I had been told he was forty-six. Clean-shaven, with soft brown eyes and long, pale fingers clasped about a cup of wine, he spoke gently to people about him.

"Gardiner hates Cranmer too, and once accused him of heresy," said Katherine. "But the King spoke for the Archbishop. Gardiner's temper is unpredictable, but he is the brains of the conservative faction."

"There is a sweet face," I said, trying to avoid further perilous talk. I nodded to a handsome young man at the King's elbow. "I met him, too, at Calais. Someone told me he was a favourite of my husband's."

"Thomas Culpepper," said the Duchess. "A sweet face indeed, and a desire under it to break the hearts of all the women at court, Majesty."

"He is a… what do the English say? A rake or libertine?"

"A charming one."

Culpepper was richly dressed that night, showing off fine, muscular thighs in tight stockings and a graceful, long body in his doublet. His face was perfectly formed, graceful angles and high cheekbones, a long but not overlarge nose, and sparkling eyes, full of mischief. There was some wildness in him, I could see it, but to my eyes he looked so young. I was not much older than him, if I indeed was, but to me he looked young of mind. I do not mean he was simple, but there was something in his air of a boy who never did grow up.

"He is a great favourite of the King's, indeed," Katherine went on, "owns property in Kent and a townhouse in Greenwich." She put a hand on my arm. "Although I am most fond of him, I should tell you he is a great flirt and showers many women with attention, some true but much false. Many a poor maid has lost her heart and head over him, but he has lost his to no one. He is one of those men all women stare at and adore; a man born to break hearts but never risk his own."

"That is most sad, for him," I said and looked to see many of my maids staring at this young man with admiration. Catherine Howard in particular could not keep her eyes from him.

"For him?" asked the Duchess.

"Of a certainty for him," I said. "One who never risks never can win, they only can lose. It will catch up with him in the end, the loneliness of the state he chooses out of fear."

"Fear?"

"One who never risks their own heart, their own feelings, this is a person who fears love. They hide from it, ignore it, thinking that will keep them safe, but it cuts deep in its own way, never allowing the person to understand the glorious highs and terrible lows which are possible when one is brave enough to love."

Katherine was looking at me a little oddly. "What is it?" I asked in English.

"They said you lived a sheltered life, Majesty," she said. "The people who told you of us."

"I did, the Frauenzimmer and my father's court, then my brother's were vastly more restricted than the English court."

"Yet you seem worldly, wise to the ways of the world, the hearts of men and women."

I smiled. "One man could meet all people of the world, every soul who walks on this earth, and yet know nothing of them if he pays no attention," I said. "And one woman could have met few, yet know much, having paid attention to each and every one."

Katherine smiled back at me. "We will have to keep an eye on you, Majesty," she said in a manner most friendly. "You are a lady who sees all."

"No one need fear the eyes of a friend on them," I said, "and I have no enemies here."

There was a fleeting expression on the Duchess's face, which seemed to say I had foes, or would have soon enough, but she smiled only wider. "Of course, Majesty," she said.

## Chapter Fourteen

**Greenwich Palace
London**

**January 1540**

The wedding was due to take place the next day, but when I rose I was informed, via a great deal of unwieldy hand signals and bizarre facial expressions, that there had been a delay.

"For what reason?" I asked, but my women all stared at me blankly, since I was speaking High German. I sighed. It was so easy to forget that they could not understand me.

My translator was not present, for this conversation was taking place in my bedroom, whilst I was dressing, but I tried again. "Why?" I asked, in English this time.

It was hard for me to understand what was said next. But in a jumble of many ladies all trying to explain something at once, I heard the word, "Lorraine."

"Lorraine?" I asked and they all nodded as though I was a genius. I certainly wished for higher power of the mind, for what followed I did not comprehend at all.

In the absence of my wedding dress, Mary Howard and Margaret Douglas tried, and failed, to get me to wear a French gown that morn, but although I admired it, it was too revealing for me at that time. I was not yet wed and felt I should not abandon the clothes of my homeland until I was. When married, when truly a woman of this land as well as my homeland I could try other clothes, but until that time I was officially still Anna of Cleves, not England. They tried again to get me to bathe in full, but I refused a bath and washed my hands and face and allowed a wet cloth to be passed over the rest of me. Jane Rochford kept trying to throw perfume on me, and I moved away, but little Catherine Howard gave me a golden ball, called a pomander, which I liked very much. The scent inside the ball was subtler, musk and ambergris, than the noxious perfume they kept trying to cover me with. Many of the people of court were so highly scented I had trouble standing near them without feeling a little faint.

When finally I was let out to see my translator, being by that time dressed, although not for my wedding, Olisleger explained the King had brought up my old pre-contract with the son of the Duke of Lorraine and was delaying the marriage until he was sure I was free to marry. "I thought all this was settled months ago, before we departed Cleves?" I asked, a squeak of nervousness entering my voice.

"The King states he but wishes to be sure that we are doing all right by you, my lady," he said. "If you went through a form of marriage thence to a marriage bed, then it was found out your pre-contract was still valid, you would have committed adultery with the King."

I was fairly sure that whatever this delay was, it was not being done so all was right with me. "Let the King have all the information he requires from my men," I said, trying to control the hammering of my heart. "I want his mind at rest about our marriage, but ensure he understands, I *am* free to wed, and I *am* now in his country. It would be a disgrace, surely, a high insult to Cleves, to my brother and me to leave me unmarried much longer. I am promised to be his Queen and have come here in all good faith that this will go ahead."

My ambassadors told us the King had asked for documents proving the betrothal was null and void to be presented before the wedding. The ambassadors did not have them.

"We did not think them needed, my lady," Carl Harst explained, looking both fraught and irritated. "The English are a very strange people, for the King brushed over this matter months ago with ease. He accepted our word and your brother's that the engagement between you and the Duke of Bar was null and void, but now seems to want proof. We have offered to stay as his hostages here, until the matter is resolved, but all of us have sworn, upon all our property, our titles and our souls, that it is no more an issue. We have even told him it was not in any way a true contract in the first place, for you never formally agreed to the match."

"Do all you can," I said. "I can ask no more of you than that."

That afternoon, as my ladies sang for me and tried to amuse me with games, a messenger came to the door. When he came before me and recited his message, Olisleger frowned. "What does he say?" I asked.

"Apparently you, my lady, must go before the Privy Council and make unto them a solemn declaration that you are free to marry."

I stared at him a while, baffled and not a little frightened by this nonsense, but I nodded. "I am free to declare myself so," I said.

In trooped the Council, and with the aid of my translator, the declaration was made.

*

By the next afternoon, I still was unwed and was growing increasingly concerned. I was not sure what honour and duty meant to the English, but for the sake of my dignity, my country's dignity and my maiden state, I should not still be here and be unmarried.

"The King does not like me," I said to Olisleger.

"Even if he did not, Majesty," he said. "Which we by no means know for certain, he cannot refuse to marry you now. It has been agreed, you are here, in his country, sent on the agreement of marriage and in perfect trust. No prince has ever refused a bride in such a manner. Your brother would make war, like as not, and I have no doubt your sister's husband would aid him. Your brother might even join forces with the Emperor, as unlikely as that sounds, for you are a Duchess of the Holy Roman Empire, and such an insult to the Emperor's people would give the Emperor the excuse the English believe he long has wanted to act against the King and revenge his aunt."

I was not so sure about that, but then, suddenly Harst brought news. I was to be married the next morn.

It was the 6th of January when I came to the altar at last. This royal wedding was not to be a grand occasion, I had been told, but most of the King's and other royalty's nuptials had not been. In England they were private affairs. The only exception had been the wedding of Prince Arthur and Katherine of Aragon. Since my wedding was taking place on Twelfth Night, the Epiphany, gross celebrations would be seen as ungodly in any case, even if it were not for the excruciatingly obvious reservations of my groom. It was clear to me the delay had been an attempt to get out of marrying me.

We rose early, for the wedding was due to start at eight of the morning. My gown, a beautiful creation of cloth of gold covered with embroidered flowers crafted from pearls, was glorious. Like the others, it had no train, leaving Margaret Douglas, my official trainbearer, with nothing to hold. "We do not wear such things in Cleves," I tried to tell her, but she still looked disgruntled.

My long hair, shining fair and bright after being combed a hundred times, was loose and topped with a small coronet, glimmering with diamonds and pearls, to demonstrate my purity. About my throat was a collar necklace shimmering with jewels. Count von Overstein came to the door to give me away in place of my brother. He looked anxious, as though expecting the King might send word of another delay.

"Calmly, my lord," I said to him as I took his arm. We were already late for the ceremony, but I had wanted to look my best.

"These English," he said as we started walking. "They are quite odd, my lady."

"I am sure we appear so to them, too, my lord," I said.

"If your brother were here, there would have been trouble by now."

"Then I am glad you are here to give me away, my lord, for I do not want trouble on my wedding day."

He squeezed my hand, locked in his arm. "It is my great honour to give you away, Majesty. All men should be aware what a prize they have in you, as a Queen, a friend or a wife."

I had the impression from his tone that my soon-to-be husband did not know what he had in me.

When finally we appeared, the King looked displeased to be left waiting at the altar, even though he himself had caused the true delay in our union. Dressed in cloth of gold decorated with silver flowers, with bands of black fur about the hems, cuffs and collar, and a cloak of crimson hanging from his enormous shoulders by diamond clasps, the King did not smile as I processed towards him. Anyone would have thought this a funeral procession, to gaze upon his face.

Sticking a bright smile on my lips, I was brought to stand on the left side of my husband, placed there to remind us all that women had been made of the left rib of the first man. The smell of rosemary woven into my dress, symbolising fidelity in marriage and love, rose into the air as the first notes of the Mass fell upon the warm air. Asked if there was any impediment, the King sullenly replied there was none.

I kept smiling.

My household stood in the gallery leading to the chapel, listening to the nuptial Mass as it was sung, and I concealed all the shame and fear I felt. *Calm, Anna*, I said to myself. *Courage, Anna. If this is not as you would have wanted, we can make the best of it.*

As the service came to a close, the King put a golden ring onto my finger. It was engraved with the motto *"God send me well to keep"*. It was my motto as Queen.

We processed through court, then to the wedding feast. All eyes were on the King. Dressed in a doublet of tissue of gold and crimson velvet, he barely said a word to me, and there were no signs of affection. It was customary for a groom to fill his bride's cup or feed her dainties from his plate. Nothing of that kind happened, but I refused to be daunted, and continued to persevere, smiling and expressing joy at each new dish set before me as though blind to the dissatisfaction of the King.

That evening my women helped me to change into a gown of crimson trimmed with ermine, with sleeves bunched becomingly above the elbows, and took me to Evensong. I bowed my head over my hands as I prayed, asking God to help my husband to find affection for me, and for courage to sustain this marriage. "Were it not for my people," I told God, "I would run away, even now."

We feasted that night, watching mummers perform and tumblers twist and bend, and before me the courtiers danced. I kept smiling as at my side the King drank deep, and often.

Later, I was taken to the nuptial chamber. My ladies from Cleves flapped about, offering hints on what I was to do to please my husband. "I know," I said to them, smiling. "All of this my mother explained many years ago."

Eventually they left me in the bed. The King had not asked for witnesses. At other courts it was routine for girls to be surrounded by witnesses as they were deflowered. I could not imagine it was a happy experience for either party. If the groom was young and inexperienced, he would feel shamed, and there was a great deal of pressure, which I had heard men did not respond to well. For a girl, being mounted by a man whilst others looked on, and for her to have witnesses to her pain and discomfort of the first time I could only imagine was a nightmare. *And that pain you will discover soon*, I reminded myself.

I tried to distract myself by looking about me. The bed was ornate, carved with royal ciphers, entwined *H&A's*, and two lewd carvings at the head of the bed, over where we, the new couple would lie: one of a cherub with a huge erect shaft, and another of a female cherub with a fat, swollen belly. They leered from behind me as I arranged the sheets about me. I tried not to look at them, truth be told, after that first glance. They were hideous.

The drapes were drawn, and my women retreated as the King and his men came to the door. The King entered in silence and the others left in silence too.

Eventually, there was a sigh, and he opened the curtain and tried to smile at me. That smile wobbled on his face, as if it might fall off. I smiled back, lying down, and with some effort and a few grunts of pain or discomfort, he climbed into the covers and lay in the bed with me. The scent of his leg was overpowering this close up and I tried not to breathe through my nose, since that made it worse. I lay, waiting for him to do all I had been told a man did on the night of a wedding.

There was another sigh.

Then there was a hand, roaming up my nightgown. I tried to lie still, not stiffen but in truth it was a hard task for I was unused to such a touch, and I did not desire this man in any way. I found him off-putting, in fact, in every way I could think of, for he was rude of character and foul of form. Visions of him eating, stuffing meat and bread and fish and comfits into his face filled my mind and I tried to set them out again. *Courage, Anna*, I told myself, closing my eyes. He felt my breasts, one by one, squeezing them in his hands, then my belly. His hands were hot, sweaty, and I tried not to move away, even though all I wanted was to flee this bed and this man. I thought he was to roam lower, but abruptly he climbed on top of me, between my legs. The movement was so swift, and he was so very heavy, I let out a noise, a little whimper, and screwed my eyes shut.

His heated breath was rank against my cheek. I lay there, trying not to gag as the scent of lemon lozenges floated above the smell of decay from impacted food in his teeth and his leg rotting away. I opened my eyes and tried to smile at him, but he was not looking at me, his head was twisted to one side as he heaved on top of me. I thought I might break ribs under the crush of his huge body.

I cast my eyes from his legs, swollen and hot, veins standing out like ridges along a hillside. I ignored the flab of his belly slapping against my soft skin, ignored too the corset he was still wearing under his nightshirt in an attempt to dupe me, or perhaps himself, into thinking his stomach was tight and firm as a young man's. Bulges of flesh popped out in strange places from the corset. In many ways, this made me pity him.

He thrust at me a couple more times, then rolled to one side.

There was silence for a moment, then he kissed me on the cheek and muttered something, which I think was "Goodnight, sweetheart," and with that, the King departed my chamber.

He had not even been there an hour. And I was still a maid.

For hours that night I lay there, wondering what was going on. The marriage had not been consummated; the King had barely even tried. I wondered then if the rumours all were true, and he was not capable of the act. If this was so, perhaps there was another reason he had not wanted to marry me, perhaps he was ashamed of his incapability to sustain what my mother had called a pike. If this was so, I could not tell anyone. It would add to his mortification, and it would hardly aid me to admit that my husband did not want me. No, it would have to be a secret.

If another reason was true instead, that he was not consummating the match in order to not legalize it, if he was planning to find a way to be rid of me, I did not want it widely known either. Opponents of the match would already be rubbing hands with glee over his dislike of me, to add to that this problem could make my position untenable.

Everyone assumed the deed was done when they came to collect me in the morning. The King had been there an hour or so in the night, and then left, which was not abnormal, although on a wedding night the groom normally enjoyed his wife until dawn. Ladies from my homeland tried to find out if I was sore. They sought out ointments from my chests and indicated – with knowing giggles – where I was to rub them, but I waved them away. They asked me about the night, but I simply told them the King was a fine man, and I was satisfied to be his wife.

But if I was careful in my speech, another was not.

I heard much that afternoon from Mistress Loew. Cromwell had asked his master how he liked his new Queen, the King had replied, "I liked her before not well, but now I like her much worse." His men were saying that the King had spoken loudly of my breasts and belly, which he had called *slack*, and announced he thought I was no virgin. The King had said I smelt evil and declared he had left me as good a maid, *"if that was what she was,"* as he had found me.

I stared at my woman. "The King thinks I am a whore?" I asked. I swallowed, my throat dry. The King had not only spoken of our time together, but had insulted me in all ways possible, and why? Why treat me so? Even if he did not like me, he did not have to be so cruel.

"Did he not consummate the match?" she whispered.

"He tried, but nothing… rose," I murmured, my cheeks flaming. "But you can tell no one that."

"Madam, the whole court knows, for the King is telling everyone he could not complete the act because of you."

"I see not it has anything to do with me," I said. "It was the King's body which failed him, not mine."

Later there was more. When I heard I was so humiliated I could have wept. Doctor Butts, the King's physician, had been brought to the King and not in private, for *all* his men knew of their conversation, and my people had enough English to understand the chortling exchanges which were taking place in corridors all over the palace. The King had declared he had been unable to perform, an astoundingly honest statement, which sent waves of amazement through court. No man admitted he was at fault in the bedchamber. It was unheard of.

But this was not quite what the King was saying. He claimed he had had two dreams that had brought him to a state of ejaculation in the night but could not find any desire for his new wife. He was blaming me. I was so unattractive he was rendered impotent when it came to performing with *me*.

In truth I thought that if he could find satisfaction in fantasy and yet not in reality this said a great deal about the sanity of the man who was my husband.

I tried to remain calm, but all I was told was so crass, so unfeeling and cruel. This man was revolting. He had plucked me from my homeland and brought me all the way here only to humiliate me? What kind of man was this?

"You will tell all my people to act as though we are all in ignorance of this," I said, lifting my chin and trying to blink back tears of shame. "I am sure the King was unable to perform, for he is old and often ill, and these slanders are being put about as a way to excuse his own failure.

Therefore, if we pretend we know nothing, we may instil some form of dignity upon this court which demonstrates none, and save what is left of my pride." Tears washed into my eyes and my women of Cleves flowed about me, enraged on my behalf. They all promised to do as I asked, however. None of them spoke too kindly of the King that day but thankfully they spoke in whispers and few could understand them. I would have liked to say a few things myself, but I bit my tongue. I would not behave badly, no matter how sore I was tempted by the bad behaviour of others.

The King was said to be in a perilous mood, his temper easily roused. Cromwell had been called, sent away, and recalled almost every hour, as the King berated him, not caring who heard, about his unhappiness. To all this, I had to pretend I was unaware. I kept court in my rooms, praising my women for their singing and dancing and spoke brightly of the charms of England. I started a game, getting my ladies to hold up objects found about the chamber and name them, so I could echo the names back and learn them.

"I wish to please mine husband," I said to Anne Bassett. "So, I learn."

"You are doing wonderfully, Your Majesty," said Anne.

I was doing all I could to be pleasing, accommodating and refined, but it was hard, the hardest test of my life until then, I think. By the end of that first day of marriage, the whole court was afire with talk about how the King was utterly repulsed by his wife, and they were all laughing at me.

It was being said my country was nothing; a poor, mean state neither wealthy nor powerful. This, it was whispered, could be seen in me, for although richly dressed, I looked like a commoner playing Queen. "She is no Katherine of Aragon," was a murmur heard. I was compared to the women who had come before me, but even against Queen Anne and Queen Jane, women with no royal blood, I was found wanting. The King did not care that I was regal, dignified and kind. I was not the promised fantasy he had dreamed up in his own fetid mind.

People all about court were mocking me, but I lifted my head high and continued on. The English had no idea what decorum or noble behaviour was, but I did, and I would show them.

"Other rumours are circulating," Olisleger told me. "It is being said you, Majesty, before you came here had declared you would not come to England whilst one abbey was left standing."

"What does that mean?" I asked.

"That they think you a Lutheran, of the most radical sort."

"I am a Catholic, born and raised."

"Whoever is putting these rumours about, Majesty, is trying to make you look like an enemy to those of the Catholic faith. In truth, it is not you they are aiming to discredit, but Cromwell."

The King did not come to my bed on the second night, but when I was told this I merely thanked my women for the message as I settled into bed with my ladies from Cleves. The King tried on the third and fourth nights, but what happened was a mirror of the first night. A hand in the covers, a few unwilling thrusts and something limp hanging slack against my leg. I shuddered on the fourth night as he mounted me. I did not mean to, but in all ways now I found the man repulsive.

And I think he knew that.

## Chapter Fifteen

**Greenwich Palace
London**

**January 1540**

Days followed, each just as uncomfortable and insecure as the last. Every morning in the faded light of dawn, I rose, trying to forget dreams where I had been at home and none of this frightening farce had happened. I washed hands and face and was dressed. I processed to Mass, casting my eyes upon the young wolves of court who were watching my girls as if they were sheep. I made sure they saw me watching, a warning. If I was to be the Queen, I would be one who protected my women.

Many of them looked away when they saw my eyes rest on them. Some pretended interest in the sermon. Some glanced at their friends, said something under their breath – no doubt some insult inspired by the King's uncouth treatment of me – and laughed quietly.

I ignored them as I ignored all else I heard, at least on the surface. Inside, I felt shamed and not a little outraged. I could barely believe this man was a knight, a king or a lord. This man had no breeding, perhaps all who had said his father had no right to sit on the throne were right. He was boring and boorish, uncouth and obscene. If he did not want to be wed to me, I had little wish to be married to him.

And yet we were married, and it was done. He had sworn a vow before God and so had I. The best had to be made of it, and that meant I had a mask to wear. I was not about to show my true feelings to the people of England, even though I was sore tempted to. Every ill-disguised titter and sniggering face I walked past I wanted to slap. Sometimes I thought something in me would break, and I would scream. But I did not. I held my head high; my chin was not allowed to drop. I smiled and I inclined my head, I walked as a Queen.

After Mass, we sewed by the fire, my ladies and me, a time when I heard much gossip. They did not think I understood what they were saying, but although some words and references still eluded me, I could understand more than I could speak. The words of the English, the patterns of their speech, were in one way not unfamiliar, some sounded the same as my native language, but I felt shy to try to speak at times, my tongue stumbling, sounding awkward. I kept trying, but I found I learned well just by listening, too.

There was plenty of talk for me to hear; my ladies, thinking I did not understand them, were perhaps more outspoken than they would have been had they known just how much I was picking up. There was word of plots, gossip, intrigue. Fights broke out daily amongst young men, I ascertained. Outside the bounds of court – for swords were not to be drawn inside, although daggers were often enough – these fights were always over some insult over pride or property. One man would slight the house or parentage of another, or dare to court their lady, and would be challenged. All Englishmen carried blades and were quick to draw them, they seemed wilder of temper than the men I had known in Cleves. Ladies of course went unarmed, although after all I had heard since coming here, I wondered why. It seemed to me a knife up a sleeve would be a good thing for most women at court. This was a predatory place where women, even the Queen, were little respected.

Yet I also found court thrilling, in a way. Perhaps it should seem odd that I thought so, for I had been brought here and humiliated by my new husband, I did not understand the people well, I was an outsider, and yet here, though there were dangers and perils of all kinds, I felt free in a way I had never encountered before. It had nothing to do with my husband, but much to do with my household. Many of the restrictions that had been part of my daily life had lifted. There was wild talk here, wild men, but there were also kind women, my household was proof of that for they spent much time trying to conceal the King's revulsion towards me and teaching me to speak England, and though that was their task, of course, they did it also I think out of affection for me.

There were also many women here who were well educated, who were allowed to write poetry, play musical instruments or play cards in public, hunt with the bow, women who were outspoken. Although there were still restrictions upon them, of course, there were many freedoms here we had not enjoyed in Cleves. And the women here, those of an intellectual bent, had continued to learn in adulthood, thriving on books and words, honing their educations. There were many women here of wit and good humour, and I was drawn to them as the sea is to shore.

It was a strange place, this England. Though repulsed by its King, I felt mildly addicted to his country, though I had not been here long. The women were interesting. If by the King I felt not welcomed, it was not the same with the women. I felt they had wrapped about me, forming a guard, and I marvelled at their kindness. It is easier to see how caring and compassionate some people are, when we are at the same time confronted by people who are selfish, rude and uncouth, like the King.

"Harris and Clairvaux met for a duel just the other day, but were chased off by the King's guards..."

Another tale of swords and honour began. I tried not to smile. The clash of swords was apparently as regular in London as the pealing of church bells, and men met just outside the bounds of court to satisfy hurt honour and pride. It seemed to me the honour and pride of these men were fragile creatures, if so easily wounded.

But still, my women appeared to admire these tales, and many stories I had to admit *were* daring even if they were, at the same time, ridiculous, so I did understand why my women sighed to hear two men battled for the love of a lady, even though we all knew they did not, in truth. They battled to be superior to the other man. The lady was just the excuse.

At eleven many of my people went to the hall to eat, and I would eat in my chambers, and after there would be more sewing, or I would watch my ladies dance, something I became most fond of doing. They were so graceful, all of them, like swan maidens dancing in dead of night, about a fire, unconcerned and lissom, as if they thought no eyes were on them. I admired them all greatly and told them how beautiful they looked in the dance. I was trying to learn the steps, for I had been told the Queen could dance of course, if she wished, just as my sister had danced into the early hours of the morn on her wedding day. But I did not want to dance badly and disgrace the King, so I watched, and I learned.

The King came on occasion. The more I saw of him, the more I wondered about him.

I had, by that time, heard more rumours. Everyone tried to keep them from me and my people of Cleves, but they had heard, and I had been told. The King did not like the way I looked, something I thought ironic in a way. He was hardly what I had been promised either.

Yet I would have accepted him as a husband out of duty, no matter what he looked like, if he had been a man of pleasant character, or even bland character. I was aware we do not all get what we want in life, and was willing to compromise, bear his weight and the smell of him in bed, even if I did not desire him, but from a dislike of the way I looked the King seemed to have drawn conclusions about my temperament, character and even my virginity. He had dared to call me not a maiden.

It was my looks which mattered, apparently, more than anything. A little rhyme had been heard at court, nowhere near the King of course, but loud enough for us to hear. It was about my portrait, and apparently had begun to be sung before I even arrived.

*If that be your picture, then shall we*
*Soon see how you and your picture agree!*

Enemies of the match were no doubt behind it. I wondered about the English. Some were so welcoming, and others reacted to me as if I was the one-woman beginning of a Cleves invasion of this country. I had been nothing but gracious and friendly, yet to some I was some incarnation of the antichrist.

And their King led this foul behaviour. No matter if he did not like me, the King and I were now married and unless he meant to set me aside, something I tried not to think about, we had to make the best of this match. I fought down my hurt and dislike of him and I tried to learn more about him. The King was obsessed with the art of medicine, I was told, always searching for ways to improve his failing health. He thought himself an expert in remedies and lectured his doctors. He also seemed overly paranoid about attack, too.

I heard how the King's bed was prepared each day, how the bottom hay mattress and box were rolled upon by one of the gentlemen to check for hidden daggers, poisoned pins or swords, how the top mattress of feathers was tested in the same way, and how his men ran their hands over the perfumed sheets and soft blankets, testing for danger. The King's sword was placed at the head of the bed once it was made, and the gentlemen would kiss the sheets where their hands had touched them, in reverence for being permitted to caress something that would lie against the King's sacred skin.

I thought of his leg, of the risen veins and the pungent, noxious odour that rose from him, and I wondered about the idea he had sacred skin. Scarred, certainly, sacred I was not so sure.

If I was to make anything of this match, I had to become more attractive to him, it seemed. The King was not concerned with soul, comportment, or personality when it came to women, apparently, only looks were important. When I noted the King's gaze, and where it lingered, it always seemed to be on ladies who certainly were pretty, although none of my women were hard to gaze upon, but they were always dressed in a similar fashion too. The more French the style of their clothing the more he watched them, and so, taking another deep draw on my courage, on the fifth day after I was wed, when they brought a French-style gown and hood to me, I inclined my head and allowed my ladies to dress me in it. They were so pleased I thought they might start skipping about the chamber.

"You are beautiful, Majesty," said Mary Howard, and I was startled by the shock in her tone. She sounded genuinely surprised. I knew I was not beautiful, so I was not sure what to make of this.

When I looked into a mirror, I could hardly stop my blushes for it was more revealing than anything I had ever worn in public before, yet the transformation was admittedly remarkable. I did not look plain, but pretty, the tight waist and tapering sleeves suiting me much better than my own gowns. The crimson of the dress and its purple underskirts went well against my light brown hair and warm eyes. With a French hood on my head, rimmed with pearls that made my slightly ruddy skin, marred by travel, appear lighter, my ladies took me to the tilting yard. As I passed through court, I could hear everyone remarking how fair I looked, and I accepted compliments with calm pleasure. Some of the men sounded quite astonished.

In truth, I was more than a little nervous. It was not just the gown, cut to display a little bosom. It was that the hood on my head showed some of my hair, and I never had done that in public before aside from at my wedding, but that had been a more private affair than this. I felt almost naked.

We came outside, the light blinding after being within the place, and I was taken to the stands. The King sat with me a while, pointing out the best riders, advising me where to bet my money – the English placed a wager on anything – then soon enough he was away again, off to chat to Brandon about the challengers and their odds. But as we watched the joust, there were rumours shifting through the stands, flowing under the cheers for the knights.

Olisleger told me what was being said. It was whispered that on the day of the wedding, the King had taken Cromwell aside and told him he would not marry me for any earthly reason, were it not vital for the security of England that he do so. There was talk of the King's desperation to find a path out of the wedding. Cromwell was not there that morn and for the rest of the joust I sat there, applauding and smiling, handing out prizes and trying to conceal that I was anxious.

"Cromwell is on edge," said Olisleger that afternoon as we returned to my rooms, "as are his men. The King is blaming him, for he told the King such tales about you, Majesty, that no woman, no matter how perfect, could live up to."

Cromwell was so alarmed, I heard, that he sought to shift the blame for the match onto the Earl of Southampton, Admiral Fitzwilliam, who had of course seen me in the flesh before I came to England, as Cromwell had not. Fitzwilliam told anyone who would listen that it had not been his task to assess the beauty of the future Queen, but merely to escort me to English soil, and the marriage had been agreed upon long before he played any part in it.

"They would all abandon me," I said, feeling not a little sad. Fitzwilliam and I had got on well together in Calais, but now he was distancing himself from me and from all his approving comments about me. No men here stuck to their own opinions, apparently, they took on only those of the King. "I wonder that any will be my friend."

But despite the King's dislike, Harst told me the Privy Council had told the King he must stay married to me. They feared war with my brother if I was set aside. But the principal reason for marriage, children, was clearly not going to come easily from this union, and that had more tongues wagging.

My English women worked hard to conceal all this from me, and I gave no indication that I knew anything, not just that day but every day after. Every day I woke with dread in my heart, and I could only share my feelings with a few. I could not write of my unhappiness to my family, I was sure my letters would be opened. Even in code, with my sisters, I was nervous to make the attempt, and so I did not. I thought it safer that way.

Throughout January, my women sang for me, showed me the steps of English dances, selecting slow ones more often than not, which were easier for me to learn. We played cards and I won with great regularity, much to my delight, and we sewed by the fireside.

Outside, wind howled, and snow fell. Tempests shrieked and ice gathered like the fronds of fern against the glass. Inside my chambers I bent my head over embroidery and spent my hours thinking of how to make the best of this hard hand I had been dealt by fate.
I did not know a storm was gathering, though at times my scar upon my eyebrow would ache, promising something cold, something of winter, to come.

# Chapter Sixteen

**Greenwich Palace**
**London**

**January 1540**

Not long after my wedding day, I was sent a note. When the more complicated sections had been translated for me, I showed it to my women with delight. It was from my new stepdaughter, the Lady Elizabeth, child of Anne Boleyn. I had not met her, nor either yet the Lord Edward. Both were housed outside of court, it being thought country air was healthier for children.

The Lady Mary I had met, and I had gathered with swift understanding that she did not like me. At the time I could little understand why, even though the English in general seemed to need little persuasion to hate someone they did not know. It was explained to me that Lady Mary believed me to be a Lutheran, and that was why she disliked me.

"I must have some time with her, in private," I had said to Harst. "We must ask the King for this, for it must be explained to my elder stepdaughter I am nothing of the sort, and even if I was, she would have no need to loathe me so."

"She is of an extreme sort of Catholic faith, Majesty, though she pretends to follow the religion the King has set in place here in England. She equates Lutheranism of any kind with heresy, and since you are the Queen, she thinks you will corrupt the country."

But at least my younger stepdaughter was not so quick to loathe me. In fact, she was all politeness.

*"Permit me to show, by this billet, the zeal with which I devote my respect to you as Queen, and my entire obedience to you as my mother. I am too young and feeble to have power to do more than felicitate you with all my*

*heart in this commencement of your marriage. I hope that Your Majesty will have as much goodwill for me as I have zeal for your service."*

I wondered if she had just learnt the word "zeal" and smiled at its repetition, but I was admittedly impressed with the missive.

"How old is my stepdaughter?" I asked after the letter had been read to my women. I suppose I must have been told her age at one point, but the letter confused me, it was so mature. "Twelve... or thirteen?"

"She is six, Your Majesty," Catherine Howard replied.

"Six!" I exclaimed, staring at the note in shock. I smiled, shaking my head. "She had help."

"Pardon my boldness, Your Majesty, but I think the note the work of Lady Elizabeth alone," said Katherine Carey. "I was once in her household, and the Lady Elizabeth is a vastly precocious child, far ahead of her peers in her studies. She already speaks Latin, French and Spanish, and is a devotee of the works of Cicero."

"This learned, and so young," I said, wonder in my tone as I thought of all Wilhelm had been taught and all we had missed out on as girls. In England it clearly was not the same. Even though our education had been advanced in some ways, for girls, Sybylla had taught me more of the world than our tutors had. I thought of all the books we had been forced to hide from our parents, from other people, but the Lady Elizabeth had clearly read and absorbed so much, so young. I could not imagine being six years old and writing like this. "My father did not..." I paused, searching for a word "... consider great learning a good thing in women, but I think it can be." I stared at the note, shaking my head. "Six..."

Looking up, I beamed. "I must meet my daughter. I will ask the King."

My women looked uncomfortable. They said nothing discouraging but I had the impression I would not be meeting my stepchildren who were not at court. This was another bit of evidence as to the instability of my position and I did not welcome it. But I would go ahead with my plan to try, I thought. These children were now my children, by law. One of them had had a mother for at most three years of her life and the prince's mother had died but ten days into his. They deserved to have a surrogate mother, one who would offer love to them, if they could not have their own mothers with them.

When I had this thought, I experienced a feeling so strong I could not have imagined it. It was as if someone standing behind me had put their hand on mine and squeezed it. I turned in my chair, twisting away from the dancers in my chambers, but there was nothing but a wall behind me. Was it my own personal ghost, or that of the prince's mother who came to me then, drawn to me for my having kind thoughts for their child? I knew not, but I did know that something of past approved my plans of present and was grateful to me.

I made my request at dinner one night and the King muttered that he would think about it. Later, Olisleger told me that the King had handed Elizabeth's note to Cromwell and told him to write to her. "The King said Cromwell was to tell his daughter she had had a mother *so different from this woman*, that she ought not to wish to see her."

I stared at my man. "He would compare me unfavourably to the woman he beheaded?" I asked, my voice a squeak.

"Some say he speaks of her at times," said Olisleger. "When deep in his cups. Sometimes he weeps."

"He loved her, once," I said. "Me, he never has loved."

I was starting to feel most afraid.

# Chapter Seventeen

**Greenwich Palace**
**London**

**January 1540**

Had I not been married to the King, I might have been happy in England. I had a household of one hundred and twenty-six, only a few fewer than Katherine of Aragon who had enjoyed the largest household of all my husband's Queens. My native women were still in my household, although there was word they would be sent home soon, and I had a Clevian physician, Doctor Cornelius, as well as Olisleger, Master Schulenberg, my cook, Harst, and a footman, Englebert. Had I not been married to the King, but still had been able to retain this household, I would have been entirely merry, for my women, both of England and Cleves were good women, my other servants lively and sweet. They were protective of me, and I could feel their warmth. Yes, if not for being married to this crude man, who I was becoming more and more afraid of, I would have been content.

As January came to a close, I was told to prepare my household for a move to Westminster. We had been a month or more at Greenwich, and the halls, once so fresh, were ripe with the scent of bodies, piss and food. Rushes needed to be cleaned out and walls scrubbed, so we would go to Westminster, and there I would be presented to the men of the capital at the same time. Worryingly though, I was not to be granted the traditional state procession into London.

I came to believe it was punishment.

I had objected, through my translator, to my new husband about the Lady Mary being granted rooms on the Queen's side of the palace. I had not been consulted about this arrangement, and it was up to me to decide who had chambers in my domain. I thought it a slight and told my husband so. He, not at all concerned with my happiness, said little and did nothing.

I did not want Lady Mary near me, for she did not show as much respect to me as she should. Rumours that I was Lutheran had much to do with the Lady Mary's lack of respect, but with the King acting as though I was an inconvenience at best, a portent of doom at worst, the King's daughter had no reason to pretend affection. She was in fact quite rude to me.

If she continued to spread word that I was a Lutheran I might find myself in trouble, too, for although I did not understand all the laws of England, I knew there was a possibility of being accused of being a heretic if the King came to believe I followed any expression of faith not his own. This could be dangerous for me.

We had passed each other at court, Mary and I, met briefly at feasts, and every time she acted as if I was not the Queen and would not be there long.

"*That* was a brief curtsey," I noted to my women when Mary saw me, bobbed as if I were a lady lesser, and walked on.

"Too brief," said the Duchess of Suffolk, her eyes narrowing. "That was an insult, Majesty."

"I have tried to invite her to my rooms," I said, shaking my head. "Attempted to converse with her, but each time there is an excuse, and she must be away, or she is ill and cannot come."

"She is of a delicate constitution, Majesty," said the Duchess, "but I think she is also using that as an excuse to avoid you."

"I think so too, my friend."

I was well aware the King did not like me, but to have a lesser member of the royal house, one declared a bastard at that, acting with scant respect was not to be borne. I already had to pretend I saw nothing of the King's vile behaviour, nothing of his court's discourtesy, but Lady Mary was most obvious in her disapproval and, feeling slighted already and not a little afraid, I could bear no more. I was well within my rights to be consulted about the Lady Mary taking apartments in my section of court, and I wanted no more enemies close to me. I had enough as it was.

But the King did nothing, except to punish me for protesting about something I was entirely within my rights to protest about. Mary got away with much, but for speaking out I was not to be granted the Queen's traditional state procession into London.

Perhaps the way Mary treated me had too much truth in it for me to bear. I had a feeling I would not be Queen long either, and I did not like to think about the way I might be removed from this position.

*

At the end of January, my ladies from Cleves were sent home, along with most of the officers of my old household. Sent away with gifts of plate and money, jewels and horses, the officers were merry, all except von Overstein. "I would stay, Majesty," he said, "Were I permitted. I do not like to think of you alone here."

"I have Ambassador Harst, and others, my friend," I said. "I would keep all of you, but we knew from this start this was not to be."

"God keep you, Majesty," he said, kissing my hand. I was touched to see the fatherly man had tears in his eyes.

Writing letters to send back with my old household, I sent word to my mother and Wilhelm, saying I was happy, and the King contented me well. I did not want them to know the truth, for it would do nothing but scare them and humiliate me. Besides, I knew not if my missives were being opened or not. I dared finally to send word to Sybylla, however, in our old code, telling her I wished I had a cloak of feathers to offer me wings. I did not say I wanted to fly away, but that was in truth all I wanted.

"I think it a good sign, though, my lady," said Olisleger, as we watched the preparations for the dispatch of my household. The chambers were in a flurry as maids hastened here and there, collecting personal items left about my chambers. "Your household are being sent home, so you are to integrate with the court, that is a sign of your permanence here."

I was not so sure of that. There was rumour of a change in the shifting wind of politics. Harst told me both the Emperor and the King of France were eager to make friends with England. Both wanted the King of England as their ally, which seemed to indicate trouble brewing between them. It was whispered that England had never been as strong as it was now. I wondered if that made the King regret his marriage to me only more. My brother was opposed to the Emperor. With friendship with other countries becoming likely, the present alliance with Cleves could well become undesirable, and worse, potentially dangerous.

"I am glad you are to stay with me," I said to Mistress Loew.

"I am too, my lady," she said. "You need some people about you in possession of sense and decency."

I smiled. "My other women, and those in this household who know me, they are decent."

"Yet many here are nothing of the kind."

I knew who she meant. The Catholic, or more accurately named anti-Cromwell, faction led by Norfolk and Gardiner had been quick to speak about the benefits of Spain and flaws of Cleves, but the King did nothing. His men said he was waiting. Often the Emperor and the King of France had pretended to be friends to England when they were not. My husband wanted to be sure of their intentions. But he did send away the erstwhile suitor of the Lady Mary. Phillip of Bavaria went home without promise of her hand. Almost that same day, Lady Mary magically recovered from a strange illness, which had always struck her the moment Phillip came to court – much as it struck her anytime I invited her to my chambers – and was seen gaily laughing with her friends again.

There was a grand feast on the night before my retinue went home, with much singing and dancing, and fine foods. A select few, such as Olisleger and Mistress Loew, and Harst of course since he was an ambassador, were permitted to remain in England, a special favour from the King.

What was worrying was that there seemed to be no plans for my coronation. It was supposed to be taking place in February, and I called my new English officers to me to discuss what it was I was to do during the ceremony and after. "I am not familiar with English custom," I told them. I was becoming more confident with my English and was not stumbling through my words anymore. I had to speak slowly, but I was happier about my competency. "I need to know what I am to do and say, at each step and in each moment, during the ceremony."

Red-faced and trying to mask abject discomfort, they told me it had been decided the ceremony would be postponed; in February the weather was unpredictable, and the King did not want his subjects prevented from attending due to rain or snow. There *was* to be a civic reception, they told me. I frowned a little but nodded. "When there is a date for my coronation I would know at once."

They promised and fled. I was no fool. I knew their excuses were thin as any ice formed in June. If the King ordered his people to turn out, they would.

They feared him, you see, just as I did.

## Chapter Eighteen

**Greenwich Palace and
Westminster Palace
London**

**February 1540**

The day before we left for Westminster, the Privy Council sent word to commoners of London to put on their best the next day and come to cheer their new Queen. "This is good," I said to my women, then noted little Catherine Howard hovering close. "You wish to see me, Mistress Howard?" I asked.

"Majesty," she bobbed a charming curtsey, "I would ask permission to be absent for the day, to visit my grandmother at Norfolk House."

"Norfolk is far," I said, for I had been looking at maps of England of late, getting familiar with the country, but she smiled.

"Norfolk is indeed far, Majesty, but my grandmother's house, Norfolk House, is in London, just over the water from here."

I smiled. "I see. Of course, visit your grandmother. She raised you, I understand?"

"She did, Majesty."

Through court rumour I knew it had been a difficult time for Catherine's family. Harst had told me that Cromwell had struck at Norfolk. Thetford Priory, the traditional burial site of the Howards, was to close on Cromwell's orders. Thetford, I had been told, was where the husband of this dowager of Norfolk as well as her son and many other Howards rested with God.

Norfolk had tried to save the place and had failed. It was one of the last monasteries left in England, and had survived until now largely because of his family, but no more. Norfolk wanted to re-found it as a college of priests, to sing Masses for the souls of his family, but Cromwell would not allow it. The monastery was to be completely destroyed, and the bones of these Howard ancestors were to be moved elsewhere, to Framlingham in Suffolk. This was not only the destruction of one of the last monasteries in England, but a calculated assault on the Howard family, and on Norfolk's pride. I had no doubt that was why Catherine's grandmother wanted to see her.

What had surprised me even more was to learn that Henry Fitzroy, the King's bastard son and apparently the great joy of his life had also been buried there, but this had not saved the priory either. Fitzroy's body was being moved, like all the Howards. The King's son was laid to rest in Framlingham too, I was told, at the Church of Saint Michael the Archangel. Some claimed the King was a sentimental man, but I did not think this was true.

"Come back soon, my little dancer," I said to Catherine. I was growing most fond of little Howard, as people at court called her. She was a sweet girl, and one of the best dancers I had seen there. She could sing like a lark too, and when I played her at cards she always lost; she was not talented at any of the games we played, but that never put her off playing and she never seemed to mind losing. The kind of person who does not mind losing and does not mind either that people know they are not good at everything, is a rare kind of soul, especially at the English court where everyone had a mask and a part to play. I think that was what drew me to her the most, she seemed entirely honest about herself, her talents and her pleasures. She had little guile, which made her stand out in this band of tricksters.

"Barges have been ordered out onto the water early tomorrow morning," said Olisleger as Catherine curtseyed and departed. He was speaking of my ceremonial entrance to London. "The King wants the waters full, and the banks, to make a spectacle to please the Duke of Cleves."

I would rather the King wanted to please me, but pleasing my brother was a start.

The next day, after Mass, we made for the waterfront. Barges were to carry the entire court from Greenwich to Westminster in a parade. When we reached the heart of London I would be presented to my people.

The river was busy; every barge of every noble, of the King and many smaller crafts of merchants had indeed been called upon to turn out with their finest regalia fluttering from masts and sails. It was a glorious sight, with colour and music and movement everywhere. Beside the boats bobbled flocks of swans, elegant and white upon the choppy water. There were so many it looked as if it had snowed upon the Thames. I stared at them a long time, thinking of every story told before a fire when I was at home, where I was loved and respected by all, where people had valued my mind and soul and not judged me solely by the features upon my face.

*It is not all people here who do that,* I told myself. *Only one, and the others follow suit for they fear him.* If the King were a better man, his people might have the opportunity to explore the best virtues they possessed, rather than the lowest of their flaws.

It was freezing, the February air as cold as homesickness as we stood on the water steps, little waves slapping stone near our feet. "Let me aid you onto the boat, Majesty," Cromwell said to me, and I took his hand, huge against my small one. It felt clammy, though the day was cold, as if he was nervous.

We headed into the water, grey, bearing small white-crested waves, and sailed for Westminster. Boats containing all the nobility of England were there, music drifting from their decks along with thick clouds of incense burned to mask the stench of the river. Refuse of the city went into it daily, and people washed clothes in it, and themselves. All this along with the leavings of the many thousands of birds upon the water and the general smell a large river flowing will possess, granted an often high and pungent scent, although it was not that bad that day. I was given to understand in summer it was far worse.

The slippery banks, thick with reeds in places and bare as the King's balding head in others, were crammed with people, cheering and waving, trying to catch a glimpse of their Queen. Children sat on the shoulders of their fathers, craning their little necks. I stood on deck, wrapped in furs, lifting my hand to each section of people I saw and every time I raised my hand anew a fresh cry would go up, caressing the air. The people of England welcomed me, and I felt tears in my eyes and throat, tears of gratitude. Considering the way some of court had 'welcomed' me, I had thought I might be taunted through London, jeered at on my boat, but it was not so.

As we passed the Tower there was a crack of gunfire in the air as cannons shot to welcome me to London. Guildsmen cheered from their barges as we floated on, and men shouted blessings from shops along the riverfront and on London Bridge. "We should be stopping here," I mentioned to Katherine of Suffolk, "the Tower is where Queens stay before their coronation."

"It will come in time, Majesty," she said, sipping warmed wine, the spices reaching out from her cup to tickle my nose. "Perhaps when you are with child. That was the tradition for some past Queens."

"Jane Seymour never was crowned," I said. "Yet she got with child. Perhaps the King does not mean to crown another Queen."

I looked to one side, seeing Jane Rochford and Catherine Howard in what looked like a deep conversation. They were utterly absorbed. "Another speaks to Jane Boleyn," I said, nodding at the couple.

"I believe they have family in common, if by marriage," said Katherine. "Catherine Howard was cousin to … the Boleyn Queen." She whispered the last words.

I looked to the Tower again and shivered, suddenly thankful we were not stopping there. That was where this Queen had died, where her bones lay. I remembered the look on my mother's face when she had told me how Anne Boleyn's women had guarded her body after death so men would do nothing to abuse the dead Queen. *I hope you rest now in some peace*, I said to the voice ever floating at my side.

Breezily, as if nothing had been said of death, Katherine went on. "It used to be that a queen was crowned when she married the King. It was that way for Katherine of Aragon, and most queens before her, but you should know, Majesty, that the King's father delayed crowning Elizabeth of York. He did not want the people to think his claim rested on her rather than his own rights, so waited until she had borne a son. And our King..." her eyes flickered to the King's boat, "... he follows his father, and crowns wives when they are with child."

*It seems I never will have a crown,* I thought. The King came often to bed with me now but did not attempt even to mount me. He lay there with me, would try to talk at times, and at others would just kiss my cheek and say, "Goodnight, sweetheart." Sometimes he would spend the night, snoring away next to me so I got no sleep, and in the morning, he would say, "Good morrow, sweetheart," kiss me, and leave.

In truth, the nights when I slept alone but for my women were much pleasanter than any moment spent with my husband. I had never known that with some people, being with them is lonelier than being alone.

Being by myself was less worrisome too, in other ways. I knew, for example, that I was not about to insult myself, spread gossip about myself or my country, or hurt myself. I did not know that about the King. With myself I was safe, with him I was always on edge.

At Westminster, the boats stopped. Cromwell, who had been talking to the King on his boat, stepped away from his master with a furrowed brow, and the King looked none too pleased either. The King left his own barge and helped me from my boat, extending his hand and guiding me gently to the steps. From there, we all walked to Whitehall Palace, just up the water a little, where we were to stay. "I have news for you, sweetheart," the King said, attempting a smile which did not reach his eyes. "The coronation is set for Whitsun."

This news trickled down the line of people following us, and I was glad of it. Perhaps it would cause some to cease looking at me as if I were the greatest jest ever told in England. I had the feeling, however, that the King had been talked into this by Cromwell, perhaps with threats about my brother or the Emperor. However he had been convinced to go ahead with my coronation, it was clear the King was not happy he was to do so.

# Chapter Nineteen

**Westminster Palace and
Whitehall Palace
London**

**Winter – Spring 1540**

"People speak well of you, Majesty," Katherine told me. "All over court I hear them. Queen Anne is so gracious and charming, they say. Queen Anne is so poised and serene. People are saying how beautiful you look now you are in English clothes and your hair is grown back upon your brow. I even heard one old lady compare you to Queen Katherine of Spain for your composure."

A compliment indeed, since as far as I had heard Katherine of Spain had lost control of herself so rarely that each time it had happened everyone remembered it.

I believed my friend of Suffolk this time, for others had said the same. If tongues had wagged about me and my mean, poor country of late, a rival wave was forming in my favour, speaking of my gentility, grace and regal bearing. About court even my enemies spoke of how I was good at heart. Some were even saying they knew not why the King thought me ugly, for I was a fair lady made fairer still by having a good and virtuous character.

Though still not secure in my position, I was feeling happier. There were other things I was finding joy in, besides the improving behaviour of the loutish English. When they were of a mood to be polite, I found the English most charming, but other privileges of my position I was discovering to be enjoyable too. My royal wardrobe was becoming a daily discovery of new dresses, and it seemed I could order what I wanted from tailors and seamstresses too. It made each time I got dressed into a little adventure, seeing how this colour or cut or hood looked on me. Although I was rather new to the art of dressing, I was enjoying it immensely and so were my women, who seemed to take delight in bringing items to me. At times I felt as if I had become their favourite doll.

My chambers were lively with dancing each day, which my ladies were most pleased about, and I had regular nights of cards too. I ensured that a certain amount of time was given over during the day to sewing and embroidery and had a lady reading from the Bible at such times, and I made sure we all were seen going to Mass twice a day. I wanted diversions in my chambers, but I did not want my enemies at court to start spreading tales that the Queen was bent only on flighty fun. I had enough problems as it was.

But there were things to entertain me and enjoy here. I had even formed my own troop of musicians, including members of the Jewish Bassano family, brought from Venice for me by Cromwell. They had brought along a new instrument and shown it at court. It was called the violin.

"I love nothing more than music, I think," I said to Katherine of Suffolk as we listened to my musicians.

"And Your Majesty has impeccable taste," she said, admiring the violin player. I did wonder if she was admiring his skill on the instrument, or the perfect line of his jaw. He was a striking man.

I chuckled a little, and when she asked me why I was laughing, I told her it was happiness to have found her. "You remind me of my sister, Sybylla," I said. "You have that same independence of spirit I admired in her, and the confidence that seemed to come so easily to her."

"Confidence is a mask, Majesty," said Katherine. "There are plenty of times I find myself unsure, but then I lift my mask, and no one knows of my quaking heart but me."

I smiled.

"Why do you smile so, Majesty?"

"Because Sybylla would have said the same."

My English was progressing rapidly, and I only used my translator for long or difficult subjects or conversations now. But if I understood much of some things, I still had to at least appear wholly in ignorance of others. What happened at night between the King and me, or rather what did *not* happen, was one of those things. Others suspected though, and this I knew because of a conversation which my ladies sprang upon me one day.

We were in my chambers, my women and I, sitting about a bright fire, all with sewing in our hands. It was cold and wet outside, a most unseasonably chilly day for spring, as if winter was clinging on, unwilling to slumber. Gusts of wet wind splattered through the grounds and the trees heaved in the parks. Not wishing to attempt a walk outdoors we had stretched our legs that morn in the long gallery and now were happily at the fire, warming our legs with the flames and our minds with conversation. I was making a new shirt for my husband, hoping to please him with such womanly skills. I was proud of it; the seams could barely be seen. My ladies too had admired it, acclaimed it as excellent work and I knew it was, for even with a certain amount of humility I knew my needlework far exceeded even the best at the English court.

As we worked, I saw a glance pass between the Countess of Rutland and Jane Rochford, and they launched into what clearly was a prepared conversation.

"I hope soon, Your Majesty, you will be turning that delicate needle to make other clothes," said Jane, nodding to the widow of Edgecombe, also apparently in on this little pageant.

"Does my husband require more clothes than I make?" I asked, carefully noting the glances between them and wondering what they were up to.

Jane smiled. "I meant clothes of a smaller kind. We all cherish hope that soon you will be with child, Majesty."

"The country would rejoice for a Duke of York, Majesty," added the Countess of Rutland.

"Then I sorrow," I said, tucking my silver needle into the cloth, narrowing my eyes upon the line of the stitching to ensure it was straight. "For I am sure I am not yet with child."

"How can you be sure, Majesty?" asked the Dowager of Edgecombe.

"I am sure."

"Unless still a maid, Majesty, you cannot be sure," said Jane.

"I think I am not with child." They were clearly trying to get details from me.

"By Our Lady," jested Jane, teasing. "I think Your Grace must be a maid still indeed to speak so sure!"

"How can I be a maid and sleep with the King every night?" I asked, affecting a chuckle.

"A little more than *sleep* is required, for a prince to be born, Majesty," said Jane, laughing.

"When he comes, he kisses me and takes me by the hand," I said, examining my work. "He biddeth me 'goodnight, sweetheart', and in the morning bids me 'farewell, darling'." I looked up, steady eyes on Jane. "Is this not enough?"

Smiles fell and the laughter stopped. I glanced down as if noting nothing and kept my eyes on the cloth in my hands. I was attempting to carefully explain my lack of a child but also trying to conceal the King's inability in bed by expressing innocence of what was required to make a child, a rather thoughtful gesture on my part since he had slandered me about court as the reason he could not perform, and although if I returned the favour and spoke ill of him it would only be me who suffered for it, I was also not unkind of nature and had no wish to humiliate him as he had me.

But the other women saw my subterfuge not. They thought I was entirely serious and was indeed a complete innocent in the ways of the bedchamber. I was clearly a better liar than I had thought.

"Madam," Lady Rutland said in a strangled voice. "There must be more than that, or it will be long ere we have a Duke of York."

"I know no more, and am satisfied," I said, brushing a hand over my embroidery as though what had been said was of small importance.

"Perhaps Your Majesty should discuss the matter with Mother Loew?" said Lady Rutland hesitantly, for from my tone the matter was closed.

"Fie!" I said, looking scandalised. "Marry, for shame. God forbid!"

My ladies exchanged glances, weighted with worry. They seemed to think I was completely ignorant about what was required to make a child. I had no way to assure them I was not, not without revealing the King to be incapable. But I had tried.

This was my way of avoiding intense mortification, for the King and for me. I was carefully informing my women the King had not consummated the marriage and was making myself appear innocent so *he* would not be disgraced, but it was also for my protection. I was pointing out if he had not bedded me, I could not be blamed for failing to bear a child.

I am sure some of the women understood, as I am sure many went away thinking I had never been informed what passed between a man and woman in bed. It is odd how intelligent people can be duped by the supposition of ignorance in others. Because I was new to many English ways and customs, they thought me ignorant, when I was in fact widening my mind by learning many new things, and because of my ignorance in one area, such as the language, they supposed me ignorant in others.

Even the wise may be made fools, by assuming they know more, and another less.

*

At the end of February, we heard Marie de Guise had been crowned in Scotland. When I was told, I frowned. "Are customs so different in that part of England?" I asked.

Jane Rochford pointed out Scotland was another country, and said things were indeed different there. I sighed inwardly. I had not really meant to call Scotland England, I was aware it was another country, but had not quite known how to refer to it as another part of the island I was presently living upon. My English was much better by that time, but still, there were matters and words and ways of expression which eluded me.

"All the same," I said, deciding that trying to explain myself would only take longer than simply going on with the conversation. "I find it odd I have not been crowned. I mean to raise it with my husband and his men, for my brother will ask soon why it is not done. I will not know what to tell him."

I saw some women lift their eyebrows, just slightly, and knew they had noted the reference to Wilhelm. I wanted security, and if the only way to gain that was to mention my brother, and his power, then that was what I had to do.

In truth I was anxious. The King did not spend time with me unless forced to, and only came at night sporadically. To all who asked, I said I had as much of his attention as I wanted or needed, but day by day my anxiety was growing.

I was the sister of a foreign duke, my position as a noblewoman and born duchess should have been protection enough, but Katherine of Aragon had been a Princess, and she had been left to waste away in a castle whilst her husband took a second wife and cast off their daughter Mary.

I tried to make appointments to see my husband, at dinner and during the day. "Tell the King he is always welcome in my chambers," I said to Culpepper, whom I had called to take the message to the King. I thought sending missives via his favourite gentleman might aid me. "But of course I understand he has much to do."

"The King is most busy, Majesty, but I will inform him of your invitation."

"I know he adores music, and I would have him hear my new band of musicians. I think he will love the sound of the violin, this new instrument to England, as I do."

"The King indeed adores music, Majesty, I shall make sure he knows what delights wait for him here." As Culpepper turned, I noted his eyes on little Howard. She was turned, could not see him, so she missed how his eyes lingered on her back.

I tried to reach out to my husband, but gently, and with care. He was polite when we met, but that was as far as it went. I felt I was getting nowhere, but at least he was not as rude about me as before. I even heard he had said I was dignified and gracious. I suspected Cromwell was singing my praises, although I saw him little too. He came to me from time to time and always dropped hints about how to please the King. My women, too, had taken up my cause, as I discovered one day when they launched yet another prearranged conversation in my presence.

One day, again by the fire, some of them decided to advise their Queen. Jane Boleyn, Catherine Howard and Anne Bassett, were my little allies. They all suddenly, and quite out of nowhere, struck up a conversation as we sewed on how to please men. They probably thought they were being subtle.

"English women laugh at all their husbands say, Your Majesty," little Howard said. "Men like to know they are amusing."

"Like to *think* they are, Mistress Howard," Jane interjected, making Catherine giggle.

I smiled gently. "The King is witty. I have no need to pretend." Well aware that anything I said would get back to him, I was not about to share a great deal with these women. I was not entirely sure of their motives at that moment.

"You are most fortunate, Your Majesty," Catherine said.

"All Englishmen are little boys, inside, Your Majesty," said Jane. "They want us to be as mothers, sisters and wives, all at the same time."

"And they like to be praised, Majesty," added Anne. "All men like to know they are noticed."

They kept the conversation general, as if simply talking of all men, not just the King. I listened, whilst maintaining a regal distance. As the bell sounded in the chapel for a feast that night, I smiled. "Your words are kindly meant, I think," I said, actually rather touched for I knew they were trying to aid me. "And will not be forgotten."

They were not. I took their advice, ludicrous though it was. I started laughing if the King made a jest, no matter how poor. Each time he entered a room, I told him how fine his clothes were and how handsome and young he looked. He did seem a little happier in my company.

But as March came in, there was a new whisper about court. The King's conscience was paining him. The pre-contract between me and the heir of Lorraine was on his mind, allowing him no rest.

"The King's conscience," I said. "I have heard it mentioned before, whenever he is tired of a wife."

Katherine of Suffolk looked uneasy when I said this and put her hand on my arm. I stared at her face and in those pretty eyes I saw fear.

# Chapter Twenty

**Westminster Palace**
**London**

**Spring 1540**

As I dropped more and more increasingly desperate hints about my coronation to the King's men, and crocuses peeked from the borders of forests, the abbeys of Canterbury, Christchurch, Rochester and Waltham surrendered to the King. "They too are closed now?" I asked Jane Rochford.

"They have submitted to the King, as Head of the Church." Her tone was balanced and careful, almost bland, yet there was a dimmed light in those green eyes which spoke of sadness. I saw that darkened radiance, that shadow of a sunlight once dazzling, in other eyes too, and in others I saw a shining zeal, sharp as a winter flame. Some held that zeal because they were devoted to the Lutheran way of the faith, and some because they served another god entirely, that of greed. Men knew if they pleased the King, riches of land, property or goods could become theirs, as such things were stripped from the monasteries. To some the richness of life lay in matters spiritual, and to some gold was the only wealth. The assets of the abbeys flowed into the King's coffers. Huge swathes of land were handed out as gifts to lords, ones in possession of itchy, greedy hands.

Yet these men did not know the truth, that this sickness for gold could never be cured by adding more gold to their purses or hands. It only made things worse. It might seem easy for a woman of my position to say such; my father had been a Duke, my brother was one and I had been raised in wealth unimaginable for many people of the world, wealth they could only dream of. Yes, it was easy to say such and yet perhaps it was easier for me to see what greed for gold did to a person because I was so close to it. Once within the veins of a man it did not feed him, it sucked the essence of his soul, the sickness of greed leeching all from that man until greed was all that possessed his mind. It was a demon which crept into the skin of a person, removing all of that person until all that was left was a shell. I could see this even if these men with their outstretched, trembling hands could not.

With these closures the dissolution of the monasteries was complete. The King went about court in a most unpleasantly buoyant mood, wearing the ring of Saint Thomas Becket on his thumb as if it were the head of a traitor set upon London Bridge, a trophy. That ring once had adorned the saint's shrine in Canterbury, Jane told me. Even I had heard of Saint Thomas, the tale was known all over the world, but this famous man was no more a symbol of greatness, of the Church ruling over the monarchy, no, now he was an example of sin. The King's namesake, Henry II, had been forced to crawl to the altar on his knees to do penance for the death of Saint Thomas, but Henry VIII would have the Church crawl before him.

"The nobles are now tied to the crown by coin," said Jane as we stood at a window, looking out on the world as life returned to it with the washing, cool breeze of spring. "These gifts of land and money, this is how the King will keep order."

Even I, by no means fully learned as to all that went on in this country, could see the power of this. No one with a mind on his purse would think to oppose the King, and at court there were plenty of them. Support of the King meant huge rewards in this life. Dissent would bring about a brutal trip to the next.

People said this last step in the dissolution of the monasteries would lead to the Lutheran element of court gaining more sway, but it seemed this was not so. The King kept all the old traditions of the Catholic Church in place, upholding them as cardinal truths even as he pillaged institutions that had kept them alive. Many at court held reformist ideals. Charges for heresy were harsh, and so people kept radical beliefs quiet, attending Bible-reading meetings in secret. Katherine of Suffolk was one of those people.

Without a word said by me on religion, I was coming to be regarded as a symbol for reformists, even though I was Catholic and had expressed no opinions on faith. The fact that I was seen in such a light made the Catholic party position themselves firmly against my marriage to the King. Norfolk, who had recently returned from France with promises of support from François on his lips, was apparently urging the King to separate from me, and Gardiner echoed all Norfolk said.

But I would not be daunted and had continued to ask after my coronation. I had also continued to complain about the Lady Mary. After one conversation with me, the King complained I "began to wax stubborn and wilful".

"You need to step with more care, my lady," said Olisleger.

"I am Queen, until someone decides otherwise, and I will press for my rights," I insisted. When I looked down at my hands, I noted they had bunched into fists without me realising, clutched at my sides. When I unfurled them, the palms were covered in sweat.

Olisleger was not the only one warning me. Others, Cromwell most prominent amongst them, told me the same. "The King prefers sweetness of temper to strength of spirit in women, Majesty," he instructed me during one rushed visit to my chambers.

I was not sure the King liked any virtue when it rested on me. All he saw were vices.

Although Cromwell was officially my ally, I did not like the man, and it was clear even to me that he was in trouble. Cromwell had been in high ascent, with the reformists at his back and the King's approval in his hands, but since my marriage he had slipped from the seat of favour and Gardiner was busy parking his generous behind on that comfy cushion. Seeing this, that April Cromwell went to war. During Lent a radical preacher called Robert Barnes, who all knew was an agent of Cromwell's, accused Gardiner of being a papist. Gardiner had initially opposed the break with Rome and had almost been sent to the Tower for it. If the King thought a man loyal to Rome, that man would end up dead.

"What will the Bishop do?" I asked Katherine of Suffolk.

"Gardiner, understanding the mortal danger he is in, has gone straight to the King," she said, "and told him all."

"Ah," I said, understanding. "Being the one to bring Barnes' accusation to the King's attention is clever, the Bishop avoids others taking the tale to the King's ear."

"Indeed," said the Duchess, petting her hound, aptly the one called Gardiner. "He never was a complete fool."

Gardiner protested the slander in the strongest terms and demanded to be permitted to bring Barnes in for questioning. The King, to Cromwell's abject horror, approved Gardiner's request.

By the beginning of April, Barnes along with two of his friends were taken to the Tower. No doubt under threat, if not reality, of torture, Barnes confessed much. Not only had he slandered Gardiner, but had insulted the Virgin Mary, saying she had only been worth something when pregnant with Christ, but otherwise "was but a saffron bag."

"The men of England sometimes sound as if they like women not at all," I said to Mistress Loew. "Even the holiest of us."

Barnes attempted to deny the charges, but when it was found he had said the King's government had no right to make changes that would rule men's consciences, he was in serious danger. That kind of radical thinking was poison to the King.

Another, William Jerome, was a preacher who had bellowed dangerous sentiments from the pulpit. He had spoken of predestination, the radical idea that men were preselected for Heaven rather than access being granted for prayer, good works and confession. Predestination was seen as heresy in England. He was easy to arrest, therefore, and once he was in the Tower much came from him that seemed to point to Cromwell.

That Easter reformists and evangelicals at court were on edge, fearful they would be implicated in Gardiner's counter strike. One of the men Gardiner had arrested had taken his own life in the Tower, many said because of torture used to extract information. It was said, every day, that Cromwell would not last another day. The King was angered against radicals on the reformist side of the faith, and now he had the wealth of the abbeys was swinging back towards Catholicism in a manner most fearful. Secret Lutherans were afraid they would burn. People started to distance themselves from Cromwell, certain his end was nigh.

But then Cromwell was not arrested, taken to the Tower or disgraced, but was made Earl of Essex.

The last Earl had died at the end of March, falling from his horse and snapping his neck. Everyone had supposed the title would go to his son, but in April it was announced Cromwell would become a member of the higher nobility for good service to the Crown. It was but three weeks since his allies had been marched to the Tower.

"Gardiner is terrified," I heard Jane saying to Catherine Howard. "He thought he had Cromwell by the throat. With Cromwell's protégés in the Tower spilling secrets, he thought he had Cromwell plucked, ready for the pot, and worse, he thought he had the King on his side."

"So why did the King ennoble Cromwell?" little Howard asked, looking baffled.

"To keep power balanced," said Jane. "The King is a Catholic, who is Head of the Church. An enemy to Rome, who upholds its ways. When the King broke with Rome everyone thought he would make England a Lutheran state, but the King despises Luther. England has a religion all its own, neither Lutheran nor Catholic, radical nor conservative. The only rule in this faith is the one men find hardest to abide by; think not for yourself, obey the King."

"So," Catherine said slowly, "the King keeps each in power to balance the other?"

"That is the way of things."

"So, because Gardiner was growing more powerful, Cromwell is rewarded?"

"You have it," Jane said, smiling. "There is also the fact that Cromwell is far more useful than Gardiner. The Bishop has a good mind, when not distracted by his temper, but Cromwell is always calm, collected and is more intelligent than Gardiner. The King knows that." She paused. "There is one last reason. The King is at his most powerful when he is unpredictable. If men believe they can predict him, they think they can control him. If he keeps everyone guessing, no one becomes too secure. This is his greatest power; to do what no one expects."

Jane glanced my way suddenly, perhaps aware I was listening. I shifted my gaze and lifted my hands to applaud Anne Bassett and Mary Norris, who had been dancing. Out of the corner of my eye I saw Jane look relieved.

On the same day Cromwell became Earl of Essex, he was also made Lord Great Chamberlain. Lands that once had been monasteries in Essex became his for life, and the new Earl was so proud of his title he began signing letters "Thomas Essex".

Soon after, a bill securing my dower rights as Queen passed in Parliament. It seemed Gardiner's plot to unseat me along with his greatest enemy had gone awry. The night Cromwell was elevated, the King dined with me in my chambers whilst Cromwell ate with his fellow magnates in the Council Chamber. The radicals arrested by Gardiner were punished, but Cromwell, it seemed, remained untouchable.

I watched my husband over the table; he looked so pleased with himself, like a child who has a secret he thinks no one else knows. I could not help but wonder what on earth was churning within that mind, that mind so haunted and pestilent, that brought such a smile to his face.

*

"Your Majesty *must* hear my songbird," I said to my husband as he and his men entered my chambers.

In an effort to win the King's affections, and under advice from Cromwell, I had ordered an entertainment. Sybylla would have been proud of my sneakiness. I had sent the invitation when the King was in Council, meeting the last remaining officers of Cleves about my dower. He therefore had no polite way to refuse.

I swept out a hand to little Howard, who was to perform, and noted the King looked pleased for the first time since entering. *He likes her*, I thought.

She was the kind of woman he often stared at, young, dressed in a fashionable French way, and in possession of a witty, lively spirit. He might have ridded the palaces of all portraits and memories of Anne Boleyn but from everything I had heard of that woman she had been the epitome of all the King looked for in a woman. He looked now for a ghost, an echo, and wanted someone who reminded him of her, the great love of his life. I suppose it should not be baffling that Catherine, who possessed many of the same traits which had made Anne Boleyn so enticing, and was indeed a blood relative of her, should have attracted the eyes of the King.

Perhaps they looked alike too, I knew not for I had seen no portrait of Anne Boleyn. The palaces had been stripped of them after her fall. I had heard, however, she was dark, famed for her raven locks where Catherine had fair hair, a sweet honey colour.

But Catherine had something else which perhaps made her more attractive, or perhaps it was a lack. From all I had heard of Anne Boleyn she had been most learned, educated as benefited a boy rather than a girl, and in her youth she had served in two of the greatest courts of the world. Catherine, although certainly not as foolish as she pretended to be when before the young lads of the court, who often warmed to women who were a trifle simple, was not highly educated and therefore in conversation she sometimes appeared a little ignorant, and certainly innocent in many ways. It occurred to me that the King might like Catherine because in body and in her light and witty conversation she reminded him of Anne Boleyn, and in her simplicity and perhaps ignorance she reminded him of Jane Seymour, who some had told me barely had known how to read.

Perhaps I reminded him of Katherine of Aragon, towards the end of their relationship, or perhaps I reminded him of none of them and therein lay the problem. It was said that each of his wives had loved him, some with all their hearts. I believe the King was more than aware of my revulsion towards him. He wanted someone who adored him, and I could barely stand him.

With Anne playing the virginals, Catherine stood before the King and his men. As she lifted her voice to sing a ballad of love, I could see many eyes watching her, and the King's were fixed on her. Norfolk, Cromwell, and Thomas Culpepper, the King's favourite serving man, all of them stared at her, but not as hard and long as the King did.

As her song ended, the King applauded loudly, hands bashing together like drums. His face was flushed, his eyes were alight with lust. As little Howard went back to her place at the back of the chamber, I saw Norfolk staring, as though his niece were a lonesome sheep on a hill, and he a wolf, slinking in the undergrowth.

*Norfolk notes the King's interest*, said the voice in my mind. *He will try to get her into the bed of the King.*

# Chapter Twenty-One

**Hampton Court
London**

**Easter 1540**

Easter was spent at Hampton Court that year, and there finally, yet only briefly, I met the other children of the King, my new stepson and daughter.

It seemed an event undertaken with great reluctance. I gathered the King did not particularly want me to meet his children, his heir in particular, but I had so wanted to meet them. Ever since I had received Elizabeth's letter, I had been consumed with curiosity about her, not least because she was the child of Anne Boleyn, whose presence I seemed to feel everywhere I went.

The King had visited his children at Richmond and, at their urging, had brought them to Hampton Court where we were spending Easter, for a day or so. They were to be sent back again after this, but at least I had a brief time with them.

Lady Elizabeth, a pale-skinned nymph with a long body and face, high cheekbones and bright red hair, curtseyed low and deep before me when she was brought into the chamber. She moved elegantly, in a way that spoke not of grace taught by courtly instructors, but inherited. It was in her bones and blood. She held her hands, pale and long fingered, before her so they would contrast with her crimson dress, bringing them to attention. And they were beautiful, her hands, so I understood why she wanted people to see them. She had pale, tapering fingers. Her skin was more than fashionable pale; it was almost translucent, and most becoming next to her bright hair. But those eyes… I almost recoiled when she looked up. I had expected to see the green eyes that so often matched with red hair, but her eyes were black. Black as her mother's. Black as the eyes I had seen in my dreams.

It was as if I had been greeted by my ghost.

I could see her father in her, certainly in that hair, for it was red as fire, and even though the King was spare of hair and running to silver I could tell his once had been bright and flaming like hers. There was something in her nose and jaw too, in her pretty mouth, a rosebud like the King's. Upon his face, that mouth often looked petulant. On the Princess it was sweet. The King was upon her face. There was no denying she was his daughter, no matter what some people whispered, but I believed her mother was there too. The King did not have high, sharp cheekbones, and those long fingers as well as that elegant neck were not his either.

It was more than simple resemblance. The woman of my dreams seemed to hover on Elizabeth's features, like the reflection of two faces in a misty pool of water, one behind the other. The face of Anne wavered, half there, half not. Half seen and half hidden. Anne was with her daughter.

*Where else should I be?* asked the voice.

At Elizabeth's side was Mistress Champernowne, her governess. She looked like a lioness guarding her cub and I was glad of it. From what I had already seen, Elizabeth was not the one fussed over by all, that was Edward. She seemed in fact a trifle neglected, so at least she had someone caring for her.

"I am so very honoured you wished to meet me, Your Majesty," Elizabeth said, sweeping into yet another deep, elegant curtsey. "Although my studies keep me much occupied, knowledge of your marriage to my gracious royal father caused boundless elation in my heart."

"I... thank you," I said, my tongue stumbling, my mind trying, apparently, to forget all English I had learned as I was astonished by the sophistication of her speech. "I am delighted to meet you, and must thank you for your letter to me, it was beautifully written."

"My gracious father has insisted on a bountiful education for me, Your Majesty," she said. "One for which I always will be grateful."

I did not have long with her, for what everyone believed to be the most important person was brought in not long after, Prince Edward. *How fat he is!* was the shocked thought that flashed through my mind.

Prince Edward was little more than an infant, with fair hair carrying a touch of red, curling under his pale ears. He looked remarkably like Lady Elizabeth in some ways, but his jaw was not as strong as hers, his features less defined. He was handsome enough and certainly well fed, a little too much so. His chubby arms and cheeks were not those of a normal child his age. Edward had a big belly and a pallid, unwholesome cast to his face. Obviously his servants stuffed him as full of food as my husband did himself, trying to keep Edward alive at all costs. To my eyes it was having the opposite effect. He did not appear sickly, but he did not look hale, either.

Edward was wearing a tiny doublet, just like the King's, along with a floor-length skirt. It was usual for infants to all be dressed in the garb of female children for the first years of their lives, but this mixture of masculine and feminine looked odd on the young Prince, as though his father wanted everyone to be in no doubt of Edward's flourishing masculinity from the first moments of his life. Masculinity was something my husband was much occupied with. One only had to glance at his outrageous codpieces to understand he was insecure about something in that area.

Edward was shy about me at first, until his older sister encouraged him to bring a toy ship to me. "It is your favourite?" I asked and the boy nodded, beaming suddenly. As the interview went on, he sat on the floor near me, playing with his ship.

"He likes you, Your Majesty," Elizabeth said to me. "Often, my royal brother is much reserved with new people, he does not go so close to them, but not so with you."

"I am glad of it," I said. "I would like both of you to be close to me. I am your stepmother now."

I was not quite prepared for a glint of moisture to appear in Elizabeth's eyes. I had said such a small thing, and yet I could tell it meant a great deal to her. "I would like that too, Your Majesty."

When the Prince and Princess left, bound again for Richmond where the air was healthier – although I saw no problem with the air of Hampton Court – I felt sad. The King saw them at times, obviously, but it was plain to me he saw them not often. They were hungry for affection, both in their own ways. Elizabeth made me sadder of the two. Edward was fussed over, perhaps too much, but she had an air of neglect, not in her clothes for they were rich, but in her eyes.

I wondered if the parts of her I supposed came from her mother were noted too by the King, and if seeing those features alive, on another person, indeed on a person whose mother he had killed, was too much for him to bear. We tend to avoid that which makes us feel guilty, and I would imagine Elizabeth brought many pangs of that uneasy emotion to the King's heart. I was not the only one who saw a ghost when I looked on her. The King did too, and that ghost, as I realised then, was not only haunting me. Anne Boleyn haunted him too.

# Chapter Twenty-Two

**Whitehall Palace
London**

**Spring 1540**

A day after we returned to Whitehall, little Howard came to me, asking permission to go again to Norfolk House, which was granted. She came back later that day, looking pale and worried. Noting this and thinking of all I had seen when she had sung to my company, I surmised that her family, Norfolk most of all I suspected, had asked her to become, or more likely told her to become mistress to the King, and the girl had no wish for such a position. If she did want to become the King's mistress, surely she would have seemed merry. Catherine looked like a corpse when she returned to court, grey of complexion and lacking all zeal for life, something entirely alien to her normally buoyant character.

All the next day she appeared distracted. Normally a careful, skilled member of the household, she kept dropping things, making the senior ladies of the Bedchamber round on her with harsh words. I felt sorry for the girl, but as if to confirm my suspicions, Catherine suddenly appeared to be the centre of her family's attention. Before this time, most of them had ignored her in general, but now they were all about her, fawning, all the time. Her sister Isabella, who had until then kept a lofty distance from her half-sister who was of a lower court station, was constantly at her side, laughing at all Catherine said and flattering her. Jane Rochford, too, seemed to be hovering about little Howard, in a slightly protective manner.

I wondered if they were acting as chaperones, perhaps protecting her? Was this to protect her from the King, or *for* the King?

If the King was to take a mistress and had selected little Howard, I certainly felt sorry for her, but I took my mother's advice, given so long ago, and ignored the situation. It was the only defence I had, after all, for it would do no good to accost him, but even then, that voice which came to me from time to time returned, whispering that the King had found wives from amongst the women of his wives' households before. Was he thinking to set me aside? If that happened, where would I end up? Jane Seymour had died in childbed and that was not likely to be my fate, so I was left with accusation of treason and public death or being sent from court to die in the marshes, perhaps by poison.

*It would be poison,* I thought. I was not as highly titled as Katherine of Aragon had been, but I was a born duchess of another country. Kill me in a way obvious, or arrest me, and there would be protest from my brother at least. And yet, I was being spoken of as a Lutheran and this was not permitted in England. Would the King dare dream up a charge of heresy and lay it at my door?

Or would I simply drink something, eat something one day, and go to my bed never to wake again?

Thoughts of death and disgrace haunting me, I kept an eye on Catherine. Little Howard started vanishing at times, and I had no doubt she was with the King. I thought of it with revulsion. She was not yet sixteen, and he old enough to be her grandfather! She was a tiny little thing, and he a great, lumbering ox. Catherine was a bright light shining away merrily, whilst the King was a dull, dark, aching cavern, barren and miserable.

She started to appear in my chambers and about court in clothes more costly than before. Gifts from the King or her family, trying to buy her way into the King's bed by dressing her so he noticed her more? I knew not, but I liked none of it. My nerves were on edge. I started to shy away from food and wine, not knowing what or whom I could trust. My sleep became reluctant to visit, and when it would come it was plagued by dreams of faces grinning at me, as hands worked ill behind me. The dark-eyed woman, she who had come to me when I needed help, when I was most scared, was there again but always in the background of these dreams. I could not reach her, nor touch her. I could not hear the warnings she whispered.

Everyone was remarking on how young the King suddenly seemed. He had a lightness in his booming, limping step, and was always ready with a merry jest. Although he was almost fifty, people said he looked thirty again. His temper, which I had not seen outright but many spoke of with terror, seemed to have vanished. I pretended to be nothing but happy at the alteration, and accepted people's compliments when they said I was the cause, but I knew I was not.

When little Howard came, asking to go to Norfolk House regularly to care for her grandmother, who was sick, I knew. This was an excuse for the King to meet with her away from court.

"Of course you must go," I said in a kind tone, "your grandmother must be old now, and needs your tender care." I smiled, and the girl looked wretched. "But I will miss my little songbird."

"Thank you, Majesty," she said. Catherine was not clever at concealing how she felt. She did not like this role, did not want it, I could see that. I had always had the impression Catherine liked me, and now she was being forced into the position of lying to me and taking my husband to her bed. I had no doubt she had no choice. All the same, I could not afford to be a fool about this.

"I want eyes on the King," I told Mistress Loew and Olisleger. "I want to know where he goes at night."

The King's barge, the *Lyon*, was easy enough to recognise, so when he went to Norfolk House it was put about court that he was visiting Cranmer at Lambeth Palace nearby, or paying his respects to Catherine's poor sick grandmother, who had been his friend and supporter a long time. Whether anyone believed this I had no idea, but the more the King's barge alighted on the water steps of Lambeth, the more tongues wagged.

Later I heard from Mistress Loew that Catherine was being shipped frequently by night to Winchester House, Bishop Gardiner's London seat.

"There are tales of feasts, where the King and Catherine Howard sit close, as if married," Olisleger told me. "The Howards are flocked about them."

"Speak to Cromwell of this, and warn him," I said.

The very next day I heard Cromwell was trying to get Norfolk banished from court. It seemed he too was panicking more than a little.

One of Norfolk's men had died, Olisleger told me, and Cromwell had spoken to the King, telling him the man had been infested with plague and Norfolk along with his entire household should be sent into the country to avoid infection. Considering how paranoid the King was about sickness, it was a true mark of his feelings for little Howard that her uncle had not been banished. Norfolk had gone to the King and told him that his groom had been living with fourteen other men, in the same room, when he fell sick. None of them had died, protested Norfolk, and he, the Duke, had been far from this man at the time of this sickness in any case.

But Cromwell had not stopped. Rumours that Norfolk was plotting to murder Prince Edward suddenly were all over court, and although there was, as far as I knew, no truth in them, everyone was speaking of it. "What good would such an event do Norfolk, in any case?" I asked Olisleger.

"If Edward were to die," he whispered, "it is likely that Lady Mary would be returned to the succession. She could take a husband and breed. Their children could rule England, continuing the Tudor line. Everyone knows if Mary came to the throne, the Catholic faith would return in truth, and England would be restored to Rome. Norfolk is a traditionalist; he would want that."

Turning on Gardiner next, Cromwell arrested one of his allies, the Bishop of Chichester, accusing him of being loyal to Rome. There were hints more arrests would follow. Norfolk was concerned Gardiner would be one of them.

But he was not.

Court was becoming a strange and dangerous place; everyone was on edge. Something was coming and all knew it.

And every day she was at court, little Howard had a new dress.

And every day, I formed a new fear.

I wondered if the conservatives would strike back at Cromwell and those he supported. I wondered if I would be arrested and sent to the Tower, charges of heresy upon me, or if I would be ordered from Whitehall to a castle in the moors, or the mists, and there left to die, just as Katherine of Aragon was.

There were many tried and tested means to remove a Queen from the throne in England. The King had used many and who was to stop him using them again? He was Emperor and Pope in his own kingdom. There was no one who had the power to stop him.

# Chapter Twenty-Three

### Whitehall Palace
### London

### Early Summer 1540

I sat in the stands at Whitehall, waiting for a jug of wine that little Howard had gone to fetch for me from the man serving from a barrel of it below us. Out in the tiltyard, pennants of knights were streaming in hot air, slapping and snapping as warm, dusty wind blew past. I sighed. I knew not why or how these men were jousting in this weather. In French hood and English gown I was, and I was baking like a cherry pie, set to dissolve into my own skin. All those men in all that armour must have been roasting as meat in an iron pot.

It had not rained for more than a week, a strange occurrence in England where, as far as I had learned thus far, no day was complete without a touch of rain, mizzle, or grey, slinking fog. But the day was dry, as was the earth. After a week without rain and with much heat it was rising up in clouds of dust as knights thundered across it, hooves of horses beating the broken earth.

We had watched jousting for five days, as well as mock tourneys of sword when the knights were resting, or it was too hot for them to engage. The Earl of Surrey was leading the defenders that day with William Howard as his second. Sir Richard Cromwell was leading the answerers with Sir Thomas Seymour as his second. Even when we watched entertainments, politics and faith were present, at war with one another.

In truth, though I clapped and smiled and handed out prizes, I found the whole endeavour trying my already strained patience. All this playing at war, it was as my father had said, foolish. Overgrown boys, who never had seen battle in truth, rode out onto this fake field of war with such exuberant pride, as if they thought themselves Achilles, or Hector. They all looked more like Paris to me, and I had always thought him a vain peacock.

My mind had been hampered with other matters too. The Emperor and Wilhelm were still at odds most perilous over Guelders, and Wilhelm had agreed in the spring just passed to go to a secret meeting with the Emperor, which my brother of course informed family about in case he did not return, to attempt to reach a resolution. Wilhelm had not, however, informed my husband of this, but I had no doubt the King knew of it since my brother had sent a letter to me, and I was sure my missives were being opened. The trouble with Wilhelm not informing his ally directly was that the King might well believe Wilhelm was up to something duplicitous with the Emperor, or might sign an agreement with him which would not benefit England. I doubt my brother considered a great deal that what he was doing, or that writing a letter to me about it might cause more trouble for me, but Wilhelm sometimes was not given to great consideration before he acted.

He had gone ahead with the meeting, and although negotiations had gone nowhere and no resolution had been reached, I had been relieved to hear through Harst as well as Olisleger, who had had word from Cleves too, that Wilhelm had arrived back home safe, and had not been captured or detained by Charles V. There was still trouble over Guelders, but my brother was home and unharmed.

I tore my thoughts from my home country and tried to concentrate on my new one.

It was May Day, the English celebration of the start of summer, the end of spring, and summer had arrived with vengeance on its mind, apparently. I knew not what the world had done to summer, but whatever it was, summer was enraged about it. The skies baked and the earth was hard already. The air smelt of dust, horses and perspiration, as well as stale wine. The stands were packed with sweaty nobles and courtiers cheering and wagering on the challengers and answerers. When I came to the lists that day and every day I had attended, I had been cheered by the ranks of commoners allowed in, separated from the nobility of course. They were to one side, the commoners, and there were thousands of them, packed tight into their stands. No less excited than the nobles, the ordinary people of England wailed as favourites fell and screamed hysterically when they won.

*It was this day, not so long ago, that marked my end,* said the ghost.

I started a little, for I had not been thinking of my own personal ghost and her fall, but when I did think on it, I remembered May had been indeed the time she had fallen. Had this event, this Mary Day joust, marked the last event she presided over as Queen?

Would it mark mine? I knew not.

Little Howard returned and filled my cup. Rewarded with a curt nod rather than the gentle smile she once habitually received from me, Catherine fell back, holding the jug in her sweating palms. Much as it pained me to be curt with her, I had to be. I could not be polite to the King's mistress. There had to be distance between us now.

I felt sorrier for her still as I saw her staring at but one knight, Culpepper. I had been told the two had something of affection for each other once when first she came to court, but it had soured in some way, and yet Catherine seemed to pine for him still. She often watched him at dances and feasts. No doubt she would rather be his mistress than that of the King, or better yet, his wife. They were of an age. From the way he sometimes watched her, I could ascertain whatever affection had been between them still was there, and perhaps this lad who I had been told never risked his heart had in fact risked it. They liked each other, but something was preventing them admitting such, and not just the fact that the King now was clearly laying claim to little Howard.

Culpepper was magnificent in the joust. Even I who thought it a silly spectacle could admire the best knights. I could see why Catherine admired him. His armour shone, glinting in the sunlight and when he won he took off his helmet, grinning at the crowds, those engaging blue eyes glimmering like water in the clearest ocean. But for all the acclaim the crowds offered him, and for all his skill, his final match that day he lost to Sir Richard Cromwell. When I happened to glance at little Howard after, I noted she looked ready to beat Richard Cromwell to death.

As this particular match ended, I saw Lady Mary, standing not far from me in the stalls, regarding me with a critical eye. I went to her. As I approached, she bobbed into another of those low curtsies I had come to hate so, but as she rose I smiled at her. "The people of England are welcoming," I said in my slow English, extending a hand to the crowds, who having cheered the knights were now cheering me once more. "I am glad of their affection. I understand your mother, when first she came to London was cheered too, by the King's people."

"Of course, she was a Princess of Castile and Aragon, Your Majesty," said the Princess who was not a Princess. She spoke stiffly, with reserve.

"And a glorious beauty, as I understand it," I said. "In my country of Cleves, the people there speak well of your late mother. It is always said she was as wise as she was beautiful, and I think that a greater compliment. Beauty, it is an accident of fate, is it not? Wisdom, however, this is something honed and refined by the one who possesses it, and it requires work and dedication to maintain and increase. Therefore, it is good to be beautiful, but more worthy it is to be wise. Your mother was fortunate in her looks, and more fortunate still to understand the wealth of cultivating the virtue of greatness of mind."

Mary seemed unsure how to respond and glanced about. "Thank you, Majesty," she said, that stiffness easing a little. "I did not know she was spoken of so, in your country. I would have thought..."

"That in a country where Luther's works are read by some, your mother would not be spoken of so?" I asked. "No matter what you may have heard, my mother and father were Catholic, my lady, my good brother remains so, and all of we children of the great house of Cleves were raised in the Catholic faith. Yet we were also raised to understand even the Church is not an infallible institution, as your father has ascertained too. And yet in Cleves, people are appreciated, valued on their own merit, and not because of the path they take to the faith." I paused, allowing this to sink in, and returned to a safer subject, in one way at least. "My country, as part of the Holy Roman Empire, knew much of your mother, and knew there was much in her to admire. Her death was mourned by our court. My mother had Masses sung for her soul."

"Thank you, Majesty." She looked unsure a moment, but as I went to leave, she flowed into a curtsey that was low, deep, and respectful, and I smiled to see it. It was a start.

The joust came to a close, and I walked away with my ladies, back to the palace to prepare for the evening's entertainments. Once, I might have asked Catherine to walk close by me, to sing when we reached my chambers. But those days were done. The King had set a wedge between us, and it saddened me.

We went to the feast at Durham House that night, and I watched as the King handed out rewards to the knights. One hundred marks and houses in which to live were their prizes. Culpepper, felled at the last, was not rewarded. Little Howard seemed sad for him, but she did not take a step near him, nor he near her.

I watched the dancing as it began, but Catherine was not amongst them. Before, she had danced every dance and always had a partner, for she was skilled and graceful, but now she stood alone, on the edge of what had been her favourite entertainment. Everyone knew, you see, that the King had claimed her as his, therefore she stood, not joyous in the dance as she usually was, but looking scared, and isolated.

My heart echoed hers.

*

A day later, and I rose from my bed to find it was all about court that I was soon to be crowned. "Cromwell is spreading the rumours," Katherine of Suffolk said as she helped me to dress.

"He thinks to force the King's hand?"

If so, I would aid him. I called my personal advisor, Carl Harst, to me and told him to go to Cromwell to talk about the arrangements. Harst did, but without success. Cromwell wanted the court speaking about this triumph that was apparently mine, but to actually go ahead with plans when he knew his master was against the idea was tantamount to signing his own death warrant. That same day there were further rumours that France and England were now allied, no doubt put about by Norfolk and Gardiner, counter-rumours to offset those begun by Cromwell.

I did not know if these rumours were a lie, but this left my country in trouble if they were true. England was supposed to be Cleves's ally and the Emperor had demanded that Cleves surrender Guelders again. My brother was showing signs of aggression in response, but he was not rebelling outright yet. The treaty between England and Cleves was mutually defensive, but the King of England was not a man to keep his word, that I had learned. My marriage, meant to bring safety to my people, was meaningless if it meant England was not to be our ally, and if it brought no good to my people, what was this marriage for?

# Chapter Twenty-Four

**Whitehall Palace
London**

**Late Spring 1540**

"Why does Mistress Anne Bassett look as if she is half in the grave?" I asked Katherine of Suffolk, as I watched the head of my maids of honour drifting about the chamber, face pale and eyes wide. She looked as if she had seen a ghost, but then, when I came to think on it, such a thing was not impossible. There seemed to be plenty of those roaming the halls of court.

"It is her stepfather, Majesty," Katherine said. "He has been arrested in Calais and is being brought to London, to the Tower."

"What happened?" I thought of Lord Lisle, this man who was my uncle by marriage who had been so polite and welcoming, so good to me, and I felt anger. Why should good men be treated so badly? I could not believe he would have done anything to deserve arrest and imprisonment, and what of his poor wife? Lady Lisle would have remained in Calais, perhaps facing alone any repercussions which came from this arrest of her husband.

"It is Cromwell," Katherine breathed in my ear, her breath on my cheek smelling of mint and warm lemon. "He has accused Anne's father of being a papist, Majesty, of communicating with foreign powers, but many say the man is innocent. It is said Cromwell has been filling Calais with radicals who like not the King's stance on religion and desire further reform. That may be why he has attacked Lord Lisle, for Lisle is a conservative."

"And this man Cromwell, who attacks my friends, few though I have, is supposed to be my ally," I said, liking Cromwell even less than before, and I had not much affection for him to begin with. Something about him set my skin on edge. I could feel the hairs on my arms and back rising when I heard his voice. I did not like to be in the same room as him. I did not need the whispering voice in my mind to tell me to distrust this man, I did already.

"You have many friends, Majesty," said Katherine, setting her hand on mine. "And at court, allies often are not the same thing as friends."

"But Lord Lisle is a good man, and his wife a fine woman," I protested. "And he is the King's own uncle, by a bastard strain, but blood nonetheless."

"Being closely related to royalty can be perilous, Majesty," said Katherine, and I shivered. "But rest with greater ease, for I hear Norfolk has already gone to the King to defend Lisle, saying the King's uncle may well be the innocent victim of 'another' who is trying to cover their crimes, by which he means Cromwell, of course. There will be an investigation into crimes of heresy in the Pale of Calais, for the King hears from Norfolk that it may be possible that Lord Lisle has been arrested to conceal the fact that 'someone', and I think we can all guess who, is shipping radicals there, men who would work ill against England."

"So, in this matter I find myself allied with Norfolk," I said.

"Agreeing with him that Lord Lisle may have been unjustly accused is one thing," said my wise friend. "Being an ally is something entirely different."

That made me feel better. Norfolk was another I did not like and certainly did not trust.

Not many days later we heard that Lisle was safe, but he remained in the Tower. He was not in a cell, and Anne was permitted to go to him, taking baskets of food and books. When I asked after him, Anne said he seemed well, and had told her not to fear. "I am glad to hear it," I said. "I liked your father a great deal when we met in Calais."

"Thank you, Majesty," she said, and tears sprang to her eyes.

"Courage, Mistress Bassett," I said in a gentle tone. "Repeat the word to yourself, when times are hard. Always there will come trying times, this we cannot avoid in life, but we can steel ourselves to face the tests that fall upon us with all the strength and resolve we have within us, and often that strength and our own resilience is far greater than we believe it to be." I smiled. "Often, we... what is the word? Underestimate ourselves."

"You give me hope, Majesty, thank you."

"You are a strong woman, Mistress Bassett, and your father is too in possession of strength. You will endure through this, both of you."

But for all the rumours that Lisle was safe, the King remained sufficiently paranoid to want to investigate both sides. He trusted no one. Soon Cromwell was fighting back, claiming Gardiner was in league with Lisle, and they were conspiring to bring papism back to England. Gardiner responded in kind, telling the King that Cromwell was part of a league that wanted to bring about radical reform, that he denied the Real Presence of the Host, and was a heretic.

It was like watching a pack of rabid dogs tear each other apart, biting their own legs from time to time in their frenzy. I wanted no part of this fight. These men, all of them would name themselves Christian, and yet I saw nothing of the teachings of Christ in what they did. They served power, not piety.

I started to tell Cromwell I was too busy to see him when requests to meet with me came to my door, for I did not want him to attempt to draw me into whatever plans he was making to strike at his foes. I would not be used to attack Lisle, would not be responsible for any of the chaos and death these men seemed to be aiming for in their frenetic struggle to be closest to the throne. Katherine of Suffolk might tell me I had many friends, but I knew I was still much seen as an outsider at court, and in many ways I would rather be outside this maelstrom of madness these men created than inside it.

Fortunately, however, in some areas there was a change to the wind.

Lady Mary had been telling people she had come to believe I was not Lutheran and was a woman of high intelligence and grace. Apparently, one could not be a woman of high intelligence and grace *and* a Lutheran, but her change of heart was a start. It demonstrated that my resolution to gently ignore all the hurtful comments and indelicate sniggering about me was having some effect. I might not be liked by all, but respect was flowing my way.

*The English need some model of behaviour to follow*, I thought, *for their King only brings out the worst in all of them.*

Lady Mary and I had, in fact, been on three highly successful walks in the gardens by that time. They were not of long duration, but the conversation had been pleasing and sweet. I had praised her mother, which evidently was the way through her cold façade and into her heart, and she had asked me much of my upbringing. "I am the second of three sisters, though we have a brother too, Wilhelm, in England you would say William, who now is Duke of my homeland," I had told her. "My elder sister, Sybylla…" – I was not about to mention that Sybylla was a Lutheran with high intelligence and grace since Mary and I were getting along at last – "… had all the beauty of the family, and she told us tales of magic and mystery when we were young, and Amalia is the youngest, and the most rebellious of us. She wanted to be Joan of Arc when she was a child."

Mary had smiled. "I too loved the tales of the Maid of France," she said, a wash of frightening zeal, a fierce love flooding into her eyes. "To be spoken to by God Himself, such a blessing I can only dream of."

"I think God speaks to all of His people, my lady," I said. "Sometimes, it is not in ways we can hear, as words, but there is a message there, trying to reach us."

"I think you are right, Majesty."

I glanced about, checking I would not be heard. "And your mother too, she sees you, I am sure, and she would be proud to have a daughter like you, as I am."

We were, in truth, almost the same age, but Mary smiled and suddenly reached out to touch my hand. "I am glad you are my father's wife," she said. "He needs someone of sense and calmness to be his Queen. I think my mother would have liked you."

"If that is true," I said. "Then I am most pleased. Your mother was a woman of wisdom, and if, in the time I am given, I can be anything like her then I will be satisfied with my role as Queen."

"You are like her in some ways," said Mary. "Like you, she was usually calm, faced the storms of life with grace. Even death she stood before and was not daunted."

I chuckled. "I think you believe me to be of higher courage than I truly am."

She looked into my eyes. Her stare was odd, in a way, it seemed to penetrate the skin, so she could see your soul. I had been told Mary was short of sight, could not see far away, and perhaps this affliction granted her this ability to appear to be seeing straight through a person. Perhaps she truly could. I have often noted that those who have known suffering can see it in others.

"I think you have more courage than you know, Majesty," she said.

*

On the 22nd of May, we had news from Scotland. A prince had been born to Marie de Guise and King James. Celebrations went on, but the King barely looked at me during them. He was busy, staring at Catherine Howard.

"This son of Scotland could be a fine match for you," I said to Lady Mary, who had come to stand near me as we watched the dancers.

"I would be twenty years and more his senior," she said. "I think he would be a better match for my sister, Elizabeth."

"I was impressed with your sister," I said.

Mary's face, often so dour, brightened. "Elizabeth is a lovely girl, Majesty. She is precocious, I rarely have met a brighter child. Not for her the tales of Aesop, but instead the works of Erasmus and Cicero. Languages she learns without seeming to even try, and she plays the virginals beautifully." Mary sounded proud, and I warmed to her all the more. She could easily have resented or indeed hated this child, the fruit of the union which had destroyed her mother's marriage to her father, yet there was nothing in her tone but love and affection.

"She is fortunate to have you as her sister," I said.

"I love both my siblings," she replied, sounding a trifle defensive, as if she knew the thoughts which had floated through my mind. "That we each came of a different mother matters not. We share a father. They are not to blame for what happened to my mother."

"I understand you were close to Queen Jane," I said.

"I was, and mourn her still. She was a good woman." She turned to me. "But another good woman has come to the throne now, and I hope in time we will be close."

"I think this hope already is true," I said, and was somewhat startled when Mary reached out and took my hand, squeezing it. There were tears in her eyes. She did not allow people to see her true self, not easily and often not willingly, that I could see, and I felt honoured I was one she was starting to trust enough to allow in. Those who do not trust easily, it is a hard thing for them to open just enough to let a new person into their circle. Mary was, slowly and carefully, welcoming me, and I cherished the trust she offered, hoping that she might be allowed to love another person, one who would not hurt her.

It struck me that all the King's children were, in their own ways, most lonely.

Harmony was entering some aspects of my life, yet at the same time it felt as if the court might fly apart, chaos taking over. At the end of May one of Gardiner's allies became Bishop of Westminster, and Cromwell counterattacked, arresting many of his enemies on charges of papist loyalties. War raged in the halls of court. Reformists were being arrested, then conservatives in retaliation. No one was safe. It was said something must happen soon, or Hell would break loose upon England. To my mind it already had.

"It is like a baiting pit," I whispered one day to Katherine of Suffolk.

"The dogs of England fight hard, and bloody," she told me. "I think we are nearing a time when one will fall, again."

She did not need to say why she had said "again". This was not the first time the court of the King had descended into war and madness, one faction pitted against another. These people, so capable of greatness they were, yet they were so brutal with one another, barbarous in many ways. I tried to think of any scandal of my father's court which had played out as this one I witnessed in England, and I could not think of any. Unless I had been protected from such things, and I did not think I had, this was not the way of all courts.

But it was the way of this King's court.

By pitting them against each other, playing them, teasing and keeping them guessing, by keeping everyone on edge and insecure, he made situations like this occur. Perhaps he even wanted them to, for then he could thin the ambitious men about him, take some of them down, reduce the number vying for prestige and power.

The corridors of court fell silent, but murmurs were behind each door. People looked pale and afraid, rabbits in a captive warren attacked by foxes. I was reminded of the Peasants' War in my own country, and something told me I should be afraid.

And I was.

# Chapter Twenty-Five

**Whitehall Palace**
**London**

**Summer 1540**

It was the 10th of June. Heat gleamed as a waving prism in the air above cobbles in the courtyards. The world was become a haze, as if the eyes I used to see it were drunk. I woke feeling groggy, stale air pushing down upon me, and the weight of sleeping badly, the room too hot to allow deep sleep, pressed on my temples. A breeze, hot and rancid, blew in the grounds, fluttering through blooms desiccating under the angry, sullen sun. The grass, the flowers, the plants, even the trees were wilting and dying, despite the best efforts of groundsmen who watered them by night.

"Is it always like this in summer?" I sighed to Jane Rochford as she dressed me.

"No, Majesty. This is a strange summer."

I stood by the window, trying to keep cool as layers of clothing were set upon my body. These gowns I had liked so much before now seemed a hindrance, too many parts, too many layers, too much of all, like the King's court. Layers of pressure, anger, vengeance, resentment, they all piled upon the soul tying it to the earth.

I stared from the window. Birds came to rest in the gardens by what water they could find, beaks open, panting, trying to cool down. Deer, no more concerned about man or any other predator, sat panting too, under trees in the parkland. Dogs lay down in the courtyards and whined. All I could hear that day was the flapping of fans, as my women went about their tasks in a daze, befuddled by the heat. I pitied those working in the kitchens, where roaring fires still burned despite the warmth of the day in order to roast meat and bake pies. We heard of maids and young lads, as well as old men, being carried out, having fainted in the unrelenting heat.

That day, Cromwell made for Council, as usual. Yet just as Jane had said this summer was strange, so this day was not a usual day.

Before Cromwell was seated, Norfolk stepped forwards, shouting, "I arrest you in the name of the King!" Other men leapt to action. The symbols of the Order of the Garter were torn from Cromwell's clothing. Cromwell threw his hat on the floor, challenging the men there to name him a traitor.

Oh, they were more than happy to do as he wished.

The end had come. Cromwell had served the King for ten years, making his every desire a reality. From separating the King from Katherine of Aragon to breaking with Rome and the Pope, from making Anne Boleyn Queen to removing her from life, Cromwell had succeeded. But in this last, fatal affair of the King's marriage to me, Cromwell had failed. The King was disappointed, and Cromwell's enemies had been able to persuade the King his best man was guilty of much.

Cromwell should have seen their plot. He had once used the King's disappointment to kill another Anne.

Arrested for links to heretical preachers, suspicion over the number of retainers he kept, for a dereliction of duty in the King's marriage, and for not supporting alliance with France and Spain, Cromwell was taken to the Tower, cries of "Traitor!" marking his every step to the boat. His London house was surrounded by archers in case of looters, his plate and goods were confiscated by the King.

With his arrest I found my last powerful ally at court was gone. I did not know how to feel. I never had liked the man, certainly never trusted him and many times, especially of late, I had not wanted to be associated with him, and yet he was leading the party of court which supported me as Queen. Conflicted I felt, as I heard of his arrest.

Others were happy, however.

That night bonfires blazed all about London and people danced about the flames, celebrating the fall of Cromwell. In the distance I saw them, red fire against dark night. They danced for his fall, for a future coming which they hoped would be better without him in it, they danced for freedom, just as the Swan Maiden had.

I wished I could be one of them, these people removed from this dangerous world of which I was now Queen. But Queen for how long? I knew not.

"Wish upon me a cloak of feathers," I whispered to the night's sky. "That I might fly away."

*

Gardiner and Norfolk worked fast, securing Cromwell's treachery in the King's mind. All knew the King was displeased with Cromwell, but charges of heresy and treachery were what sealed his fate. It seemed that once the King thought ill of someone, anything bad said of that person he would believe.

It was said Cromwell had been about to suppress preachers who possessed the King's support and was keeping an army of men ready to attack the King. He was a zealot disguising himself as a loyal subject and meant to plunge England into an ocean of heresy and lead his sovereign into sin. Cromwell had had knowledge that I had been betrothed before I came to England, it was said, and had kept it from the King. It was also said Cromwell had tried to confound plans to marry Lady Mary to a foreign prince, as he wanted her for himself, so he might make himself King.

I could almost feel Mary's terror, that her father might think she had agreed to such a plan, leeching through court, so palpable it was like a snake shifting through the passageways of stone and tapestry.

The only ones left on Cromwell's fast-crumbling side were the Archbishop of Canterbury, who had only dared speak for his friend a little, and the Lord Admiral, an opponent of Norfolk's. I could not speak for Cromwell, what influence did I have? I was not sure I wanted to, in any case, even if it might aid me. How many lives had this man destroyed? How many would he destroy in the future if he escaped? How long can a man serve himself at the cost of all others, before retribution comes to him? I would not speak against him, if anyone even asked anything of me, but I would not speak for him either.

The same day Cromwell was arrested, a Bill of Attainder was drawn up and taken to Parliament, the charges against him heresy and treason. "An Act of Attainder allows the King to move against an enemy without the requirement of a court of law," Katherine of Suffolk explained. "It makes Parliament the judge and jury, allowing them to pass sentence."

"So, Cromwell will not have a trial?" I asked.

She shook her head. "Parliament will decide his fate, although all know the King is the one truly judging Cromwell."

Not long after that, little Howard left court, for good. It was said she was to nurse her grandmother, but I had grave doubts this was true. The Dowager Duchess of Norfolk surely had people enough who could do such a thing without sending for kin from court. Besides, the girl could not look me in the eyes as she requested to leave my service. I could only suspect, but I suspected much.

Cromwell had fallen, little Howard had been taken somewhere. Something was coming, I could feel it, and I did not think it boded well for me.

That night I sat by my window. I could not sleep, my heart and mind both dull and flat and alive and manic in the same moment. I was so tired, yet I feared to close my eyes. The night air was stifling. Little relief came even from open windows, bare of shutters, left open in a vain attempt to cool the chamber. Still there had been no rain. The streets were sticky, and London reeked as streams of offal and blood from butchers, fish guts and scales from fishmongers, and ones of dog shit and fetid water from tanners, poured slow and heavy down the roads, pooling in dusty swells, transforming into vile-smelling vapour which floated up in the hot air.

The river, too, was malodorous. The city was fusty with the rank perfume of sour sweat, rotting waste, shit, piss and festering meat. Above those smells but doing precious little to remove them was the scent of incense burning in the gardens of the palace. Fragrance from pomanders and the slick, highly perfumed skin of courtiers rose too, only adding to the putrid fug.

Sweat inched down my spine, a warm, tiny worm slinking down my back. But the sweat was only partially caused by the heat. Some was formed for fear. What would happen to me? I had some friends here, it was true, but if something came, some order that was I to be removed, to be arrested as Cromwell had been, would they stand for me and even if they did, would they have any power to aid me?

I had never felt more alone than I did that night. That was when she came to me.

I must have gone to my bed and slept, for when I opened my eyes, I was in a place I knew I could not be. I was home, in one of the forests of Cleves, standing at a bonfire made on the shores of the Rhine. There was no one else there for a while. The forest was dark and perhaps I should have been afraid but I was not. Leaves whispered about me, a soft, emerald light shone, and the forest was cool and sweet. I walked to the fire and there I found a heaped mound of cloaks, all made of feathers, as if they had just been discarded by the swan maidens, readying for the dance. I put my hand to them, the white feathers glistening a brilliant, beautiful light upon the skin of my hand, as if ice and stars danced there. I stroked them, and found the softest down caressing my palms. From the cloaks there rose a sense of contentment and purpose, of security, discovery and wonder, of which, in life, I had only ever dreamed.

I looked about me, but I could not see them, these magical beings who guided people from one world to another, these feathered creatures who became women upon the removal of their cloaks. "Is that how we become women?" I asked no one. "We take away that which gives us freedom, remove that which gives us purpose?"

"Such things are taken from us, not discarded by us," said a voice and I turned, not shocked or afraid, but certainly curious. "They never can be entirely stolen, you know. Only taken away for a time, only hidden from us, and what is hidden, it may be found again."

She was standing by the fire, on the other side to me. I could not see her face through the flames, but her dark hair flew, unbound and uncovered, in a light breeze drifting through the trees. Black eyes shone, the fingertips of flame reflected in their darkness.

"You are here," I said.

"I have been with you, always," she replied and reached out a hand to the flames. Red lights flickered about her fingers, on her skin, but did not burn her. "The time is coming," she said. "And you must be ready."

"Ready for what?"

"To do what none of the rest of us achieved," she said, and there was a smile in her voice. There was also fear.

"Which is?"

"You must survive."

"How?"

"There is a way, if you are strong enough to take it. It does not come without sacrifice, but all choices of life ask us to sacrifice something."

"What do I sacrifice?"

"What you can, in order to survive."

I woke in my bed, covered in sweat. My hands were grasping the covers as if they were arms trying to throttle me. I lay back, gasping in the hot air of the night. She had come, she always came when there was trouble on its way. Something was on its way for me, and that something meant me harm.

"How do I survive, Anne?" I asked my ghost, a whisper in the darkness.

There was no answer.

\*

The next day, orders came. Harst came to give them to me. My household were to be moved to Richmond Palace, and me with them. It was said this was to keep me safe from the ill airs of London, as plague had been sighted in the city. Actually, the plague had not come, despite the heat. I knew this. If it had, the King would have shifted out of the city, and he did not. He stayed at Whitehall. I was told the King would soon join me, for summer progress was to begin, but when I saw the route planned, I saw it did not take the King past Richmond.

I wondered if Richmond was but a start and I was to be sent to another house, as Katherine of Aragon had been.

This was how it would begin, how it had begun before, with the Queen's removal from court. All our stories, all our tales, they ran in circles. The circle had come about again, and the wheel was poised to crush me.

# Chapter Twenty-Six

**Richmond Palace
London**

**Summer 1540**

Richmond was a pleasing place. Though my nerves were ragged as a doll played with by too many generations of angry children, I still could not help but admire this palace I had been sent to, although for what purpose I knew not.

Richmond was upstream, on the opposite bank of the Palace of Westminster which stood about nine miles to the north. It had not been long named Richmond, but had once been Sheen Palace, and had been altered and expanded by my husband's father to become a new residence. Richmond had been his title once, Earl of Richmond had Henry VII been known as before he had become King, so it was named to honour him. The area too had been altered in name from Sheen to Richmond, but people still used both names, which I found a trifle confusing at first.

The lodgings were three storeys high, with fourteen turrets and there was too a round tower called the Canted Tower which, although it looked not a great deal like my childhood home, reminded me in a way of the Swan Tower of my father's castle. It was something about the shadow it cast, and it brought me comfort, as if some echo of my family was with me at that testing time.

There was a long gallery which adjoined the gardens, a pleasing way to wander from the outside perfume of the grounds to the inside if it happened to rain or one simply required shade, and the palace had piped water, brought in from three pipes which ran from conduits in the park and nearby fields. The Great Hall was perhaps one hundred foot in length, I knew from walking it, and one side entire of the palace looked out onto the waters of the Thames.

"Sheen Palace, Majesty, was almost entirely destroyed by a fire," I was told by Mary Norris as we toured the halls. "The old King, Henry VII, and his Queen, as well as their children and the King's mother, only just escaped, for a ceiling came down on the old King as he tried to escape. It was after this Henry VII decided to rebuild it and make it more glorious than it had been before."

"From the ashes, comes the phoenix," I said.

It had a great park, Richmond, rich with deer, for when it was Sheen it had been a hunting lodge. The stones of the walls were white and black, the towers were octagonal with pepper pot chimney pots and charming ornate brass weathervanes sparkled in the sunlight even on a dun day. There was a great library, a beautiful chapel, and the windows were panelled, which allowed more sunlight into the palace. It was ten acres in total, just the palace itself, and the gardens were a joy of walled areas which kept in the sun, as well as orchards which held peace and serenity.

"It was here Queen Katherine had a boy, called Henry," I was told by Margaret Douglas. "And here too he died."

I wondered what would have happened if that little boy had survived. Elizabeth might never have lived, or might have been but a child of the King's mistress. Would Mary be here, or would the royal couple have stopped at a son? Edward would not be prince of the realm, and I would never have come here.

I was not sure what I was doing here now.

"Is the King to join me?" I asked Harst almost every morning, and every morning I was told he was busy. From London proper we heard the news. It seemed the King was busy indeed, arranging the death of his friend.

*

On the 29th of June, the Act of Attainder was agreed by Parliament. Cromwell was condemned. He was judged a traitor, his goods and estates forfeit to the Crown, and he would die. Some said the King had only made Cromwell an earl in order to claim the lands of that title for himself when the time came. His offices were distributed to others, those of Norfolk's faction, and Cromwell was now to be known not by any noble title, but would be called "Thomas Cromwell, shearman."

Cromwell wrote to the King, begging for mercy, and was ignored. Archbishop Cranmer attempted to intercede, and also was ignored. Norfolk and his allies rejoiced. In the end of Cromwell they saw the light of the old faith returning to England. "There will be no reprieve, Majesty," Harst told me. "Cromwell's foes know that if he escapes now, they will be the ones on the block in a month or so, and so they will not allow him to escape."

Norfolk and his allies wasted no time. Cromwell's policies, every last one of them, were being unpicked in the King's mind. Norfolk had used his embassies to France well, gaining support from Catholic countries and their ambassadors. Norfolk wanted England in league with France and Spain again, and Cleves to be forgotten. The King's deeply conservative nature would be played on, and with Cromwell gone, all further reform in England could be brought to a halt. The only strong reformer left standing was Cranmer.

People in England rejoiced. They thought the end of Cromwell was the end of the changes to faith and country they had endured for years. Monasteries would be re-founded, life would return as it was supposed to. Peace with Catholic countries would come, and perhaps even with Rome.

There were whispers too that a new Queen was to sit on my throne.

I felt a hand at my throat, fingers tightening.

# Chapter Twenty-Seven

**Richmond Palace
London**

**Summer 1540**

At the start of July, as England sweltered in unyielding heat, the King was working hard to rid himself of me. People thought I was unaware, but I was not. I was entirely aware, and terrified. Reasons for the annulment of his present marriage poured from the skies like the rain all people of England dreamed of, and at the same time, he was preparing for his next.

This was why little Howard was vanished from court. The King meant to get rid of me, by what means I knew not, and wed her. She was being taken from court so as to remove her from the eyes and waggling tongues of court and country so that she could not be blamed for him setting me aside when the time came. The Queen had to be above reproach, and so she would be. I knew this pattern, for I knew this had happened with Jane Seymour, before Anne Boleyn was arrested. Anne too had been sent away for a time when the King was first pressing for an annulment from Katherine. All these tales I had been told since I got here and now I was here, in the centre of one myself.

Catherine was the woman my husband was protecting, and that meant he was about to attack me.

An Act had been passed at the end of June. Any marriage contracted and consummated would now be upheld as valid, whatever pre-contracts existed. The Act also condemned dispensation, saying it had been used by Rome as a way to extract money. Cases were listed that would no more require dispensations. Kindred or affinity between first cousins was one, along with "carnal knowledge of the same."

I saw through this in a moment. The King had bedded Anne Boleyn, and Mary, both cousins of Catherine Howard. Jane Seymour, too, was some kind of cousin to the Boleyns and therefore was probably related to the

Howards. This Act would mean he was not related to Catherine, as Rome would declare he was. I felt a shiver of terror in me all day and night. He was working to make her his wife. I was in the way of his new dream of a perfect wife, a perfect life.

By the fifth day of July, I was ready to climb the walls and leap from a window. I could not sleep; I was barely eating. Waiting patiently at Richmond for a husband who would never appear, I had been assured by the Earl of Rutland, my Chamberlain, the King would do nothing but that which "should stand by the law of God, for the discharge of his conscience and hers, and the quietness of the realm."

I was not assured.

On the sixth day of that month, Parliament petitioned the King, asking, for the sake of his conscience and theirs, his marriage be investigated. The King agreed. "But what does this mean?" I asked Harst. "The King thinks his marriage to me is no marriage?"

"Calm yourself, Majesty," he said, though he looked none too calm himself. "We will discover the truth behind this. I will not allow you to be insulted in such a public way."

Harst left again to find out more, and, perhaps knowing I was without my ambassador, that was when the Council, all of them, appeared at my door. They trooped in, their steps on the floor matching the hammering of my heart, and told me there was to be an investigation into my marriage. If that investigation found the union was illegal, they wanted my consent to start proceedings for an annulment.

How I kept myself from fainting, I do not know. The air was so hot, the world was closing in about me. I rose from my chair, fighting to keep control of my voice. "I am content for the matter to be examined by the King's clergy, as they are competent in such matters," I said in a voice so strong and clear it surprised me. "I am certain the King will deal fairly with me, as will his men."

I understood the danger I was in with perfect, awful clarity. This was a moment most perilous, a moment where a choice had to be made. I was not Anne Boleyn, nor Katherine of Aragon. There was no other person, no child, who was relying on me hanging on to my position to protect their own. There was no one at risk here but me, and I was not about to risk my life for the sake of my pride. I would not fight, would not offer any resistance. The defiance of Katherine of Aragon and Anne Boleyn had cut the King deep, for they had questioned his authority, shamed him before his people. But I would submit.

*You do well,* said the voice. *We who came before, we were not as clever as you.*

*You had not the examples I have to stare at in terror*, I said, watching the Council men file out, whispering to one another. *You loved him and thought the best of him. You did not know what he was capable of. I do.*

*Yes, you do.*

# Chapter Twenty-Eight

**Richmond Palace
London**

**Summer 1540**

"I will protest in the strongest terms that you were questioned unjustly, and without your ambassador at your side, Majesty!"

Harst was almost beside himself, outraged by the conduct of the Council and King.

"Do nothing to annoy them, Lord Ambassador," I said, feeling fragile as glass. "I know not what the King is thinking, but I wonder if fighting such a man is a good idea."

Harst, however, listened little to me and went to complain to the Council about the treatment I was receiving. He complained about me, a lone woman, being approached by so many men when I had no ambassador with me, and asked if it was the custom of England to bring a young woman of noble birth to its lands, a woman of high status, only to then try to send her away?

"I have demanded that the Council approach the King, Majesty," he said when he returned, "for I cannot believe this state of affairs has been sanctioned by the King, who has called himself your devoted husband in dispatches often enough."

I could believe it, however, and soon enough there was further proof.

The next day, the King sent a written declaration to the Council appointed to investigate his marriage. He told them he had been troubled by his conscience from the first moment we had met. His men said the same, and claimed this was why the King had been rendered *temporarily* impotent. Doctors testified too, and ladies of my Bedchamber were brought in to talk of my absolute innocence of the marital bed. The King's men spoke of how the King was revolted by my slack breasts and belly. My personal habits, such as my scent, clothes and upbringing, were discussed in this semi-public forum and all were found wanting.

"And all this, they are talking of in public?" I asked Harst who had been running back and forth like a crazed bumblebee, trying to find out what was going on and what it meant for me.

"They are, Majesty," he said. "And there is more."

The King declared I had come to him a virgin and remained in that state. He had shared my bed for four months but had never had carnal knowledge of me.

"But this at least is good, my lady," said Mistress Loew later, trying to sound bright though her face had been pale for days. "The King admits you are a maid still."

"There is no word of my being a heretic," I said, "that is what comforts me the most."

"Why would he think you a heretic?"

"To be rid of me, as he once rid himself of another Anne. For her, charges of treason and adultery, but he cannot accuse me of that. Heresy would seem the most likely way to be rid of me, permanently."

She grabbed my hand and clutched it. "He could not do such to you. There is no word of displeasure so deep."

"Other than with anything that might render a woman attractive. That is what he objects to. He wants a wife who he desires and more importantly, one he thinks desires him. He knows I do not want him, he knew that from the start when I mistook him for a poor man, an old fool. He knew that every time he climbed into my bed. That is why he wants me not; I saw through the façade of fantasy he has wrapped about him and saw him for what he was. All the rest of England have blinded themselves voluntarily, they have held a red-hot iron in their hands and plunged it deep into their eyes, affecting their very brains too, and all to keep from seeing the truth of what their King is, in form and mind, but I saw it, and he will rid himself of me, because I do not pretend to be blind."

"My lady, your brother is a Duke... The King could not harm you."

"Katherine of Aragon was a Princess, her father a King, her nephew the Holy Roman Emperor, and still she was set aside to die in obscurity and loneliness. And who amongst them, all those men so powerful, so feared, came to save her?"

I shook my head. "There is no one coming to aid me, Mistress Loew, no one. I am alone in terms of who can help me now, and since I am alone, I alone will aid myself! I will not pray for some knight of swans or lord on a fast charger to come and rescue me, for it will never happen. I will not stand in defiance hoping my position will aid me or my titles will protect me, for they will not. I will not hope the King will show decency, because nothing thus far has shown me he understands such things. I am alone here. No one can save me, but me."

"You are not alone, my lady."

"I am. And I will save myself."

"How, my lady?"

"I must be ready to survive." I thought of the dream, of Anne. I was sure it had been her, standing on the other side of that fire in the woodlands, the cloaks of feathers at our feet. She had said there was a way. I had to do what none of the rest of them had, and I knew what I had to do.

"The others, all of them defied him. I will not. The King wishes me to step aside? I will, gratefully and with grace. I will not make trouble. I will not scream and shout. I will lay down my crown. What do I want of this position in any case? I never wanted to be a Queen, I never wanted to come here, or wed this King and if he wants me no more then he shall have me no more."

"But, the indignity, the humiliation..."

"Are nothing!" I shouted, finally losing all control of my temper. "They are nothing, do you hear me? These things we create and take inside ourselves, these things we cling to and call pride or honour, they are meaningless. They are ideas we have made up and called real, yet there is no substance to them. These things, they have meaning only if we think they do. They are baubles, shining so bright we think they are the sun but they are shimmering surface reflecting only candlelight. They are shadows. Their light is a lie created by man, reflected back at us to dazzle our eyes and confuse our minds. And we come to stare at these false lights, these reflections so long that when we in truth see the sun, we know not what it is. That is this idea of pride, like this court, things that bedazzle the eyes so well we think we see greatness, we think we see truth, when we do not. This idea is a bauble, and I will stare at it no more."

"But my lady, you are a Queen..."

"The wealth of life does not rest in our position, nor in a jewel-encrusted band upon the brow. If I am to have pride in anything it will be in my conduct. I did not strike back when others harmed me. I stood against the storms the world threw at me and did not stumble in the tumult of the wind. I lived where others died and fell. I will have pride that despite what I suffer now or will in the future, that these sufferings did not alter me as they have altered people here, so men once great have become monsters who kill the ones they once swore they loved."

Mistress Loew was staring at me, dumbstruck.

"These things such as pride or humiliation, they do not mean anything. Life means something, my life means something to me, and willingly I will reject the callings of false emotion and feeling within me, I will humble this false creature called pride in my heart if it means I will not die. I am twenty-five years old, Mistress Loew. I am not ready to die here and now for the sake of pride and a crown I wanted not in the first place! Let the King humiliate me, let the world laugh at me, let them giggle how the King of England thought me ugly and wanted not to lie with me. *Let them!* What do the opinions of those who know me not mean to me? What does their censure matter? What do I care if the world thinks me ugly or my scent ill, or my breasts slack? What does any of this matter when one faces death? If I am able to survive this, I will smile at every laugh which is hurled my way, I will welcome every sly glance thrown by fools for I will be alive to hear those laughs, I will be alive to see those glances, and I will be alive to know that every fool who chuckles at me never has had to face such a test as I have at this time. Let the world laugh at me. Let them find amusement in the pain of others. If I survive, I shall find joy in knowing that I, who might be thought low by some after this, am higher than them all, for I never have threatened the life of man or woman because I did not warm to their looks, I have never laughed at another for their misfortune, and I have never looked down on one, because of the way they appear on the outside to the foolish gaze of man. I have never ignored the worth of a soul or spirit, the value of a heart, and in that I know I have virtue beyond that which this country and these people see in me."

I took in a shaking breath, my lungs, my heart, everything in me trembling. "I am more fortunate than the others for I am forewarned of what this man is capable of when he is defied," I said. "And as I am forewarned people may say I am forearmed but war will not help me here, and so I will lay down my arms and submit to his wishes. I will live to see another day."

Mistress Loew ran to my arms, and I embraced her, feeling her shake against me. "Courage," I said, and she nodded, weeping into my shoulder.

*

Whilst the King was happily and boldly declaring all manner of matters I always had been told were private to his clergy, the House of Lords were debating my marriage too. My contract with Lorraine's heir was discussed, along with consummation, or lack thereof, of my present marriage, but the final reason against my union with the King was most important. The purpose of marriage was for the King to sire another son, making England safe, and this would not happen if the couple were never bedded.

On the ninth day of July, the Convocations of Canterbury and York declared. They found the King's marriage to me null and void. The fourth marriage of the King of England, my first, was destroyed in seven days. His first marriage had taken seven long, wearisome and shameful years to bring to an end, but he had learned much since then. "The King works fast," I whispered before Harst on that day as I heard. "And now what will become of me?"

"My lady, we will fight for you," said my ambassador.

I held up a hand. "You will not," I said.

"Majesty..."

"No, my lord." I offered him a wan smile. "You will not. That is my order. This is done and there is no sense fighting for something already lost. I thank you for all you have done, you and the few men with me here, you have been the only ones who have stood for me, spoken out about the mistreatment I have suffered, but here we will cease to speak."

"But what of you, Majesty?"

"I will pray, my friend. Pray that I am treated better than others have been."

\*

That day, the Council came to me, and told me that my marriage was no more. I thought they were to tell me I was under arrest, or would be taken to a palace far away, at best I thought I might be sent home, shamed and ruined for any future prospect, but no, they had another fate in mind for me.

From that day forth, they said, the King would call me *sister*, and he would be as a brother to me.

For a moment I but sat there, my hands shaking. I did not know if I had heard them correctly. I was not to be arrested? Not to be sent away? The King of England, my husband, was to become my brother?

They were all staring at me, and I realized it must have been a least a minute since they had spoken. That might not sound like a long time, but attempt it one day in conversation, wait a minute entire before responding to a person and see if they stare at you as the Council did at me.

"I consent to the annulment of my marriage for it is the will of the King, and always it has been my duty and pride to do as he wishes," I said, my voice so sure and confident it felt like the voice of another person. "I am his servant," I went on. "And proudly will call myself sister to His Majesty."

I was rewarded for submission. As I sat there, half faint, wondering if this was a trick, it was explained to me that I would have precedence over all women of England, besides the next Queen, the King's existing daughters and any legitimate ones he might sire in the future. I had four thousand pounds per year, a mighty fortune the like of which few could boast.

I sat on my chair, staring at them. I was nothing solid anymore. I was air. I felt as if I was floating away, as if I was falling as I had when my father died. "I am to have... all this?" I asked.

"That is not all, Your Highness," one of them said, and it was not. I was granted manors, such as Bletchingly, Richmond, and Hever Castle, once the childhood home of another Queen Anne, was suggested too. Two houses would be mine for my lifetime, and others I could rent from the Crown, at a reasonable rate, so I could have country seats too. I had jewels, plate, furniture and a huge body of servants. I would be master of my house, unless I chose to wed again. My throat, dry as a bone in the desert, could not form words.

But something began to sink into my brain. I was not to be killed, or imprisoned. I was to be free, as free as a widow might be. The King was to make me a royal woman of England, a Princess. I would become a woman of independent means, and since the King had insisted I was a virgin it would be easy for me to remarry if so I wished. I was the King's honorary sister, a high catch for a wealthy lord, although even then I was not sure I wanted to try again with another husband. This experience had not made me warm to the idea of marriage in general.

All this was mine, they told me, as long as I did not pass beyond England's seas. I understood. The King did not want me in another country, making trouble for him.

"His Majesty is generous to me," I croaked.

I sat there looking stupefied, and I was, but my mind was racing. It would not be a hardship to remain in England, especially with such wealth. I did not have to reside within the court of the King. I would have my own houses, and could retreat to them when this gaudy bauble became too much to bear. I could scarce believe I was so fortunate. I had thought I would die, and here I was, rich and free! I could have wept in relief and happiness.

I know not how I stopped myself from bursting into hysterical laughter.

When they left me, I continued to sit there, still as a statue for a moment, and then something broke in me. Every measure of calmness, every ounce of control I had nurtured within myself all my life broke, and to the floor I fell on my knees, my hands clasped as though praying, though no prayer could have been sufficient to thank God, crying and laughing at the same time.

My ladies rushed to me, fearful I had lost my mind or at least my wits, but I pulled them to me and embraced them. "I am happy," I told them. "I am well."

Even then I knew it might take a while before what I said was true. I felt I might fly apart.

*

Doctor Wotton was sent to inform Wilhelm that his sister was no more England's Queen, and I sent word, informing my brother I would remain in England. I loved England, I wrote, which was partially true, and its people, which also was not entirely a lie. Some of them I had come to love dearly. The King, my good brother, was my friend, I wrote, my hasty pen scratching away, my hand still shaking, and I meant to remain in this land I adored.

There was nothing for me in Cleves. If I went back I would be shut away again, kept in the Frauenzimmer until I was an old maid, never to wed because of being cast off once, an embarrassment to my house, but here, here there was much for me.

"But what will you do here, my lady?" Olisleger asked.

"I do not know, my friend," I said. "And that is a thing most wonderful."

"How can uncertainty be a thing wonderful, my lady?"

"Because, my friend, uncertainty is full of possibility."

# Chapter Twenty-Nine

**Richmond Palace
London**

**Summer 1540**

In time, we heard back from Wilhelm, who said he was merely glad I had "fared no worse". The King appeared mystified about this statement. "I wonder who the person my good brother sees in his mirror of fantasy is?" I asked myself. I suppose it is hard for any of us to think of ourselves as the villain of the piece, especially those who ever have had everyone telling them they are the knight.

To my surprise, my brother never blamed me for the end of this so short a marriage. Of course, he knew the reputation of the King, but never once did Wilhelm hold me culpable. Sybylla however was outraged. From that day to the last of my life she never stopped referring to me as the Queen of England. The Schmalkaldic League, at the urging of her husband, broke ties with England and it was widely believed on the Continent that I was being kept in England as a hostage, so the King could keep some form of alliance with Cleves despite us being no more married.

They might have been correct of course, I thought this was possible, but even more probable was it to my mind that the King did not want me out in the world, telling tales of him that others might titter at. The pride of this man was more important to him even than politics.

I had to show my family's letters to the King. This was something he had insisted on. Wilhelm's were fine, always couched in diplomatic terms. Sybylla's caused more of a problem, though I was thankful, always, that much of her outrage was told in terms of our old code. Had the King understood all of what she wrote, I might have fared worse.

Within days the news of my marriage being annulled was loose in Europe. The King of France and the Emperor declared they thought the annulment was correct and right, but they were both pursuing the King's friendship, so naturally that was their answer. Martin Luther was less kind. "Squire Harry wishes to be God," he announced, "and do as he pleases!"

The King only hated him more for those words, though I thought Luther had a point. He always was a learned man.

What shocked me the most was the sympathy of the public. England's people were incensed on my behalf. I had known the country was starting to warm to me, but I had had no idea I had made such an impression on the common people in so short a time, and by doing so little. I had waved to them at processions and the jousts, sent alms and charity from the houses I stayed at, and these slight gestures it seemed had won me their hearts. There was fury in the streets when people learned I had been set aside, and it could be heard even from the palaces.

On the eleventh day of July, I sent a letter to my *new* brother, telling him I formally acknowledged the dissolution of our marriage, and thanking him for his patience, grace and friendship. *"Though this case must needs be both hard and sorrowful for me, for the great love which I bear to your most noble person,"* I wrote, *"I neither can nor will repute myself Your Grace's wife, considering this sentence and Your Majesty's pure and clean living with me."*

I went on to say that I hoped the King would visit me. I thanked the King for all he had done for me, ending my letter by asking the Almighty to grant him long life and good health. It was signed *"Your Majesty's most humble sister and servant, Anne, the daughter of Cleves."*

"And now I am daughter, too, of England," I said to myself as I sealed the letter.

That afternoon I went over papers sent by the Council, outlining all they had offered me. I looked at the houses, the money, the estates, and I realized I never had owned anything, not in truth, in my own right. All that I had had as a child was my father's, then my brother's. My gowns, money, combs, horses, everything had been loaned to me in truth. All I had been promised if I outlived the King and became a widow had been his too, on loan to me only during the span of my lifetime and then to revert to the Crown. The same was true of much I was offered here, the houses would not be mine to give away, I would own two and rent the rest from the Crown and King, but all the same, I had much now, and it was mine for the entirety of my life.

And what need would I have for property when I was dead? I had no children of my own. The only children I had now were my stepchildren, and so property going back to the Crown would aid them.

I had never been so free, never had been free at all. That night I called my household to me, which was somewhat in disarray as some were preparing to leave me to serve the next Queen, and we all could guess who that was to be, and some were hoping to stay in my service, and I asked them to have patience. "There are times when it seems the world falls apart before us," I said to them. "And yet sometimes what is left remaining is all that we need."

I had them gather in groups about tables, brought into the great hall. That night we all played at cards, and the ale and wine flowed freely from the cellars that now were mine. I gave generously, and people began to laugh, no more fearful that I would be arrested and they might be called to testify against me, no more afraid they might be sent into exile with me. It was true not all of them knew what their futures would be, but the future was no more as dark as we had thought it only days before. The bets grew wild, there was dancing, and the laughter and merriment only grew as the night stretched on.

I went to bed a little drunk for the first time in my life, and though I awoke with a head sore from all that I had put it through the night before, my soul was merry. I had been captured, kept and bound to a fate I had not wanted, but I had found the cupboard where my cloak was kept. "It was not the end," I said to myself that morning in bed, "it was the beginning."

I was twenty-five years old, and my life had just begun. I had no idea what I was to do with that life – and that was wondrous in itself – but I knew one thing. I was going to have a little diversion in it. "Let us walk in the gardens," I said to my women that day. As we went out, strolling the paths, admiring the flowers, those that had survived the interminable heat anyway, I heard two of them talking about me.

"Our lady is light as a feather, this day," one said.

"Would you not be?" asked the other, plucking a flower to twirl in her hands. "She thought she might die, and now she is to live."

*

On the twelfth day of July, my marriage was formally annulled, and Parliament urged the King to marry again immediately, for the sake of his country. I almost laughed when I was told of his pious, dour face when he made a solemn promise to oblige them. On the thirteenth day I was sent letters from the King and my brother, along with rich presents. On the seventeenth day my household was disbanded but told not to go far.

By the twentieth day of July, all England could speak of was the wonderful grace of their former Queen. Accustomed by that time to the cast-off wives of the King causing untold trouble, England was stunned by my calm acceptance, my gentility, and my happiness. Reports of me were everywhere. I was merry, dining with the Council, playing cards with my men, and feasting and laughing as though I had not a care in the world.

The King, suspicious, or perhaps affronted — he had not wanted me, but I of course was supposed to pine and whine about not having him anymore — sent men to warn me I was not to "play the woman" and change my mind, urging my brother into war on my behalf, but the King seemed quickly assured I was not of a mind to cause trouble. "I rejoice to have become a sister to the King, and a daughter of fair England," I told his men. "The King need not have a single concern about me, or my feelings, for I am perfectly happy and His Majesty is the one who has made me so. I have nothing for him but deep and humble gratitude and abiding love."

"The King will be relieved to hear this, Highness," said one of the men.

I smiled. "I am sure he will."

I expressed a desire to remain friends with my former stepchildren, with whom I had a warm relationship now, some in person, such as Lady Mary, and some by letter, like Elizabeth and Edward.

I was declared a private person by the King; no ministers were to call on or trouble me, and I was protected under the laws of his country, and the blanket of his love and gratitude. "So now you love me, Henry?" I asked as I read this letter. I laughed.

That was love to this man, I supposed, submission. He wanted no more women with their own minds in his bed, that was clear enough. He believed little Howard was too young, perhaps, to have a mind, too merry in her ways to have strong opinions or deep beliefs. He wanted a child to marry, so he could mould her from the start into his perfect wife.

I had won the love of the people as well as, apparently, the love of my former husband. The moment I was Queen no more, the King, his court and all his people came to adore me. "Of course," I said to Mistress Loew when she told me how all at court, even Norfolk, were singing my praises. "My enemies love me for I have stepped aside fast and with ease, allowing them to place another Queen on the throne. My friends are relieved that I am alive, and not cast off, and all others, they love me because no more do they fear me. I am reduced in power, so they think, by losing my crown. People fear power, and those with it. It casts a mist over a person, so they cannot be seen and their intentions cannot be known. The mist is cleared about me now, so they fear me no more."

"You are remarkable, my lady," she murmured.

"I do not think this is true," I said. "I simply had warning, from the past, and in that I was fortunate."

On the twenty-fifth day of July, I heard little Howard had been shipped quietly from Lambeth in London to Oatlands Park in Surrey, and on the twenty-seventh day, the Bishop of London was sent for too.

"He will officiate at her wedding," I said to my ladies. "And I wish her all the joy it is possible to have."

I was not sure that was much.

In truth, though she had my throne and my crown, my husband and my title, I pitied little Howard. I was a Queen no more, but I was free of this unwelcome boor in my bed, I was rich and I was at liberty. I had all I wanted.

I could not think she had anything she truly desired.

# Chapter Thirty

## Hever Castle
## Kent

## July 1540

I pulled up my horse on the small hillside, looking down to the castle below. The hot summer air buzzed with lazy insects, and the scent of roses was on the wind, distant and delicate. I had heard there was a beautiful rose garden here, perhaps a little neglected since the one who had long tended and loved it had died, but still glorious. I stared down the sloping hillside, watching the afternoon sun play lazily on the sandy bricks of the castle, on its clipped lawns, glittering on its tiny and ineffectual moat.

It might be mine now, not in entirety, but I was riding here to see if I wanted it. The house was owned by James Boleyn, and he had offered it to the Crown for a price. The King had no wish for this castle, no desire to visit it. I would imagine there were memories associated with this place that even he could not rid himself of and ignore, and so he was happy it be offered to me. It had been suggested that I ride here, at this time, to view the property and see if I liked it. If so, the sale would go through, and I would then be allowed to lease it from the Crown, for a rent most reasonable, and it would become one of my country residences.

Since it was not far from London, I had decided to take a few days to visit it. No one minded, in fact the Council had seemed delighted I would be gone from London and had encouraged me. There was much going on in London and the palaces of the King. No one minded if the former Queen vanished for a few days, it might in fact be beneficial, and so I had sent word of where I was going to the Council and, taking my household, had come here.

They had other things to think on.

Little Howard was at Oatlands Palace, marrying the King that very day, and Cromwell was in London, losing his head.

And I, the Lady Anne, sister of the King, was riding towards a castle which once had been the family home of another Queen, Queen Anne Boleyn.

Hever Castle.

It was a beautiful house, and more a house it was, that I already could see, than a castle. It was shaped as a castle, formed as one, but the tiny moat, the lack of defences, and the beauty of the place told me it was an ornamental castle, built more for comfort than anything. This pleased me.

Much else pleased me too.

I had barely seen the King for many weeks now, so busy had he been in London, pulling apart the last strands of the end of his fourth marriage and weaving the first of his fifth. The King would claim he had only been married once, to Queen Jane, and all other marriages, dissolved by law, were not lawful. But if he counted them not, everyone else did. When the King married Catherine that day, he would become the most married monarch of Christian history. Little Howard was the fifth Queen of Henry VIII. Their marriage was to be even more private than his last.

Yet already people were spinning rumour about the new Queen, calling the poor girl a whore, claiming she had been his mistress and was already with child and that was why the King had married her and cast me off so quickly. They all sang my praises now, these strange people of this odd nation who only seemed to love someone when they were falling and never if they were rising.

I stared at the park, stretching out in shades of green, yes, but increasingly of brown and ash. Gardens could be watered, but not the whole park. It had not rained since June. The country was starting to yellow like brittle parchment. Cattle were expiring in the fields and pigs fainting in sties. The plague had come, truthfully this time, rendering London bare as some stayed inside and others fled to the country. Reports from France said there it had rained blood, a stream of gore tumbling from the skies for seven hours. Some said it was God weeping, for what would be done.

For the day of the King's wedding was to be marked by blood. At Oatlands, he would marry. In London, Cromwell would die. It seemed to me an ill omen, self-created by the King, to execute the man who had torn apart his first marriage, and his second, on the day he wed his fifth wife.

But for me, poor cast-off little me, there were no ill omens, there was no blood, no unwelcome marriage. I was arriving at a house which could be mine, making plans for a future where I was the master of my own fate.

"Come," I said, looking at my guards and ladies, who were wilting in the heat. "Let us to the castle go. There is much I want to see."

It was not just the house I wanted to see. Something had called me here, someone I had reason to be grateful to.

*

I walked through the castle, my ladies far behind me, as I had asked. It was a pretty place, not large but easily comfortable enough for me and a small household. It would be a pleasing place in the summer. The interior was cool even though it was hot outside. There were marsh lands beyond the castle, excellent for hunting and hawking, a large park, and a village not far away. The castle itself was dark, as many buildings here were, the windows small but the views magnificent. The countryside here felt soft, tamed almost. In the gardens the roses I had been told of sang a song of perfume to the skies.

I walked along the echoing long gallery, through passageways to the grander bedrooms. One had been prepared for me, the skeleton staff of the house told to get it ready for me by their master, James Boleyn. He had inherited the house the year before, when his brother Thomas Boleyn had died. There was another who could inherit, Mary, the once-mistress of the King and sister to Anne and George, but I was told she had been disinherited by her father, and lived now in Calais with her husband. As I mentioned, James had small use for the house and had offered to sell it to the Crown, and the Crown, not wanting to use the house, had offered it to me.

In a way, I felt an affinity with the building. I too was a cast-off, not wanted by the one who had come to own me. We had not been loved or cherished, this castle and I, but I would show it this was no bad thing. Together, we could find love.

I could feel love here, an echo as resonant as my footsteps sounding in the hollow house from a time not so long ago, only the span of a life or two. A family had lived here, and no matter what had happened later they had once been close. The gardens whispered to my ear of a woman with a heart that had cherished her children, the halls seemed to hold the laughter of those children too, like the end of an echo vanishing down a long, winding staircase. Yes, love had lived here, and I would make it live again. "Do not be sad," I whispered to the castle. "You are alone no more. You will live again."

Many of the rooms were still wrapped, closed, with linen stretched over portraits, beds and chairs. The servants asked me not to go in such chambers, for they had not had much time to prepare for my visit and those rooms were not ready for me, but I told them I cared not for dust sheets, I wanted to see all the rooms. I wanted to feel her, this woman I was sure had aided me, who had called me here in some way undefinable, some whisper I could not explain that had been in my head since I had come to this country and whose presence had kept me safe. I wanted to thank her.

Past rooms containing books I came, past old beds still glorious, along corridors where a trapped butterfly batted against the window, until I let her out, one of my maids carrying her in cupped hands to the door. In one of the rooms, I found there were stacks of portraits, taken down, left in a row against a wall. All were wrapped in linen to protect them. With a shaking hand I opened each one, knowing somehow that there was something here to see. Face after face I saw, Boleyns and Howards of old, people long since passed staring back at me, and then as I reached the back, I stopped.

He had tried to make her disappear. He had tried to purge all his palaces of her face, her name, her memory, I had been told the tales, but here, someone had saved something of her. Perhaps it was her mother, or her father, perhaps her uncle, maybe even a servant who remembered her fondly, but someone had hidden this portrait away. The hands of the King had not reached this far, he had failed in his mission to rid the world of the woman he once loved.

Her face I never had seen in my dreams, it was always hazy and unclear, but those eyes I had seen. I knew them so well. I put my hand to the portrait, the woman in it seeming to smile, just a little, her dark hair caught in a French hood covered in black silk and rimmed with pearls, so like mine. She wore fur dark and a touch russet on her arms. There were strings of pearls and gold at her throat, with a *B* formed of gold at her breast. Those dark eyes stared out at me, and seemed to catch on my heart, playing a mournful note, yet there was, too, joy in the song my heart played.

"You could not save yourself," I whispered to her, "yet you saved me, I think."

Anne Boleyn stared out at me, her expression gentle, and I could almost feel her merry humour too, drifting from the wood and oils. That slight smile, she looked as if she knew a secret she was about to share with me. The voice in my head was silent now, her mission done, yet all about me I could feel her, a presence unearthly but not frightening. I felt welcomed. I felt as if I had come home.

"Thank you, Your Majesty," I said and in the distance, along a dark and shadowed corridor, I almost could hear a laugh, bright and happy, which resonated in every fibre of my soul. I wrapped the portrait up again with care. I would have it hidden away, so the King would never hear of it, so something of this woman of such grace would be preserved, forever. "We will make sure he does not win," I whispered to her.

"We will do well here, I think," I said to the household as down the stairs I came. "And now, show me the roses the Lady Boleyn was so proud of. If they are half as lovely as their scent, I will in heaven be."

*

I heard of Cromwell's death that night. I sat with a cup of wine by the fire. It was not lit, it was too hot, but the fireplace was filled with the roses, red and pink and white, that I had wandered amongst that day.

"The Lady Boleyn was most affectionate with her gardens," an old lady, who had served the Boleyns, told me as I wandered. I had asked for someone who knew the gardens well to show me them.

"They have fallen a little into neglect," I said, casting my eyes about.

Her face flushed. "I am sorry, my lady, we do our best, but since the last master passed there have not been many of us here, and there is so much work…"

"Peace," I said, adding a smile. "It was an observation, not a criticism. You must learn my ways, for I am told that I speak more bluntly than the English often do. It is the pattern of speech of my country, I think, and it is not quite like yours. But I will try to be more gentle in my speech, for I am a daughter of England now, even as I am of Cleves. As I learn, however, be patient with me, and understand that often if I say something and it sounds harsh or blunt, I do not mean it to be so."

She smiled. "You are most gracious, Your Highness," she said. "The stories they tell of you in London are true, I see. I am glad you like the gardens. Sir James Boleyn, he has small interest in them, in truth he barely has come here since the house passed to him."

"Men often disregard the beautiful, unless it is in regards to women," I said stopping by a bush of roses so violently red they looked like blood. Their scent was intoxicating. "And even then, their attentions are, I think, fleeting. But women, we love such places, do we not? We know their worth, how they enhance the soul."

"The mistress, My Lady Boleyn, spent much time here, as did…" she trailed off.

"Her daughters?" I asked. "Though we must take care, I would not have you forget them. I would like to know more of them."

"That must indeed be said with care, Your Highness," she said, looking over her shoulder as if the King's guards should appear and arrest her at any moment.

"And it will be so, but still, what you can tell me I would like to know." I glanced at the skies, pure blue and glaring gold. A wild falcon swooped in the skies, gliding on her wings, hovering on the heat. She crested against the sun, black on gold, and vanished into the marshlands.

When people leave life, they do not die, not unless we allow them to, not unless we cease speaking of them. In memory we hold them, and there they live. This woman whose ghost had saved me was gone, yet I would keep her alive in my mind, and when I had the chance, I would tell her daughter of her. I would bring Elizabeth here, and I would show her the portrait and the places her mother had loved. "My promise to you," I whispered to the vanishing falcon.

*

"Tell me of it, then," I said to the messenger, come riding to Hever to let me know Cromwell was dead.

It seemed fitting somehow, another part of her final victory perhaps, that I should be here and here I should be told Thomas Cromwell had died. Perhaps that was why I had to come here, other than to thank her; so that Anne Boleyn's ghost could hear the tale of how the man who had engineered her fall had himself come to meet death.

The messenger bowed, and the story was told. Cromwell left his prison in the Tower, walking out to the open space just north of the Tower walls. Not for this man a private, quiet death. No, Cromwell had been stripped bare of titles and would die a commoner, crowds of thousands screaming in his ears, baying for his demise.

Cromwell stood in the full light of that summer's day, blinking against the sun. A thousand of the King's guard stood about his place of execution. There was no escape. Did he think of Anne Boleyn, brought to death in disgrace, her name defiled? For now the same was so of him. He was a traitor, a heretic and an unholy friend to the King, his master. I doubt the irony of fate escaped this man.

Cromwell faced the crowds.

"There were noblewomen there wearing veils, both to shelter delicate skin and hide their identities, Highness," said the messenger. "There were noblemen, bare-cheeked and undisguised, unafraid to see him fall."

There were commoners too, of course, resentful of his policies, his destruction of the monasteries, and no doubt of his treatment of Queen Katherine, and, perhaps of his treatment of the disgraced Queen Annes both. And the common people were there, too, because they hated him for once being one of them and leaving them to dwell in poverty as he bathed in riches. They despised him for the favour he had won, the talent he had possessed, and for the people he had killed.

*It could have been me standing there, this day,* I thought.

"Cromwell comforted the man who was to die with him, Lord Hungerford, condemned for four counts deserving death, including sodomy, witchcraft and treason."

In a dry, emotionless voice, I was told, Cromwell addressed the crowds.

"Good people, I am come here to die and not to purge myself, as some may think I will, for if I should do so, I would be a wretch and a miser. I am by the law condemned and thank my Lord God that has appointed me to this death for my offence. For since the time that I have had years of discretion, I have lived as a sinner and have offended my Lord God, for which I ask Him heartily for forgiveness. And it is not unknown to many of you that I have been a great traveller in the world, but being of base degree, was called to high estate. Since the time I came thereunto, I have offended my prince, for which I also ask him for hearty amnesty. I beseech you all to pray to God with me that He will forgive me. O Father, forgive me, O Son, forgive me, O Holy Ghost, forgive me. O Three Persons and one God, forgive me.

"And now I pray you that be here to bear record, that I die in the Catholic faith, not doubting any article of my faith, no, nor doubting any Sacrament of the Church."

"I wonder if he thought that would save him, a final reprieve?" I mentioned.

"Perhaps, Highness," said the messenger, "but there was no reprieve."

Cromwell, interrupted several times by Hungerford, who was demanding that the executioner get on with it and put him out of his misery, finished by saying, "Gentlemen, you should all take warning from me, who was, as you know, from a poor man made by the King into a great gentleman and I, not contented with that, not with having the kingdom at my orders, presumed to a still higher state. My pride has brought its punishment."

Thomas Cromwell knelt, praying to the Almighty to accept his soul. When he rose to make for the block, he saw Wyatt crying for him. "Gentle Wyatt, goodbye and pray for me," he said. "Do not weep, for if I were no more guilty than you were when they took you, I should not be in this pass."

He asked the headsman to take his head off with one blow, so he would not suffer. The man was unable to obey this last command. When Cromwell knelt, his head on the block, lips muttering his last prayers, and the man swung, the aim was poor. He may, in fact, have been *chosen* for his lack of experience, or paid to make a poor job of it by Cromwell's foes. It was a revenge I could see Norfolk taking delight in, certainly. The executioner bit deep into the back of Cromwell's head with the axe. It took several blows to take the head off. Some said Cromwell was alive, gurgling in pain until the last.

"How did Hungerford fare?" I asked.

"Hungerford died swift, and clean, Your Highness."

I nodded to the man, wondering if this ill death had indeed been a last punishment since the axeman had improved his aim so swiftly. "Thank you, refresh yourself with ale and spend the night here, if so you wish. There are other men lodged in the stables who can show you to a bed."

"Thank you, Your Highness," he said.

I sat back by the fire, alight with roses, a cup of wine in my hands, and again I seemed to hear that laugh, throaty and welcoming, echoing in my mind.

## Chapter Thirty-One

### Hever Castle
### Kent

### July 1540

It was night, a hush had fallen upon the world. Birds in the trees kept their last notes sung to the gloaming to a murmur. There was a stillness in the air, the faintest breeze I could hear in the trees closest to the castle, a washing sound, as if of water. It reminded me of the sea, on the one journey I had taken to come here. I lay in my bed, wide awake, my head awash with the wine I had drunk that evening, thinking on Cromwell's fall, on Anne's, on how narrowly I had avoided such a fate.

Of course, I had only avoided it *this* time, I reminded myself. I was now the King's sister, a subject of his Majesty and was, although in a wealthy and polite way, a prisoner in England. In some ways this changed little about my situation, other than the country I resided in. I had, although I had not known it, never really thought of it, been a prisoner of my father, country, family and duty before. I was now a prisoner of the King of England. The difference was, I supposed, that my father had been a benevolent gaoler, and at least part of his efforts to shelter me had sprung from an urge to protect me, out of love. The King did not have those instincts. He wanted to keep me close because he did not want me running home, taking tales of him to other lands, spoiling the fantasy he thought the world believed in, about him.

I wondered if anyone but the King believed the tales he told in his own head about himself, that he was a good man, a good ruler, that he was godly, that he had been unfortunate in marriage, all the problems with all the women he had encountered not his fault at all, but theirs and he had simply been a plaything of fate to have met so many women all bent on making his life so hard. *Poor* King Henry.

His ideas of himself were false. He was no knight, no great King, no good man. His fantasies were as false as his court, a gaudy show concealing a rotten centre. The King had trapped not only his wives and children in his marriage of many abuses, but the people of England now too. The people here, they were wed to this man as sure as any woman had been, and they were trapped with him as their master. That was why they did not look past his fantasies, this façade he had built about himself; they did not dare. They, like him, tried to blame the problems for his rule on his advisors, like Cromwell, or on wives, like Anne. It was easier to blame others, for like the wife beaten by her husband who, when that husband is attacked by another stands up for him, so the people of England did the same for their King. It was easier to blame others than to accept the stark, barren, and terrifying truth, that the one in charge of them was vicious, vindictive, cruel and cared only for himself. They kept hoping their prince of promise, the man the King had seemed to be when he first came to the throne, would reappear, but that man was long gone, if he had existed at all.

But those whom the people and the King could blame for all the ills he did were fast falling away. Others rose in their places and fell too. One day, would the King be left, stark and raw, naked before the eyes of the world, and people finally would see the fault lay in him? Would he one day run out of loved ones to kill, calling murder justice?

I, who had come from outside these lands, I had seen the truth of him. I truly believed that was why he had such an aversion to me. It had not been my looks so much as it had been the way I had seen him, seen right through this lunatic fantasy of himself he held so dear, and in seeing through it, I had ruined it for him, just a little, just enough. That was why his dislike of me was so immediate and so violent. No matter what other qualities I had, I *had* to be the wrong woman, something had to be wrong with me, otherwise he was indeed the man I had seen on first sight, aged, feeble, foolish, and unremarkable.

This night he would take a girl to wife, one young enough to be a granddaughter, or even great-granddaughter, and she, a woman of England already trapped with him as her King, would become trapped a second time, another gilded gate clanging shut behind her, when she became his wife. Catherine was no fool, she would pander to his fantasies of himself. If she wanted to survive, that was her task. She knew this game and its rules better than me. She had a chance to win.

Heat hovered over me, a relentless, pressing weight. The world felt oppressive that night. I could not get the vision from my head, that this night yet another girl would be lying in a bed, the King heaving atop her, her face trying to hide her revulsion at the smell of his fetid leg and his equally foul breath. Poor Catherine, truly, I felt she had the worst deal of the two of us. I knew she loved Culpepper, it was obvious to me as the stars in the night sky on an evening most clear, yet the King had looked her way and her family had noted it, and so she was Queen. Her choice had mattered not. She was a tool to her family and to powerful men who supported their faction.

I wondered what she was to the King. Another fantasy, I supposed. I did not believe he knew anything true about her.

I rose carefully from the bed, not disturbing the maid slumbering at my side, curled up as if she was a baby bird, nestled safe in a soft nest. To the window I walked, and opened the shutter carefully, just a little. One side of my room looked out onto the marshes and parkland, but this one looked inwards, into the courtyard of the castle. It was tiny, four horses would have jostled uncomfortably for room on the cobbled floor, yet that slight space seemed to hold so much, as if a space no matter how diminutive may encompass time and memory, so moments of importance seem to touch, whisper to one another, catch the end of another's breath. I could see children there, three of them, playing. Two with dark hair and one with fair. I could see a mother walking out, going to check on her beautiful roses on a dusky morn where the grey world of light indistinct smelt of dew on grass and the rain of the night before was caught in drooping petals. I could see a father mounting a horse, ready to fly to London on the whim of the King, his master, and I could see that same King arriving here, at different times to visit different daughters of this one, same house, where he had lost so much of his heart.

What man had Anne Boleyn, or Mary, seen? I wondered how different their King was to them, how different their version was, from the other's version of the man. When they had met him, he would have looked as he did in the portraits I had been sent, and I had been told that back then he was open, generous, a friend to all he met. That was not the man I had met. The husband I had encountered was bitter inside, twisted of soul and high of suspicion. The women who had lived here, they had met this man when he was full of promise and virtue, capable of all greatness. I, who had come later, when most of them were dead and gone, I had met the man this prince of promise chose to become, a man who had not followed the best within him, but in many ways explored the worst.

They had dared to love this man, I could see enough of what he had been to know he might once have been capable of stealing a maid's heart in truth, and that love had destroyed them, but it had not left him unscathed, either. Many he had loved had fallen, friends and wives, a son too, but a part of him had died as well, each and every time he destroyed someone he loved. It had to be that way, I thought. We cannot give a part of our souls to another, and not lose it when that person dies, especially if we are the one to bring about their deaths. In killing them, he had been slowly murdering himself, a little each time, a little every year, and now much was lost. What I had been presented with as a husband, this small, dark shell, so fragile and brittle, was all that was left.

I was glad, in a way, they had seen the best of him, glad I had escaped the worst. At least once, he had been worth the love of people. I sighed, standing at the window, knowing sleep was to be a stranger that night. I sat on the wooden window seat, an old cushion under me, and brought my legs up to my chin, my eyes on the stars above. I knew that I was fortunate, even to be alone, even though some laughed at me. All this I could endure, with ease, for I was not the worst off in this scenario. I knew another girl was out there in England this night, trying to find a way to endure much else in a marriage bed she never had wanted, and in which she was now imprisoned.

*

A few days later we returned to Richmond, and I heard the news. The King had mounted his new wife three times on their wedding night. "Why do you think this is news you should be speaking to anyone?" I asked my maid.

She looked a little baffled, as it seemed the rest of the world wanted to know all about the potency of the King. "This is a matter for the King and his wife, and no one else," I went on.

"Of course, Your Highness," she said.

As she retreated and I went back to my card game with my men, I shook my head a little. "Whilst I am glad the King, my good brother, may be on his way to having a second son," I said to my men, "I wonder at the proclivity in people, of wishing to speak of it so publicly. Perhaps it is my upbringing, for in Cleves such matters were to be private."

"And yet the bed of the King, where heirs are produced, is a matter for all of us to care about, Highness," said one of the men.

"Of course, but I feel for his young wife. She was a maid, innocent and sweet, and to have the intimate details of her transition to wifehood discussed by all, it seems a lot for a young girl to undertake."

"Your kindness does you credit, Highness," he said. "And perhaps you are right, and we do not take the feelings of the lady enough into question. The King, however, will be proud of himself."

"And that is good but let us at times have a moment of concern for the Queen."

Two days later, before the new marriage was officially proclaimed, a less than romantic event occurred when three men were dragged on hurdles from the Tower to Smithfield, where they were executed for high treason. Richard Fetherston had been a tutor to the Lady Mary, Edward Powell had championed her mother and Thomas Abell was Katherine of Aragon's former chaplain. Their collective crime, we were told, was "popish treason", which I supposed could mean whatever the King wanted it to. On the same day these men died, a Lutheran scholar named Robert Barnes burned at the stake. Two more of Cromwell's men kept him company. Condemned by Act of Attainder, they had not had a trial, but died by the will of Parliament and the King.

The men who burned had gone before the King and recanted their heresy some time ago. They had been forgiven, but required to make their, now conservative and traditional, beliefs obvious in sermons at St Mary Spital during Easter Week. They had obliged, preaching all that was conventional, but it did them no good.

"Gardiner had no faith in their conversions," Katherine of Suffolk, come visiting, told me. "The Bishop complained to the King, the King sent them to the Tower."

"I think it is not beliefs which are in question, here, my friend," I said, nodding to thank a maid placing a plate of wafers and slices of thick marmalade at my side for the Duchess and me to enjoy. "It is loyalties. Proving these men heretics makes Cromwell's death only more justified, to some. This way, his ghost will not cause trouble for his enemies, for all will believe he deserved to die, and therefore will not make of him a martyr."

That day was an odd day, but the message was clear for those who had the wit to see it. Conservatives died on the same day as reformists. No one knew which way the King wended on this fragile path of faith, but one thing was clear; conservative or reformer, if you opposed the King you would die. It was safe to follow the King, to do as he said, but form an idea which opposed what His Majesty believed or decreed, and you would burn, or lose your head.

"Some are putting the deaths of Cromwell's men down to Queen Catherine's influence," said Olisleger that afternoon, standing at the window, watching light stream in through the glass. Beams of sunlight hit shadowed walls, shimmering light upon darkness.

"If she is wise, she will stay away from talk of faith, it brings only trouble here." I looked up from my desk, where I was looking through piles of missives, petitions being sent to the King's sister, from people in need. Every day it seemed there were only more of them.

"All the men who burned were reformers, Highness. Queen Catherine, whether she wants it or not, is of the conservative faction, supported by them. Gardiner asked for the deaths of Cromwell's men. Barnes attacked Gardiner once, whilst preaching at Paul's Cross, you see, and Jerome and Garrett were Barnes' supporters. They were named Anabaptists, but no one believes that was true."

"Conservatives died too, my friend."

"If the King thought Gardiner was trying to sway him back to Rome it would be dangerous, so the Council, led by Gardiner and Norfolk, suggested those conservatives to the King also as traitors."

I set my quill down a moment. "You mean, Gardiner and Norfolk made sure both parties of men died, even men who were on their side, to show the King they were *his* men, balanced men? That is balance, is it? Deaths on each side of the faiths?" I shook my head. "The more I hear what men of faith do, the more it sounds to me as though they read not the Bible. Peace, kindness, compassion, this is what I find in that book, but it seems there is no mercy and peace in the men who swear they follow its teachings." I closed my eyes. "But this is not my office. I am of no faction."

"Queen Catherine's family are, though, and they are in ascent now. Norfolk can ask for much, and have it done, through her."

I opened my eyes. "I think what will be done is whatever the King wants done. The Duke may like to believe he influences the King, but the King is influenced only by himself, and the King has now the riches of the monasteries *and* the power the break from Rome granted. He never loved the reformist cause, that is clear enough to me. It was a tool, nothing more. Now the King can have all he wants, return to being a Catholic in practice whilst enjoying the wealth and power of governing a free kingdom, an ideal situation."

I paused. "But this is dangerous talk, and I have left danger behind. I am the King's subject now, and so I do as he wishes. Politics is my concern no more, pleasure is. Come, I would speak to you of the feast I am having here tonight."

"People are saying your court is merrier than the King's, my lady."

I smiled. "My household is no court, and that is why it is a merry place. Here, people may entertain life instead of dancing with death."

# Chapter Thirty-Two

**Richmond Palace
London**

**August 1540**

"The Queen has inherited your Master of Horse, John Dudley."

"She has inherited all my people, for the main part," I said with a smile, laying down a card. "I am content with those left to me; they know how to play a good hand of cards." I tossed another coin gamely into the growing pile in the middle of the table, and smiled, challenging my opponents as I wagered harder on my hand.

The man smiled, matching my coin with one of his. "I hear, Highness, the Queen's new women have the new Master of Horse selecting mounts for the Queen based on what dress she is wearing that day."

I supposed he was trying to make out Catherine was nothing but frivolous and I eyed him with a look of disapproval. "If a woman turns herself out well, people often think better of her," I said. "Certainly, if she takes no care over her appearance people will suppose her slovenly in other ways too, such as of character or virtue. But then when a woman tries hard to look her best people will say she tries too hard, is only concerned with matters physical and is frivolous, and yet these people would be the ones to judge her poorly if she did not try. If the new Queen tries to look her best, in all ways, it is most likely this effort is made in order to please the King and present herself well before her people, indeed she is a representative *of* those people, therefore she is doing her best to perform the office she has been granted through marriage to the King, and I will hear nothing but praise for a young girl, who seeks only please my good brother and represent her people and country well."

"Of course, Highness, I meant no disrespect."

"Of course you did not, but it is easy for people to misjudge others, to read into their behaviour some trait of personality which is unfavourable, when all that is going on in truth is a young woman striving to be thought well of. I am most fond of the new Queen and remember her well, with great affection. I am not surprised the King fell in love with her, for she has much in her that makes her worthy of great love, and in my house I will hear no word spoken against her. If you could make that clear to others, I would be grateful."

"Of course, Highness, if that is your wish all the household shall follow it."

"Good, and in doing so we shall lead the way by example, showing respect to the Queen, and to the King, who chose her as his wife."

The man smiled at me again. "You are a great lady, Highness," he said.

"I am grateful to be thought so, though all of us, if we are both wise and humble, know we are never wise enough, and always are learning how to be better than we were the day before. We all are students in this game of life and building good character takes constant work. We should not forget that, for then we are always ready to learn more." I looked over at the window, the skies blue and no sign of rain, again. "We shall ride today, in the park," I said. "When I have won this hand, which will not take long for you, my friend, pay no heed to your cards, we will depart."

There was laughter about the table. I am sure sometimes in the past my men had let me win, but I had become most talented at the card games of England. I knew this because the faces of men flushed with concentration and consternation at times. They did not like to be beaten by a woman, and many of them tried harder and harder every time we played to best me. I welcomed it, I needed to be challenged or how would my skill grow?

Later that morning we went to the courtyard. My new horse master bent down, cupping his hands so he could help me onto my horse. Up into my saddle of fine leather topped with soft velvet I went, my hands taking up black silk and gold reins, my crimson dress shimmering next to buttons of copper on the saddle. Waiting for my women to be set on their own mounts, I stared at stripes of gold flickering upon the cobblestones, the sun dancing across the ground. One of the men spat, his spittle thick, splattering upon dry, flaky earth, curling like a worm in vinegar. I looked to the skies. The skies were parched. They shone blue by day and pink by night. There was no grey. There had been no rain. England was desiccated.

"We will not ride them far in such heat," I said, stroking my horse. "Let us walk out and find a shady spot to rest for the afternoon."

I relished being the one who chose what I was to do with my day, every single day. Never, never would I have been allowed to be so free in Cleves, so able to command, to select what I did each hour. I had never thought I would be so free here, and yet here I was, commanding my own people, riding out on my own horses, from my own residences. At night I could command what was served at dinner, that people would play cards or dance all night, what time I slept and rose. Always I had lived by the rules of others, but not now. It was astounding. I still woke at times in the night, terrified and frozen, thinking this life I now had was but a dream. In some ways I still did not believe it was not.

We headed into the park at a walk, the men ahead of us, talking gently of nothing. Along the road we clopped, watching sunlight burst through thin, dark silhouettes of trees. The woods were cool and sweet, awash with the sound of birdsong and a breeze rippling in the treetops, making a sound like the ocean. It reminded me of my dream, in those days of danger before I had been granted all I could ever want.

The King and his new Queen were on a progress, Oatlands, Hampton Court and Nonsuch, I had been told. I wished them well of it.

I breathed in hot air, feeling sweat already running under my clothes. The countryside baked. It had been this way since before my marriage ended. No rain, few clouds, endless heat. People whispered it was a sign of God's disapproval over the annulment of my marriage and the King's making of a new one. Plague and ague had broken out in London. People fell to fever, the Thames was shallow, cattle were dying of thirst, chickens roasting in their own feathers, and crops were wilting. People roamed the streets of London and other cities praying to God for rain and to their King for aid. Their King did nothing. He was too busy enjoying little Howard.

The King's people did not love him, I knew that now. He saw them waving and cheering and thought they turned out to shout his name out of love.

But there are other reasons people put on a show. Not every pair of lips turned upwards makes a smile, sometimes it is a grimace. They feared him. It seemed strange at times that a man who had spent so long and worked so hard in pursuit of love, could have found so little of it in his life.

*Perhaps he should not have murdered all those who truly loved him,* a ghost whispered, a voice murmuring in the leaves of the trees.

And his night-time exploits with poor Catherine had become famous. As much as the people complained their King did nothing for them, they talked of Catherine Howard. Many were quick to disapprove, not of the man who had set aside a lawful wife and taken a girl, little more than a child, to his bed, but of Catherine. She was the one they would blame now. Now that I had fallen from the throne and taken up a position lower than queen I was universally admired, and now that little Howard was Queen many talked of her with tongues laced with sharp, critical slander. The English, so it seemed to me, did not much like their Queens. The marriage was not officially announced as yet, but already there were rumours she was with child. Although this was intended to be a slur upon her character, I hoped the gossip was true, for her sake. Bear a son and she would be secure.

As we rode, heading for the cool inner forest, I thought of my former maid, Mary Norris. She was to leave court soon, so I had heard, sent to wed George Carew. She had written to me, thanking me for all I had done for her. I was not sure what that was, but I wished her well and sent her a gold cup, a traditional gift from royalty of England to nobility, I was told, to aid her on her wedding day.

I felt sorry for little Howard again as I thought of Mary Norris, for Mary had been one of Catherine's friends and she was leaving court. I doubted little Howard had many friends in truth now, for now she was Queen she was removed from them all, made higher than them, so she could not be their friend for they were not allowed to be close to her anymore. Her secrets, they were now only hers, her confidences now confided to few but herself, for who can a queen trust?

We rode, the heated air brushing my face, riding my breath. Outside the woods the countryside was a haze of brown and yellow. Sometimes it felt as if the world was holding its breath, waiting for something.

*

It was some days later when I was told the King was to come and dine with me.

Although presented as one, it was not a friendly call my former husband was making to the house of his new sister. Members of the Privy Council were to be present and were to put a document before me, the formal deed of separation. It required my signature. Afterwards, foreign ambassadors would be told the King had remarried and Catherine would be presented to court as Queen.

"We will set the King at perfect ease," I said to my people. "Ensure every favourite dish of His Majesty is on the table, the musicians will play songs of his composition and all will be perfect."

The household roared into life, new sheets on beds, flowers in the fireplaces, the walls washed in vinegar, and new rushes and herbs on the floors, the old ones swept out. The kitchens were a hub of activity, baking pies and roasting meats, so the table of the King would be set with all that pleased him that night. I had books of physick sent to his chambers, new ones I had found and enjoyed. I knew well the pleasures of the King for I had been paying close attention during the time I was supposedly his wife.

I was so warm to the King when he arrived that he kept glancing at me, a sideways look to see if I was in earnest. Evidently, he wondered even now if I would bring trouble to his door, perhaps he even expected it. No woman had left him without a fight, and I had not even lifted a hand to defend myself but had neatly stepped aside. His men brought the document to me, their faces betraying their nerves, and I signed it immediately.

"You will be happy here, in England," the King said when the ink was dry and the document had been snatched up, in case I might think to grasp it and him back to me.

"I love England, Your Majesty," I said, setting my swan feather quill in its pot again. "And you, my good brother, have given it to me. I will always be grateful for this, and perfectly content to remain in your glorious country for the rest of my life."

Again, that suspicious glance, but a smile came to his mouth too. "I am pleased that you are merry," he said cautiously. "What will you do with your time here?"

"You are most gracious to ask, Majesty. I would like to see much of my new lands, and of England," I said. "But I am content enough at Richmond. This palace will always be special to me, for here I became your good sister, and I will always be your good sister, Your Majesty."

"Would you think to take another husband?"

He sounded almost hurt. He had rejected me, but I had not fought his rejection and now he thought that an affront, for I should be in love with him as all women should, and it appeared I was not.

"I am not considering marrying again, Your Majesty," I said. "I have had a husband, the best of men, and now who could compare to him?" I smiled. "I will be happy to remain a daughter of England, to serve my brother faithfully, and to honour you and your new wife."

That glance again, edged with anger and pleasure both. "The Council has said I *must* marry," he said, his tone defensive.

"And of course you should, for your own comfort and for the good of the realm." I smiled again, walking to him and taking his arm. "For duty and your own happiness, you must marry, and I wish you only happiness, Majesty. Happiness with the right woman, who teaches your good heart to sing once more, and who can provide your country with another heir, so all your people may sing with joy too."

"I *have* married a new Queen," he said as we walked to the Great Hall, thence to the gardens, the words coming out in a rush most awkward. "I wanted to tell you in person, for I knew it might pain you."

*He thinks I do not know of little Howard?* I asked myself. *How blind does this man believe me to be?*

"It is good that you have done the duty your Council and people need of you with speed," I said. "Majesty, I mean all I say. For the sake of your people and your own heart, a new wife, one who suits you in temper and mind, is what is needed and I rejoice you have found her so swiftly. May I know the name of my new sister?"

"Lady Catherine Howard," he said.

"A fine, beautiful and most agreeable woman," I gushed. "Majesty, you have chosen well, and I think with her you will be happy and content."

He stopped on the path, gazing at me with that same curious look he had, suspicious, a little affronted that I should be wishing him well rather than shrieking in pain for him leaving me, and pleased all at the same time. All these emotions fought on his face. "You are a gracious and good woman, sister," he said and lifted my hand to kiss it.

It was the most affectionate gesture I ever had from him.

We feasted in the Great Hall. Only a select few feasted with us that night. The favoured milled about, drinking wine near Flemish tapestries flanking the walls, glancing my way to observe how I ate, how the King treated me, how I responded. The King beamed when he saw the food and was surprised when the musicians struck up only his melodies.

"Who is of the new Queen's household?" I asked the King, sitting back with a goblet of wine in hand.

The six great ladies, I was told, were Margaret Douglas, Mary Howard, Katherine of Suffolk, Catherine Howard's own aunt Lady Margaret Howard, wife to Lord William, and Lady Clinton, Elizabeth FitzGerald. The other women were Jane Boleyn, Catherine's sisters Isabella and Margaret, Lady Edgecombe, as well as Lady Rutland, Mrs Herbert, Elizabeth Tyrwhitt, Joyce Lee, and Susanna Gilmyn.

"They are all much older than the Queen, she may wish for some friends her own age," I mentioned.

In truth I knew, she had no friends anymore. Allies, confidants if she was lucky, but she was alone, as I had been. Anne Basset was once again the only one left of the old maids. Her father's arrest had left her floating between worlds, for no dowry could be secured whilst his fate was undecided.

"Many of her family are at court now," said the King. "She is well served."

He seemed little concerned, and I knew better than to press the matter with him. We spent the night in merriment, feasting and watching my people dance, and the King and I spoke more than we ever had when married. "You seem content in your situation," he mentioned as we parted for separate beds.

"I will be happy all my life to remain in your beautiful country," I said and almost smiled at how relieved he looked.

"It is, my lady, your country too now." He kissed my hand.

"It is," I said.

The King left the next day, utterly assured I was not going to make any trouble for him, and he was right, I was not, but I heard plenty to make me suspect trouble was coming for little Howard. "The Queen's women, they are not warming to their new mistress," I was told by Harst. "They say she has not the manners of a Queen, nor the bearing and behaves like a spoilt child."

I had never thought Catherine behaved in such a way, from my experience of her she was a pleasing soul, but I thought that not the problem. I believed some of her women wanted to dislike her.

I was not surprised to learn that many women distrusted their new Queen and were averse to her. Catherine had risen too swift. A month ago, she had been a servant to many of the women, and inferior to all the men. One minute little Howard had been their subordinate, now was their superior. Plenty of the women would hate her for rising above them, and many men do not like the look of power on a woman, it scares them.

She also represented the Catholic faction of court, of course, which was another reason for their antipathy.

"The new Queen is odd, very childlike," Harst said with a sneer. "She gives gifts out as if they are wafers and chides her women soundly when they do the slightest thing wrong."

"She is scared, of them, and her position," I said. "You see an odd woman, my friend, where I see a scared child."

# Chapter Thirty-Three

**Richmond Palace
London**

**August 1540**

"The Queen's new emblem is a crowned rose."

We lay under trees, in the park, my park. My musicians were playing, soft notes wafting on the warm air. Thankfully we did not have to listen to only the King's compositions that day, since he was not there. People might praise them highly and the King certainly believed they were great works of art, but I did not. There were melodies far more worthy to listen to in this world, and in my house and my gardens there always was music now. It was my command. I went through my days with notes joyful or mournful surrounding me, a haze of beauty. I had insisted my musicians were, too, under shade, like me and my ladies, that day. England baked as a honey cake, one left in the oven too long, so it emerges dry and hard.

"There is nothing of her in that new emblem," I said to Mistress Loew, twirling a blade of grass crowned with a seed head fluffy and delicate in my hands. "The rose is the King, it is the symbol of his family, and he is this mythical thing, the perfect being, the rose without a thorn. He is called *the rose without a thorn*, is he not? Therefore, the Queen's new sigel is a depiction of him."

"People are now saying *she* is his rose without a thorn."

The King had ordered a medal struck too. It was gold, Tudor roses and lovers' knots entwined, carrying the message, *Henrius VIII: Rutilans Rosa Sine Spina.* One had been sent to me, a gift from my new brother and sister-in-law. The only place the poor new Queen was present on the medal was in the lovers' knots. The medal had been struck in honour of her but honoured him.

I felt more sorry for the girl than I could say. I could afford to be generous, being rich in gold and freedom both. Catherine had become a person no more; she was an extension of the King. If I needed any further proof I had only to look at the motto my former husband had selected for his new wife; *"Non autre volonte que lasienne"*, *No other will but His.* It was all about court that Catherine had chosen it, but Harst told me she had not. The King had picked it for her.

Mine as Queen had been *God send me and keep me well*, shortened at times to *God send me well to keep*, such as on my wedding band, and given my new state of happiness I knew God had done so for me. From marriage I had been sent, and I had been kept from harm.

"I think the message is, she is to have no will of her own," I said.

There were others I pitied, who were working in this hot sun. As we lay under trees, listening to music, it was time for painters and masons to become busy about England again, taking down the badges of one Queen, replacing them with another.

All over England my arms and sigels were coming down and Catherine's were going up. It was easier than some of the alterations the King's men had had to do over the years, although I heard his men had become talented at transformations after performing so many. Every few years and another woman was Queen. I had lasted but six months. The most fortunate of them all, in many ways.

Fortunate it was for the King's purse that lions could become leopards, and falcons could transform into phoenixes. This latest alteration was easiest of all; the Black Lion of Julich was becoming the White Lion of the Howards. My swan badge had not been widely used, so there was no problem there. Painters were busy, but the army of masons and carpenters who had been called in to alter Katherine's badges to Anne's, Anne's to Jane's and Jane's to mine, had less work this time. Paint over a black lion and he becomes white. A flick of paint, and this Lady of Cleves had never been Queen.

Other people had been forced to make swift changes too. A writer and translator called Richard Jonas had dedicated a book on midwifery to Catherine, but she was not the original Queen he had thought to honour.

Jonas had come to England in my train and had intended me to be his patroness. Swiftly, he altered his dedication, and I sent him my blessing when he dispatched a shamefaced letter, explaining himself. The book was apt, I thought, since the King wanted a son.

But if the badges altered with ease, it was said little Howard was not having an easy time transforming into a Queen. Even though I had stated my household were to speak only well of her, and they had obeyed, others were talking.

People of England were gossiping about this sixteen-year-old who suddenly was their Queen. It was said the Queen had no refinement, that she wore too many jewels. No doubt they were all from the King and she was trying to please him by wearing as many of his presents as she could, but the people here were harsh on her.

Catherine was to walk to Mass for the first time as Queen that day and all eyes would be on her as hawks, waiting for her to make a mistake. Some of them no doubt wanted her to.

But the King seemed happy enough and he was the one she had to please. He looked fitter, all said, and having seen him recently myself I agreed. He had never slept so well, so he told the court, making his men guffaw and clap each other on the back, proud of their King and his virile ways.

I was not surprised the King was finding slumber an easy kingdom to reach. He had not been this active for years, certainly not in the last six months with me. His waist had reduced in size since he had married Catherine, I had noted that when he came to dinner, and his many chins had not departed exactly, but each one looked tighter. Riding all day in an attempt to demonstrate he was as young and fresh as his new wife, followed by mounting that unfortunate wife through the night, was more exercise than he had taken in a decade.

But if the King had new confidence, Catherine sounded less sure of herself every day. I heard she was often hidden away in her private rooms, only Jane Boleyn with her. She was churlish with her ladies, ordering them about, and sometimes was shrill.

"The Queen did well at Mass, in the Chapel Royal, Highness," I was told later that day by Katherine Bassett, sister to Anne, who had been sent to serve as one of my new women, as we returned to Richmond for dinner and cards. "She walked in, took the King's arm and made it through the ceremony without a mistake."

"That is good," I said, handing her my perfumed riding gloves, and thinking how little was expected of women. Walk and remain silent was all she had done.

So little is expected of women, yet from that little we may come to be so deeply condemned.

## Chapter Thirty-Four

**Richmond Palace
London**

**Summer 1540**

"They say she is barking orders at her women as if they are dogs," said Katherine of Suffolk.

"She is new to her position, old friend, and insecure in it. I have no doubt some of her people, who like not her quick rise in power and position, are also of a mind to undermine her and spread gossip to paint her in the worst of lights."

"It is likely that is true, Highness."

The new Queen was at Hampton Court, and not making friends there, or anywhere else, I was told.

"She is also much younger than her women," I went on as we strolled down a corridor, our gowns whispering secrets of silk to on another, "and it can be testing for one so young to know how to behave when faced with problems. Remember, she was not born to this calling, it was placed upon her shoulders."

Not all of them were this way. Lady Rutland was kind, motherly in a way towards the new Queen, we heard, and Jane Rochford was Catherine's constant companion. I had long suspected them to be friends. But as for the others, there were many who would resent Catherine's rise in status.

Most expected me to, but I did not.

Oddly, perhaps because I had been in her position, I could see her mistakes and why she was making them. Catherine was young, inexperienced and new to her role. I could see that when she was trying to be regal, royalty being a costume she was new to wearing, it emerged from her as haughtiness, but there are many ways to interpret a trait in another, and at this time all people of England were prepared to think the worst of her, so if she was distant people called her cold, if regal she was haughty, if she acted with any confidence people called her arrogant, and if humble, people named her unsure. If people are disposed to think badly of you, there is no way you can win.

Lady Mary had also decided to dislike the Howard Queen on principle. She had come to see me and spoke of how affronted she was that Catherine had been set up as Queen in my place. "But I, whose position she has filled, am not so," I said to her, smoothing the skirts of yet another new gown I had ordered, this one in azure and silver cloth. "If I am not affronted, why should you be for me?"

"*You* are a woman of a royal, noble house, Highness," she said, her tone tart as sour wine. "*You* were trained and educated as becomes a Queen. This girl was not, and the way the chit acts about court, flouncing here and there and barking orders at her ladies, it brings the entire monarchy into disrepute."

"I would be wary about calling the Queen of England names such as that, Highness," I said.

I had a feeling, right from the first word which came from her lips, that Mary was not speaking about me, in truth. She was speaking of her mother. Although she had disliked me at first, she did not now, I even guessed she loved me a little as a friend, and somewhere in her mind, as Catherine displaced me, I had become her mother and Catherine had become Anne Boleyn. Mary did not like little Howard, because Catherine's rise reminded her of the fall of her mother.

It did not help that Catherine was younger than her, too. I had been just about acceptable as I was the same age as Mary, but Catherine was so young she could not play the mother with Mary, she could not, either, order her about as an elder.

"The King is happy, and so we must be too," I said. "Do not pit yourself against his wife, my lady. This is not a battle you can win, nor does it do you credit to enter the lists."

She had left, but I was not reassured she would be easier on little Howard, and I heard that was the case, for Mary's short curtsies resumed at court, this time to another Queen. I heard she spoke loudly of the refinements and great education of other noble and royal women, all skills Catherine had none of. Mary was trying to show Catherine was unworthy, and replaceable, and this would scare a young girl already scared.

Yet the King adored his new wife, and in that way I was relieved for her. He smothered her in jewels and she wore so many of them that people said it was blinding to look upon the Queen.

"The Queen is now trying to get her men appointments in the Church," I was told one day by Harst.

"She can do this?" I asked.

"She cannot, Highness. Even the King only suggests posts to the Church, but she has written to Archbishop Lee of York, asking him to offer a favour to one of her chaplains, Doctor Mallet, and for another, Doctor Lowe, she wants a certain appointment. The Church rarely offers appointments even at the King's request. Everyone is laughing at her arrogance and ignorance."

"Then my household will not," I said sternly. "Make that clear to all within these walls, my lord ambassador."

*

It was not only Catherine's household or the outraged Lady Mary who could barely believe little Howard had been made Queen. The marital history of my former husband was causing confusion about the world.

After Catherine's first appearance as Queen, foreign ambassadors had been told that the King had married again. The King had been attracted to Catherine's "notable appearance of honour, cleanness, and maidenly behaviour," they were told, and he was therefore "contented to honour that lady with marriage, thinking in his old days, after sundry troubles of mind which had happened to him by marriage, to have obtained such a perfect jewel of womanhood."

The message the envoys were given also hinted that he hoped for children from his new wife. Ambassadors had sent word to their masters and some monarchs were apparently struggling to keep up with the rapid changes of wife the King of England made.

"It is said King François stared at his man in bafflement," Olisleger told me. "And when he was informed the King had set aside you, Highness, he asked, 'The Queen that *now* is?'. When he was told that yes, it was that Queen, the King of France merely sighed."

"I was told François and Charles V declared it was right and good the King separate from me."

"Perhaps it is more that he has, once again, married which has caused the confusion. And the choice of wife. I heard that in Spain there has been a great deal of gossip about the new Queen's lack of suitability for the role."

"I think in time she will surprise them."

"For her sake I hope that is true, Highness."

"The King cannot go an hour without her, and I am told he touches and kisses her more than any other woman he has loved. He is the one she must keep faith with, and that task she is doing well."

"But there has been no word of a coronation," Olisleger said.

"There will not be until she is with child, but that may come soon. The King is much in her bed."

The King and Queen went to Nonsuch not long after. I had never been to this place, but I wished I had seen it.

Nonsuch Palace in Surrey was the King's masterpiece, everyone told me, so no wonder he wanted to show it off to little Howard. Not as vast as his other palaces, but unique in its distinctive beauty, it had walls of white stucco, with deep reliefs picked out in glimmering gold. Busts of emperors of Rome stood about the walls and on marble pillars in the grounds. Beyond the palace were gardens; meadows of wildflowers and formal plots surrounding quadrangles of red and white brick. Upon open ground,

Tudor roses and lions of England were drawn out in coloured sand. Ivy, honeysuckle and jasmine crept up walls and lattices, which stood about groves where seats made out of soft moss and grass stood. Trees aflame with yellow lichen glowed in the half-shadow. Reaching up to the sky were octagonal towers and all about the palace was a vast deer park, rich with forests. It was a place of romance, I was told.

Yet there was another reason beyond romance he took her away. The King did not like to be in London when ill events, done in his name, were occurring. When troubles came, he ran away.

This was a burning.

Richard Meekins was an apprentice. Accused of heresy, he had been sentenced to death, but many said it was unjust, for all Meekins had done was listen to Lutheran preachers speak against the Mass. This was permitted. It was not illegal. His mistake had been to repeat what he had heard. The King was busy persecuting the outspoken on either side of the faiths, however. Meekins had become, in truth, a sacrifice to demonstrate that religious debate was at an end. The King no more wanted to hear his people discuss and disagree. They would fall in line.

"Comment not on it," Katherine of Suffolk said.

I had never had any intention of doing otherwise. The cruel side of the King was not one to awaken.

# Chapter Thirty-Five

**Richmond Palace
London**

**Summer – Autumn 1540**

"Their progress continues well?" I asked the messenger, sent to inform me of the whereabouts of my good brother and his wife.

"Indeed, Your Highness, the King and Queen have gone on from Nonsuch, where there was much hawking and on to Reading, Grafton, Ampthill and Dunstable."

"Grafton was where the King's grandparents married in secret," Katherine of Suffolk told me later, come riding away from court and to London to conduct some business for her estates. I flattered myself she had taken a slight excuse and used it to come and see me. Much as she enjoyed court, she also enjoyed my company.

"There was a reason this was done in secret?"

"Oh, it was a great scandal. The King's grandsire adored Elizabeth Woodville," she explained, a little smile on her lips of pleasure derived from a tale of love. "And desired to wed her from the first moment he saw her. She was of the nobility, but not high, and she came to him in the forest, asking for his aid, for her husband had been slain in the Civil War of Lancaster and York, and she was friendless. He was captured by her beauty and her spirit. His men wanted him to make a profitable match with a foreign bride, but he wanted her, and so he married her, a quiet ceremony and the marriage was kept secret for a while, but there was uproar later, when he won the war and his men tried to marry him off, only to be told he was married already to the damsel he had encountered in the forest."

"A romantic tale," I said.

"The new Queen did well, meeting the French Ambassador, Charles de Marillac," said Katherine, smoothing her gown. "The King kept the audience short, however. He wanted to show off Queen Catherine to ambassadors so his brother-princes might writhe in envy, thinking of the nubile maid now in his bed, but not long enough that she might disgrace herself. I am told by my husband that her lack of experience worries the King."

"I am sure it worries her, too," I said.

"At Ampthill the Queen's ladies, her whole household in fact, were not easy either," went on the Duchess. "They were jumping at the slightest thing when I left."

"Why so?"

"Ghosts, my friend," she said. "Ampthill was where Katherine of Aragon was banished when first the King sent her from court. Some say her phantom lingers."

"But the King and Queen, they were happy?"

"Oh indeed, for the King did much hunting. Deer herded from the forest were brought to the park so the King could shoot them with bow or crossbow. At Grafton he hunted in the saddle, but it tired him."

I stared at her, I never heard of deer being herded towards someone so they could kill them.

"The deer were herded past a platform on which the King stood, so he could shoot them with ease," she explained, perhaps thinking I had not quite understood.

"This is... considered noble in England, to hunt in such a way?"

"A good kill requires skill and a steady hand, so it is still considered noble, Highness."

It did not sound noble to me. It sounded like a slaughterhouse. My father would have died of shame to consider hunting in such a manner.

"Lady Herbert has left the Queen's household for her confinement," Katherine went on. "She left just before I did."

"A good woman," I said, remembering her from court. "I hope she does well. I will send a gift. What is traditional in England for a birth?"

"Herbs for the mother to aid her in her struggles, or a chrisom robe perhaps. A rattle of silver is sometimes given, for they say it brings luck, the noise keeps ill spirits away." Katherine sat back sipping her wine. "The Queen has had a little luck, too, Highness."

"I am glad to hear it, in what way?"

"The King called in Baynton, her chief of the household to scold him," said Katherine. "Baynton and others were deep in their cups one night, and were drunk before the King, something he likes not. The King fears such a man, though he be Catherine's brother-in-law, might be a bad influence on the gentle sensibilities of the Queen and has sent him a warning."

"Why is this good for the Queen?"

"Baynton has not been welcoming to the new Queen, Highness. It is said he was sending out reports about the Queen that were unfavourable and encouraging gossip about her."

"I see."

"Some are saying someone friendly to the Queen might have slipped something else into the wine, to make the men more drunk than they were."

"So that they would disgrace themselves, and the Queen would not be governed by a man who did not like her?"

"Indeed, the name of Rochford has been floating about."

"Whenever something ill happens, Jane Boleyn is assumed guilty. I wonder how anyone can live under such suspicion."

"She is a survivor, Highness. She always was."

"It can be a lonely place to live."

"She has the Queen. They are as close as two widows in the wilderness, I am told. And it is good she has people, the Queen, I mean. She has enemies even amongst the common folk. The King heard of a man who slandered Queen Catherine of late; a priest of Windsor who spoke with scant regard. The man was arrested, and His Majesty has insisted the man be sent to prison."

"Do you know what slander he spoke?" I asked.

"It was said she had lately loved one man and then swiftly married another."

*So others know of Culpepper*, I thought.

I looked to my people. Men and women had formed opposite each other in the chamber to perform *branle doubles* and *pavanes*; regal, sedate dances better suited to the small chambers we were in. I could see the eager fire in the men who wanted to impress with high leaps and bounds. Dancing was about exhibition in England. It was a lost art without an audience.

Men impressed with leaps, speed and stamina; ladies with ease, dignity, precision and poise. Female dancing was about control and grace. Men's dancing was wilder, perhaps freer, but there was great skill in both.

I stood and took Katherine's hand. "Come," I said. "I would have you teach me to dance."

She smiled and obliged me.

# Chapter Thirty-Six

**Richmond Palace**
**London**

**Summer – Autumn 1540**

"There are even more ghosts at The More."

According to Katherine Bassett, the Queen's women were jumping at shadows. They were at the More, a house I had been told was another Katherine of Aragon had stayed in, and had once belonged to Wolsey too. The King had been ill there, which no doubt had not aided the atmosphere at court. "Is this house not a good house?" I asked.

Indeed, no, I was told. It was a grand house, most comfortable. There were fine royal apartments with Presence and Privy chambers, which afforded a touch of privacy. The King's rooms were in the northern range, connected to the Queen's, granting a sense of intimacy. The chambers throughout were beautiful, with ornate plasterwork and gilt gleaming from ceiling and wall. The Queen's watching room had white walls with details such as fruit and flowers picked out in ochre. From there one could see the moat. There was a huge gallery and there the King practised shooting. He used a bow and arrow at times, and pistols at others.

There was, too, a walled courtyard to the southern side of the moat, and corner towers which had an antiquated feel to them, according to descriptions I was given. On the north side was a garden enclosed by another section of moat, fed by a nearby river, which I surmised made this garden cool and pleasant to walk in. More moated gardens raced along the south-west of the house, connected by meandering leats and timbered walkways where honeysuckle grew thick and twisting. The King had commanded work done to improve the inside of the house after the death of Katherine of Aragon, who had spent one winter there as an outcast of court, but the outside, so Katherine told me, was still the work of Cardinal Wolsey.

Whilst at The More the King and his wife hunted and hawked each day. The King was feeling better and Catherine's family were being rewarded. Her brother Charles was granted an annual pension of one hundred pounds which would pass to his sons upon his death. Her brother George was granted one hundred marks per annum, and Isabella, too. Hers was a *fee simple*, which meant she could choose to whom it passed. Catherine's sister Margaret received the same.

"And now people are saying the Queen is too greedy, though I hear, Highness, she asked for none of these favours for her kin." Katherine of Suffolk, come visiting again, touched her headdress and inserted a loose pin a little tighter.

"I hear the King is in fine health now and gets up at five or six of the morning, is out hunting all day with the Queen and then sleeps well. The Queen is clearly good for him. And it is only natural that the King should grant favours to her kin. There is nothing odd about such an event."

I too was merry, doing much the same as the royal pair. There was hawking with my new gyrfalcons, a present from my brother, and in the afternoon, after we had dined sitting upon chairs and about tables brought out to make a great hall under the trees, there might be more hawking, but often I strolled in the gardens, watched my men and my ladies dance, or played cards.

One morning when I woke the air felt cooler, blissful. Autumn had come. The summer sun surrendered and although it did not rain, winds came more often and were colder than before. Tennis was played now there was no risk of players igniting from the heat, and having never seen the game I was entranced, it was so fast, so impressive.

The court was indoors, in a large room with a long net. The players had to hit the ball over the net, catching the others by surprise so they could score points if the others could not return the ball. "But it can be bounced from the walls too?" I asked as the game began.

"Indeed so," said my companion, the Duchess. "And points may too be scored by hitting the ball and getting it into any of the three goals in the walls." She pointed to them.

"It was once the King's favourite game," Katherine of Suffolk told me as we watched and wagered on the players. "An ambassador it was, I think, who said it was the prettiest thing in the world to watch him play."

Love had washed in with autumn winds. A dangerous love, so the Duchess told me as we stood watching the match. "Lady Margaret Douglas has an eye for Howards. Once she fell for Thomas Howard, and now she has fallen again, for the Queen's brother Charles." None could hear us over the cheering and shouting for the match.

I looked at Katherine. "Will they be allowed to marry?"

"No, he is not high enough for the King to allow it. This could end badly, as it did the last time."

# Chapter Thirty-Seven

**Richmond Palace
London**

**October 1540**

When the King and Queen reached Windsor in October at the end of progress, they were driven within the walls of that fortress rather than into London by rumours of plague in the city and the King's intense terror of all illness. They were shut in at Windsor, as I was at Richmond.

"All precautions must be taken, Your Highness," said my worried steward.

"I will bow to your guidance on this matter," I said, understanding that at least part of his concern – although I was sure he had affection for me – was that I might die and then there would be word the King had killed me secretly, leading to my officers enduring the wrath of my good brother of England. "Your word shall be my command in this house."

He looked relieved, going over precautions; vinegar and wine were to be left at all doors, in pots, so everyone could rinse their hands in it, rooms to be purified with sage smoke, alms to be given at a distance to appease God but remain safe, the household should all eat toasted bread sprinkled with wine vinegar and spread with butter and cinnamon for this was known to be a preventative, and bundles of herbs such as lavender were to be hung at every window, to stop the sickness entering the house. "And no people who have been near a suspect place containing plague are to come to this house unless they have been ten days clear of symptoms of illness," he added. "If any fall ill in the house they must be contained and separated from all others."

One of my fingers went to my throat, tracing the scar of smallpox there. Barely could they be seen, these slight pieces of evidence of my brush with death, but I remembered how I had once been one of those people contained, separated from all others.

"Messengers, from the King or Council?" I asked. "What will they do?"

"They will wait outside the gates, in a prepared room, their letters will be run over with a light wash of vinegar and smoked under sage bundles, then they will be read to you, Highness, but you will not touch the papers. You will write your response and that will be given to the messenger, still outside the door."

"Very well," I said. "But please ensure that in that room there is food and ale left for these men. They are riding far each day, taking great risks on behalf of the King, and me, and they should not be left without succour."

England was in peril, it was clear, but some thought there was not trouble enough in the world.

A man named John Lascelles arrived at court. Once he had worked for Cromwell and there was word he had returned to seek revenge on Norfolk.

"He went to Sir Nicholas Hare," Olisleger told me, who had had a letter from a friend at the King's court. "The man is no friend of Norfolk's, but he sent Lascelles away. Lascelles wanted Sir Nicholas to report Norfolk to the King as it is said Norfolk rebuked a man for marrying a nun after she left her order when it was dissolved by the King."

"But the King himself has said former nuns should keep their vows of chastity," I said. It was, to my mind, a foolish order. How were former nuns, released of their vows and sent into the world, to support themselves unless they married? Employment for women was sparse, and for unmarried women still fewer were the opportunities. Some might have kin they could go to, but many who entered religious orders had been placed there, frequently as children, because their families had too many bellies to feed. I had heard of many nuns now having to resort to prostitution in order to simply feed themselves. I could imagine little worse than going from a life of seclusion from men to having to offer one's body to them, many of them, night after night, just to eat.

"Indeed, but men like Lascelles, reformers, do not think the same way. To Lascelles this is proof Norfolk is a papist. And it is the words Norfolk used which caused suspicion."

"What did Norfolk say?"

"When the man defended his right to marry a former nun, saying God and the King had made all of these former religious folk free, Norfolk said 'By God's Sacred Body! It will never be out of my heart as long as I live!' That could be interpreted as a sign that Norfolk adheres to the old ways of Rome, that he does not accept the Royal Supremacy."

"So, this Lascelles heard this, and wants to use it against Norfolk?"

"He wanted Hare to take the case to the King, indeed, but Hare said he would not. He told Lascelles to take the matter to the King or Council himself, but Norfolk is in a position of power at the moment, and Lascelles knows that. Without noble support he will get nowhere."

"Do you think he really cares what Norfolk thinks? Norfolk boasts loud and bold that never has he read Scripture in his life, I have heard him myself. Why should men care so much what others think of religion?"

"Because religion changes the policies of a country, its laws and the freedom of men."

*Not to mention that of women*, I thought.

"Where is Lascelles now?" I asked.

"In the King's household, but a minor post, as a sewer. It is said His Majesty took him in out of pity. He does not seem intelligent or charming enough to rise far."

"Then Norfolk is safe, and how are the King and Queen?"

"His men complain they see him not, for he is always with the Queen."

I laughed. "I hear the Council have to chase him with their papers."

"He wishes to lose himself in pleasure."

"It is good he looks well; people will know Catherine is doing him good."

"She needs a child to be safe."

Others were curious, eager to watch for signs of pregnancy too; enemies of Catherine's family kept an eye on her belly, as did allies. Curiosity came from afar too. Marguerite d'Angouleme, Queen of Navarre and sister to King François, had sent a request for a portrait of the royal family to add to her collection. It was not an unusual request, exchanges of portraits were common between royal houses and she had, in fact, once asked for a portrait of me, but Katherine of Suffolk, who wrote with this news, told me there might be a special reason for her interest in the new Queen.

*"The Queen of Navarre was fond of Queen Catherine's cousin,"* she wrote. *"When that cousin was in France, in the household of Queen Claude, she spent time in Marguerite's circle of reformist thinkers and poets. They kept in touch through letters when she became Queen. Perhaps the Queen of Navarre wishes to be kind to our English Queen in remembrance of another Queen. If the King were to issue a portrait of Queen Catherine with his family, it would be a sign of favour. The Queen of Navarre might well be a friend to our new Queen, despite differences in religion."*

"Anne," I whispered to the ghost. "You are aiding your cousin, and I am glad of it."

I wondered at times if this was also why Jane Rochford had become her friend. Catherine was a Howard, kin to Anne Boleyn. If Jane had failed to save one Queen, perhaps she felt her penance was achievable within another.

Then, the very next day there came a ridiculous rumour.

And it was about me.

## Chapter Thirty-Eight

**Richmond Palace
London**

**Autumn 1540**

"With child?" I asked. "How can I be with child? I am a child of God, but not the Virgin Mary, my friend." *And the King, though he might think himself God, is closer to the Antichrist,* I thought.

Rumour had it that when the King had come to see me, his 'good sister' here at Richmond not long ago, he had got me with child. People were saying I was his mistress. I could barely believe anyone would even consider it as truth. He had made it obvious how much he loathed me, face and form.

"But people are saying how beautiful you look now, Highness." Harst looked vastly uncomfortable.

"It is most sweet of them to compliment and slander me at the same time," I said dryly.

"People are saying the King has said to some he made a mistake, and he will declare that the nullification of his marriage was unlawful, and Catherine is but his mistress."

My heart shuddered. "The King has said no such thing to any person, and I am not with child. This man is now my brother, by law. That people would suggest such a thing is revolting, and ungodly."

*And terrifying*, I thought. I had just become free, was this all to be ripped away if what people claimed the King had said was true? And if it was not, would I be blamed for these rumours starting? Defaming the name or honour of the King was surely enough to have me arrested for treason of one kind or another. What would the poor Queen make of this? She would be as scared as I was, although for perhaps different reasons.

Until this rumour surfaced the Queen had appeared to be doing well, but there were issues. Quite aside from there being no talk of a coronation, Catherine had not been presented to the officials of London as I had. Plague raging in the city was the formal excuse as to why this ceremony was being delayed, and although this was reasonable it no doubt worried the Queen that even the slight ceremony of being greeted by the city's officials had not happened. I had undertaken this ceremony quite soon after becoming Queen, but Catherine's was not even being talked of seriously. She must have felt already insecure on her fragile throne, and this would only add to it. Perhaps someone was trying to make us enemies.

"People are saying she might be cast off, and you would become Queen again, Highness." Harst looked at me as if this might be something I wanted. I did not.

"People in England are always saying much, lord ambassador, and hardly any of it turns out to be true. This accusation that I am the King, my *brother's*, mistress is a slight upon me in many ways, which I might forgive, but also upon my brother and my sister-in-law, which is more damaging. We will show ourselves to all within this house and demonstrate it is not true."

I went before my household that hour, wearing a tight waisted gown to remove accusations that this phantom child was already showing upon my body, and told them they were to put paid to any such rumour, "for it casts foulness upon my reputation and that of the King," I said.

My household, by then most affectionate towards me, swore to a man, and woman, they would do all they could to quash the rumours. They were not the only ones working on this grim matter.

A man arrived that very day, sent by the King to see what was going on. I told the man I had no idea what had happened to bring about these rumours. I had been in bed for a few days the week before after feasting with my household, I suspected I had eaten or drunk something which did not agree with me, but I was not with child and was as good a maid as the

King knew I was. "Tell the King I am ready to present myself before all his people, to make any kind of public declaration he so wishes, or to be examined in any way that is thought right and proper so this rumour I am with child, which has come from nowhere and greatly harms my moral reputation as well as slandering the poor King, is utterly false," I said.

"The King is much mortified that anyone would slight you, my lady," said the man. "And he shares not only your distress but your zeal to set the rumours down at once."

"Please send word also to the Queen," I said. "That nothing said by these malicious tongues is true. If I know anything in this world it is that the King loves her more than anyone, and never would turn to another woman."

I did not know this, but I did want the Queen to know I supported her and was not conspiring to seduce the King from her and set myself up as Queen again.

As it transpired, someone had heard of this slight illness of mine, and an enemy of Norfolk's had jested it was morning sickness. That slur was taken up as truth by malicious tongues. Many at court never believed it in any case and I was glad of it. Ambassador Marillac in particular was openly sneering at the gossip, for he said the King was so entranced with Catherine that he saw no other woman in the world.

I was most heartily relieved. I had thought I might be blamed for the rumours. It was a reminder that although I was merry now, my position was fragile still. Not as fragile as before, but pottery may smash to bits on a hard floor just as well as glass does.

"The King is to reward the Queen," said Katherine of Suffolk, finally able to visit again now the plague was dying down in London.

"I am glad, I was so worried over this affair of an affair which never was, my friend."

She smiled. "There is an Act going through Parliament," she went on, "which will set out the rights of the Queen of England. It is called the *Queen Consort Act*, and it will grant Queen Catherine the power to act as a woman *sole*, so she might grant favours and appointments without the consent of her King and husband."

"That is good indeed, yet I imagine she will still turn to him for advice, and he will expect her to do so?"

"In all likelihood, but it is a gesture of trust. She will have the freedom to appoint members of her own household, and to grant favours. It increases her power."

"It is a public sign the rumours are false," I said, nodding. "She will be relieved by that, as I am."

"There is more," she went on. "All lands once in the possession of Queen Jane are to become the Queen's."

"I am glad of it," I said.

*Glad I have escaped, again, I thought.*

## Chapter Thirty-Nine

**Richmond Palace
London**

**Autumn – Winter 1540**

"The Queen has said she knows little of such matters and would have her Council manage the estates for her," Katherine of Suffolk and I sat together after dancing. I was getting quite skilled in the art.

"That sounds wise," I said. We were talking of the Queen's new estates and what she was to do with them.

"Wise?"

"Such a request demonstrates that the new Queen understands her limitations. She was raised perhaps to look after a house, some land perhaps, as a lord's daughter should, but the estates the King gives her now are vast, the responsibilities many, her dependants numerous. If she delegates to others who know more, and will work for her well, this is wise. Taking on all that work and doing badly for lack of experience or education would be the mistake."

"I had not considered such," said the Duchess, pursing her lips and looking ponderous.

"And she knows the King's men will check on the accounts, the King himself perhaps, so these men, if tempted to cheat her, will be caught swiftly."

Katherine laughed.

"I suppose some will think badly of her for this, but would it have been wise to attempt this herself, make a mess and displease the King, not to mention what her tenants, people with poverty already their lot in life, might suffer? The King does not do all work of the realm on his own, he chooses men best suited to each task. Delegation is not dereliction of the Queen's duties, but the best way to manage her responsibilities."

It was clever in another way, for if these men managed Catherine's lands well, and they became part of her jointure, she would do well when the King died. She had plenty of clothing and jewels, and also many lands now. Some had been Queen Jane's, Cromwell's, Lord Hungerford's, and some had come from the estate of the late Abbot of Reading, whose body was presently hanging in a gibbet upon his old abbey gate. Catherine Howard was a rich woman now. I could see my former servant thinking ahead, to a time when she might outlive the King. Little Howard was not a fool, as some thought her, she was planning for her future. People thought her fancy-free and flippant, but I saw much hidden under her mask.

"Sadly, Lady Margaret Douglas is not doing so well," said Katherine as we sat, watching the dancers.

"The King has discovered where she has lost her heart?"

"Indeed, and she has lost her freedom. She has been banished to Syon Abbey and the Queen's brother is threatened with the Tower."

"Did the Queen speak for her brother?"

"She did not. She said she was in ignorance of the affair, and her brother should not have gone against the wishes of the King."

"I think it is Margaret who should have known what would happen, for this is the second time she has been imprisoned for daring to think she might love who she wishes to. Few people have that option, women fewer still."

Shipped to Syon, Margaret was warned to "wholly apply herself to please the King's Highness."

The court marvelled at how the affair had not dented the King's affection for Catherine. Some praised her for ceding to the will of her husband, as others censured her for not speaking for her brother. It was, to me, another sign of her cleverness. She had remained loyal first to her husband, not to kin who had stuck her in her unwanted position. Her husband was the one in ultimate control of her, he was the one she had to please, and she had done so. A simple enough plan it might be, to merely keep her husband happy, but it was not undertaken without effort or sacrifice, and in all honesty often the best of plans are the simple ones.

Charles Howard swiftly fled abroad, and the King raged that he had escaped, but I wondered if this escape had been arranged by the King. He might want to punish Charles for daring to try to wed Margaret, but the King would not have wanted Catherine shamed. Charles's escape granted the best of both worlds.

Norfolk escaped the wrath of the King over this affair as he was not at court. In the summer and early autumn, Norfolk had been in the country, and he only returned in November after the scandal had died down. He denied all knowledge of the affair and told the King he was scandalised by it. I wondered if he had been ignorant. Had Charles managed to marry Margaret, a Howard son could have been placed in the royal line, far down, of course, but still there, still possible as a claimant to the throne. Norfolk had tried it once, marrying his daughter to Henry Fitzroy, and he was not a man of large imagination, so might have tried the same thing again.

The King greeted Norfolk with great affection, I was told. Despite the trouble one Howard had caused, having another in his bed had made the King warm towards Norfolk. Norfolk attended one Council meeting and then was sent to interrogate Lord Grey, the former deputy of Ireland, who was in the Tower languishing under charges of treason. I also heard Norfolk did not bother visiting the Queen.

"He has what he wants of her," I said to myself. "And that was elevating her to secure his power." In truth I thought Norfolk did not like women a great deal. He always had talked to the men about me, rather than to me.

Norfolk had the post of Lord Treasurer and was rumoured to soon become Lord Lieutenant of the north. His men had good positions, secured by Cromwell's demise. Richard Radcliffe, Earl of Sussex, had become Great Chamberlain and William Fitzwilliam, Earl of Southampton, was Lord Privy Seal. "As far as Norfolk thinks, which is not far," Katherine said, "the affairs of the realm are back in the hands of the nobility, a Howard is on the throne, therefore the world is as it should be."

There were, however, hints that my former husband was not as pleased as Norfolk with the new structure at court. Since Cromwell's death I understood the King had been forced into a more active role in the government of his realm. Although attempting to spend all his time with his new wife, he had to be in Council a great deal. Cromwell had taken care of much and the King had trusted him to do so. He did not trust Norfolk or other nobles in the same way and was well aware of the limitations of their intelligence.

"Denny says the King is always scribbling away, making notes," Katherine of Suffolk said, speaking of Sir Anthony Denny, Keeper of the Palace of Westminster and Yeoman of the Robes. Denny was a rising star of court. "The King might have despised Cromwell at times, but he knew his kingdom was safe with him. Not so with Norfolk and the Seymours."

"Sometimes I wonder who in this kingdom truly can call themselves safe," I said.

# Chapter Forty

**Richmond Palace
London**

**Autumn – Winter 1540**

"The King is *completely* in her thrall."

This was said often, and with disapproval. The King and Queen were still at Windsor, and it was said if a man wanted to find the King or forget his cares he should go to the Queen's chambers, for there was nothing but song and dance.

Why should she not celebrate? Catherine was doing well, had been rewarded, had escaped censure of the King after her brother's failed love affair, but it was true that her ceremony of entering the city of London as Queen had been put off again, this time apparently because of the weather. Autumn was bleeding into winter, and now the ceremony would not happen until spring. I suspected the King was indeed waiting for Catherine to become pregnant before bestowing even this slight ceremony upon her. Yet there were no signs she was with child, and everyone was watching for them.

"Gardiner is to be sent to the Emperor Charles," said Olisleger. "Phillip Melanchthon, a famous reformer, condemned the King for setting you aside, Highness," he said, joining me at the window.

"I remember his name," I said.

"He said England was full of atrocious crimes of faith, and the King was light of morals, having set aside you to marry Queen Catherine."

"It is strange to me how many people are more interested in seeing me now married to the King than when I was married to him," I said.

"And so Gardiner is to be sent to the Emperor Charles." Olisleger said this again, so I gathered there was something important about this mission.

"Why?"

"Because the King fears the King of Spain and King François will hear such condemnations and believe them. Gardiner is to demonstrate to King Charles that the King is godly, is *not* acting for his own selfish wishes, and the Queen is to be used as an example of how the King protects the faith, because of her good and old Catholic family."

"I too had a good, old, Catholic family," I mentioned.

"Do you regret your alteration in status, my lady?"

"Not for a moment," I said.

"Lady Mary continues her quiet war against the Queen. She will not pause to talk to her stepmother in public, has continued to not bow her head low when the Queen is before her. She has spoken disparagingly of Queen Catherine's accomplishments which, although spare, are not worse than those of many other noblewomen."

"Though I love her, Lady Mary is her own worst enemy."

I was right. The King heard of his daughter's behaviour and had words with her. There was talk she would be banished from court but instead the King took his new wife and a select household and went to Woking Palace.

Woking was a small palace, and only had eight acres, but half were gardens. There were orchards surrendering last leaves to the rising wind. Bowling greens, two chapels and kitchens, miniature versions of the ones at Hampton Court, which all men said were the best in the world, were littered about its grounds. Walled gardens and a double moat stood proud about the house, protecting it from harm. There was a corn mill and a fulling-mill and fishponds. A large lawn at the front overlooked land used for hunting deer, leading into a marsh, good for hawking.

What there was not, however, was room for a large household.

Lady Mary found her father had moved on, and she had not been invited. "I doubt not it worried her," I said. "It must have seemed an echo of when he left Queen Katherine, her mother."

Mary was not obeying her father; this was the trouble. Perhaps she had done that so little over the past few years that she had fallen out of the habit. Mary was unwilling to obey her father and honour Catherine. She pretended she was, but by all reports her bows were no longer, and her smirks got only deeper. She had made no more comments about Catherine but did not stop her women making them. Although hardly subtle, she had grown a touch craftier, and the King could see what she was doing.

The King had been ill before they left, a fever brought on by his leg, but he recovered swift, and it was said this was because of the Queen's good influence upon him. She had kept him in good spirits before he was ill – he would not see her during his illness – and he was in good health.

So was I.

In chill wind we hawked, day after day. When it rained, we kept to the palace, walking in the gallery.
Oftentimes, we sat up late with my men and my ladies, playing cards, or dancing and listening to musicians sing songs of love. Sometimes I smiled, thinking how often we are sold an idea of love, and how often we find that something else is more precious.

We are lied to, often, by bards. They would teach us women that finding a husband is more important than anything, but in my case, it was being set free of one which meant more to me.

*

"She will find herself on the block if she is not careful," said Katherine of Suffolk. "The King is enraged."

The Lady Mary had been called to Woking to make peace with the Queen, but the King's daughter was not after peace. She was not outwardly rude, I heard, but avoided Catherine, keeping to conversation with others.

When the King led Catherine to her, affording no chance of escape, Mary talked of matters she knew the young Queen understood nothing of, trade disputes and land laws, the politics of other realms.

"After a while, the Queen simply lapsed into humiliated silence," said Katherine, who had also been there. "You should have seen her face, she looked as though she might burst into tears. I felt for her, Highness. It was a cruel show, intended to shame the Queen. The King was furious. They have gone on to Oatlands, and left Mary behind again."

"I did think they were due to return to Hampton Court."

"They were, but the King decided otherwise. He wants more time alone with his wife."

"And none with his daughter?"

My friend lifted her eyebrows and breathed in. "I think if Lady Mary continues as she is, she may never see her father, or the light of day again."

# Chapter Forty-One

**Richmond Palace**
**London**

**December 1540**

"An invitation," I said to my women as I opened the missives brought to me that morning. For the most part they were incidental, a person asking for patronage here, a request from one of my estates there, and occasionally there were letters from family, all bearing a few slight signs that they had been opened. The men of the King probably thought they were subtle, that the indications a seal had been opened could not be seen, but I could spot them. I was supposed to send my missives to the King, but it was clear to me that my letters were being read, probably both ways, as they arrived and as they were sent. The King did not want me sharing things with my family that he might not approve of. I did not mind, we sisters long ago had made our code and no one else knew it. Besides, I had little to complain about. I was merry in my new life.

"We are to go to court at Christmastide, for the New Year celebrations," I said to my women. "I am to be presented to the Queen."

"Will it not be strange, Highness?" Katherine Bassett asked.

"I suppose it might be, for some, but not for me. The new Queen will no doubt be nervous to meet me again, since I was in her chair before her, but now she is my sister. I have many sisters, my friend, and always I have found them to be a good thing to have, so I do not regret gaining another now. And we shall show the new Queen, and all the court as well as England that there is nothing but perfect peace and love between us. I liked Catherine a great deal when she was my lady, and the separation of the King and I as husband and wife now allows that we can be friends again, something I rejoice for."

"No doubt the King wishes all this too, Highness," said Mistress Bassett, "and hopes very much you will pay respects to the new Queen, so ambassadors can report to their masters that you are well treated in England."

"That is only the truth," I said, chuckling. "I am well treated, and aware of my good fortune, so if the King, my good brother, wishes to show this to the world, I am only too happy to oblige him."

We heard the King was almost smothering his new wife in gifts. People said they had never seen him so in love before, not even with the Queen whose name no one was allowed to mention. There was talk of a set of rosaries the King had given her, made of gilt beads and coral, and some said Catherine had asked for them for she was a devoted papist, and others said the King had simply given them to her for they were a pretty piece, and Catherine adored pretty things. I wondered, however, about the volume of gifts being showered on little Howard.

Was it a sign of insecurity that the King lavished so many gifts upon her? Was it not enough that his chosen motto was about her wrists? That she was his wife, that she was in his bed every night he wanted her? It was not, it seemed. The King would have all men know pretty Queen Catherine was his property. This was possession, ownership, dressed up to appear as affection. And so many presents he bestowed upon her. More each day. To me it was a sign the King was not secure about his marriage. Perhaps he was only too aware, somewhere deep down and buried with care, that his new wife had had little choice about marrying him, and given the freedom to have a choice, she might not have done so.

People marvelled at the King's generosity, saying he had never bestowed so much upon a wife before. Others laughed at an old man trying to buy the affection of a young girl. Some censured Queen Catherine, saying she was greedy. I found the last curious as it was the King who chose to grant presents to her, but of course as a woman, the Queen must in some way be responsible for the sin of greed in a man.

"She asked for the rosaries to demonstrate that she can guide the King back to the true faith," I heard was being whispered, too.

What fools these people were, so anxious to see politics in everything that they made Catherine either a genius at the intricacies of manipulation or a dunce being used as a pawn by her family. There was no middle way, it seemed. It was often the way with women. Devil or angel, virgin or whore, simpleton or schemer, we were one or the other. I, apparently, had become one of the angel virgins. A ludicrous notion. The Queen many saw as a demonic whore.

Plenty thought the Queen should stay out of religious matters. I heard Archbishop Lee of York wrote a response to the Queen's requests for positions in the clergy for her men that month, saying he was unable to grant her command that one of her chaplains be made an archdeacon. "It is said the Queen did not actually state whom she wanted in the post, which was embarrassing enough, but the Archbishop pointed out that he had only ever granted the right of advowson to the King, and then only once, which he regretted. The other appointment she wanted was also not available." Olisleger sighed. "She blundered in like a toddler, demanding this and that, and now the court is laughing at her."

"These demands, they were made at the start of her reign. She was insecure, and wanted to assert some authority," I said. "Was I so different, asking the King about my coronation over and over?"

"You are most different to this new Queen, my lady."

"You see all the ways we are different, my friend, but I see so many ways in which we are not."

The Queen allowed the matter to quietly drop, which is what I would have done too, so I again saw more ways in which we were alike.

\*

Just before Christmas the King and Queen came riding back to Hampton Court. That palace was where I was to go to meet them soon, and in preparation I was having new gowns made and ensuring my dancing was graceful and skilled. I had practised so much of late there were blisters on my feet, but never had I welcomed such slight irritations more. I was becoming talented at the dances of England, and I loved them. If for nothing else, I would have remained in this country just so I could dance, with my women, with my men, in public and to perform dances that required more than staid, short movement, as we had learned in Cleves. Energy and vim were a part of all English dances. Perhaps because there was such danger to life here, people celebrated life more too.

Richmond was beautiful that Christmastide and I was determined that my first season of Christ's birth in England was to be one to remember. My house was to be decorated, we would keep all English traditions, and I would show them some of Cleves and Julich, "and we are to be merry," I announced to my household, "that is a requirement set in place by your mistress!"

There was much cheering and laughing at that. People said mine was the best noble household to be in within England, for I was a generous and kind mistress, and there never was a lack of something to do.

I wanted to see the world, and so I insisted still on walking and riding out even though it was winter. I wanted to know the changing of the seasons of my new country, wanted to feel the air of each month on my face, lift my nose to it to see how it smelt. Every day was an adventure to me now. Hoar frost was on all the trees, spikes of silver like hair upon bare, skeletal branches. Snow had not come, but it was in the air, an iron tang on the chill wind. We passed villages and hamlets where the scent of pottage rose from chimneys and through whistling cracks in doors; onion and turnip on the wind, bubbling in broth. Windows were shuttered against the freezing wind, the insides lit by fires of wood within.

Sometimes we saw women walking on their way home or to market, baskets full of leeks and onions, mud clinging to the long, light roots. Shimmering like frost, those roots reflected the sun, now just a slight light in the skies above. Women and men we passed were wrapped in as many layers as they could afford; cloaks and hoods, boots and gloves keeping the blood warm. On Sundays they would go to cold churches armed with hand warmers, hollow metal spheres holding hot coals and shards of glowing wood, so they would not freeze as they prayed to God to deliver them through this season.

We came to a pool near Richmond where children whizzed about on skates of bone and wood. Seeing me, they had tried to bow and two lads had fallen over. I had laughed and thrown them coins. "I am honoured you should bow so low to me, the King's new sister," I said to them, making a jest, of course, about them falling over, and they laughed with me.

On the day before Christmas, Richmond was resplendent with greenery. Ivy and holly brought in from the park decorated each window, wound in garlands about each staircase and banister. Christmas was the longest holiday of the year, twelve days from Eve until Epiphany, and no one in England would be working during that time. Cattle, and flocks of geese, chickens or sheep would be tended and food would have to be cooked of course, but on the Eve of Christmas people set aside tools of the everyday to go to their homes, pray to God, and eat with their families, some sharing a minced *pye* of thirteen spices, honouring Jesus and his apostles.

Sometimes, lords would still invite peasants into their great hall, I was told, to eat with them on the day of Christmas. This was an old tradition, and not all still kept it, but some did. I was unsure about how the King would react to my having peasants in my hall, but I sent word for charity to be plentiful from my house. Vagabonds and homeless men washed up to my noble gates all that Christmastide and none went away without a full belly and full hands.

Christmas Eve was the last day of fasting, when not only was there no meat, but no eggs, cheese or milk. We feasted on fish that night, then gathered about the fire in the great hall. I was delighted to learn that the English kept Christmas Eve the same as we did in Cleves. I suppose some traditions are similar in many Christian countries. There were fairy tales and ghost stories to be had that night. "I would hear a story of my new land," I said, after I had told one of mine, of elves and people missing in the forest who ate and drank of the food of the hidden people and never were seen again.

"I have one," said one of my new ladies, Martha Crew née Denny. Her husband, Wymond, was acting as another interpreter for me, though I was well aware he was also reporting on me to the Council. "One of my distant cousins married a lord of Scots, and she sent me word of creatures known to live there, in the seas about the outer islands. They are named selkies, Highness."

"Selkies," I said, my tongue stumbling on the unfamiliar word.

"There once was a selkie," said Martha, staring into the flames. "Selkies may be male or female, and on land they look like humans, but when in the sea, where they truly live, they shift into the shape of seal. They do this by way of a cloak of fur, which, when about their shoulders makes them into a seal, and when taken off, makes them human."

I started for a moment, the tale so familiar yet the creature different.

"The selkies are all beautiful," she continued. "When in their human form, none may resist them. And so it came to pass that one day a selkie maid came to shore, and upon the pebbles and rocks of the beach she removed her cloak of fur and became a woman, lithe and beautiful. Upon the rocks she lay, sunning herself as she enjoyed the sun full upon her skin and not cooled by the waters of Scotland…"

"And Scotland is in the north, so the water must be freezing," said one of my maids to another, causing the teller of the tale to cast a glance of censure at her.

"As she lay on the rocks, enjoying the sunlight, a man came along and seeing her and how beautiful she was, and seeing her cloak nearby and knowing the old stories, he took her cloak away and hid it. Then he returned and told her that he had her cloak and so according to the old stories she was now his to command. The selkie maid was horrified, but she knew the tales too and knew they were true, so she was compelled to do as he wished, and what he wished for was marriage with her. They lived in a house near the very beach where she had been captured, and they had a daughter. The selkie maid was a good wife to him, doing all he said, but at times he would see her standing on the shore, reaching her hands out the sea, to her home, to which she never could return. She was sad at times, thinking of her people, of her kingdom in the depths, but he had her cloak and so she could not return."

*Is it possible this could happen more than once,* I asked myself, *or do we all have the same tales about how women are captured?*

"One day, though, knowing her mother's sadness, the daughter of the selkie woman gave herself a task. She would find the cloak and give it back to her mother. She knew that this would mean her mother would return to the sea, but the daughter of the selkie woman could not stand the hollow sadness in the eyes of her mother anymore. She watched her father, and one day she saw him go to a cave on the beach and stay within it a while, and she followed him, hiding at the mouth of the cave in an alcove. When he came out, she snuck in, and far, far in the back of the cave, where her candle barely could give any light, on a shelf of rock she found her mother's cape. Back to the house she fled, as fast as she could and to her mother she gave the cloak. Her mother took it, her eyes shining, but she looked, too, with sorrow at her daughter, knowing she, who was half human, could not come with her. 'Go,' said the child. 'I am well here, and I would you were happy too.'

"And so the woman, knowing her husband would not be gone long, ran to the beach and there she put on her cloak of fur, and into the sea she dove, transforming into a seal. She swam away and her husband never did see her again, but her daughter did, for every year the woman would return in secret. She never dared to come to the beach and take her cloak off again, but every year on the same day, the day her daughter had given her freedom, the selkie maid returned. There in the sea she would bob, watching her daughter on the beach, and her daughter would raise a hand to let her mother know that she was well. Every year, as the girl grew and became a woman, as she brought her own children to the beach to see their grandmother, the selkie maid returned, knowing the bond between them could not be broken by mere distance, and knowing each were happy where they were."

I smiled at the woman. "A beautiful story," I said.

*

I woke to bells, pealing in the skies to celebrate that this was the day Christ was born.

After Mass on Christmas Day, there was the feast. A pastry which contained a turkey, a new creature imported from the New World, stuffed with a goose, stuffed with a chicken, stuffed with a partridge, stuffed with a pigeon was brought in and cheered all the way to the main table where I sat. There was also venison, roasted hare, wild birds, tarts, saffron eggs and fine pottages. The roasted head of a wild boar was brought in, and the tongue was served to me, an honour, since it was the tenderest part.

We watched performances by wandering bands of players, called mummers, brought to my house by my Master of Revels. Greeted into the great hall with shouts of "wassail!" and "drink hail!" they did short pieces;

people and stories taken from the pages of the Bible to stand before us as flesh and blood. I watched Mary greeting shepherds and listened as the players imitated cows and sheep who stood about the Christ-child, lifting their heads to greet his arrival in the world.

There followed carols. The first of these kinds of songs, made especially for Christmas, had been sung in the time of the King's father, and that year we listened to ones of the King's composition. I applauded them, but even I, a newcomer to the English language, could see where the King forced words to rhyme which did not quite rhyme. Later I had my musicians play, and their songs were far superior to those of the King.

Maids of honour were kissed under the mistletoe, an old tradition, or so my men told me with entirely straight faces, as over them glittering lamps and candles swung gently in the heated air at the top of the chamber. We drank wassail, an ale brewed with spices and apples. Served in a large bowl, it was handed about as wassail songs were sung.

Later there was dancing, although many were too full to take part. But I did. And with glad, light feet I danced until dawn broke over my house.

*

"The King wants you to know, Highness, that he is quite overcome with the magnificence of your gift," said the messenger.

Gifts for the New Year had gone out. Mine from the King had arrived, rich clothes, plate of silver and many jewels, but my present to the King and Queen had become delayed, which I was sad for, but they could not be risked in the drifts of snow surrounding Richmond.

I had eventually, when the roads were clear enough, dispatched two large horses, with violet trappings and saddles. It was a handsome gift and the King had been touched. He adored fine horseflesh, and the saddles, flush in colours of royalty, were most attractive. Sending a matching pair, was, I hoped, a sign to the new Queen that I was in full acceptance of her marriage.

"Would it not have been better to send a smaller one for the Queen?" Katherine of Suffolk had asked as we inspected them.

"But then they would not be matching, and the King cannot possibly ride on a smaller horse. I wanted this as a sign that I accept their marriage and sovereignty. Send an unmatched pair and it might be thought I think them badly matched. I hear the Queen is a good horsewoman, I am sure she can handle such a fine animal, though he is big."

"They are beautiful," Katherine admitted. "You know the King's tastes well."

"I do not think the tastes of men are hard to gauge. Women, now there is more a challenge."

Digging my hands deep into my new muffler of black velvet and sable, hanging from a rope of pearls about my neck, I had walked about the horses, my feet crunching in the snow.

"You are nervous about seeing her again?"

I sighed, stroking the side of the horse. "Perhaps," I admitted. "More that she will suspect me of anger or annoyance at her."

"Do you have no anger? She took your place."

I looked at Katherine. "You English are strange people to me still, at times," I said with a smile. "The Queen took nothing from me. She took nothing because it was not in her power to take what I had or in her power to give anything in return. The King was the one who took my position, he gave it to another. It was his choice that I leave the throne at his side and become his sister instead. I grieve nothing lost, for I think too we were not a good match, and the position I have now is freer than any I ever have had, including the office of Queen."

"Yet you are lesser in status now, my friend."

"People think that the highest position is the best, for you have the most power and perhaps this is true, if power is all that one desires, but for me there is beauty and grace, liberty and happiness in a life of less power. If I were to carry resentment it would not be for the Queen. The King chose her and set me aside. That is what happened between us. I am content in my situation." I looked at her. "It could have been worse, remember that, old friend. Much worse could my present situation be. I could have no situation, I could be in the ground, and yet instead I am full of joy and discovery and wonder. I regret nothing, and I resent nothing."

"All the same, most women would bear a grudge against the other woman."

"Then they look to the wrong place. Are we to believe that men have no willpower, no ability to make their own choices? If so, we are in a sorry state for always I have been told that men are the more powerful, stronger in mind than women. Men are not so helpless, so caught in the thrall of a woman they know not what they do. There is always a choice. The King made that choice, he chose to pursue Catherine. That it turned out well for me too is a good thing, but this marriage, the end of our marriage, all these are choices *he* made. The other woman, as you call her, she is almost incidental. Queen Catherine has done nothing to me, and ever she was a sweet girl when I knew her. I have no cause to resent her."

"Do you resent the King?" She whispered this question.

"Although it was done for reasons of his own, to make himself happy and safe, the King has made me freer than so many women of this world, more at liberty than I ever hoped to be. It is an odd thing, perhaps, that in seeking to do selfish acts, one man can manage to do more for another woman than anyone else in her life who loved her. There are times I truly do not understand him, but I do not resent him."

"You do not mind that some laugh still, about how you were cast off?"

I smiled, remembering how I had spoken to Mistress Loew when in the throes of terror and yet now I meant truly the words I spoke back then. "Let them laugh, my friend, and I shall laugh with them. They think I am disgraced? They think wrongly. They think I am shamed? None can shame me but my own thoughts, and I have nothing of which to be ashamed. I did my best to be a wife to the King, and now I will be a good sister, and if the world should choose to titter at me I shall laugh along, but you see, my laugh is the better one, for it has no meanness in it, no censure, and it is the laugh of one who has won at this game of life, just as she thought she would lose. Therefore, those who would laugh at me, they do not understand the jest, for the jest is not on me. Sometimes I think they laugh out of spite, for me doing better than they thought I would, or as they thought a woman should, and still I will laugh with them, for nothing they can do or say can harm me."

I looked to the skies. "A falconer took me into his aviary, and, finding my feathers did not please him, he set me loose and into the skies I returned. He could have chosen not to capture me in the first place, but he also could have killed me rather than freed me, could have locked me away so others did not see me until I wasted to death. He chose the kinder path, and though many times I have heard he did not choose that way for other hawks, I am grateful that in my case, he opened the cage."

"But you never can go home."

"I am not sure what there is for me at home," I said. "I love my family, I will always miss them, but with them I would be but a bird in another cage, and I have had enough of cages too tight to breathe in."

Katherine regarded me with a steady gaze. "You still are in a cage, Anna."

"We all are, my friend, every one of us; cages of mind, of body, of position and money. Marriage is the cage for most of us, for life, but this one at least is larger, I can fly, I can do as I please." I smiled at Katherine. "I can see my friends."

I looked up to a sound of hooting, swans in the sky. Some left England when the snows came, but I had been told some remained, spending their time on any water left unfrozen. These swans were no doubt in the skies now, searching for such a place. "We all are always looking for something in this strange and often frightening existence," I said to Katherine. "And yet some of us are fortunate enough to know what we have, whilst it is ours."

*Here ends The Swan Maiden*
*In Book Three A Cloak of Feathers*
*Anna will explore her freedom, as others lose their lives.*

# Author's Notes

This book is a work of fiction, although based on research of the events and people of the time period in question. I read a great deal of sources for this book, which I will include as a bibliography in the last book of the series.

Anne of Cleves is a much-maligned figure, the Queen of Henry VIII who was cast off after he decided he didn't like her looks. But I've always wondered about her, because of all the wives of Henry Tudor, she did the best. In the rhyme about his wives, Catherine Parr is noted as the one wife who survived, but that's not really true, because Anne of Cleves survived too, and not only Henry, but Catherine Parr as well.

I think we would do better to remember her as a survivor, and a clever one at that, rather than as a cast-off wife.

Her looks will always be up for discussion, as portraits of the time might be accurate, and they might not, but I think Anne had a great deal to recommend her which had nothing to do with looks.

For the most part in this book I have tried to stick to the historical events as they happened, but a few things I have invented.

We cannot be sure how well or swiftly Anne managed to learn English, and how much she could understand of gossip about court or indeed what was happening to her when the King first started investigations into their marriage, but I have gone off the idea that she had learnt English fairly well by this point and that her people kept her well informed about court gossip and rumour. She had Harst, too, who as her ambassador was likely to be always working to keep her informed. Some have posited that the conversation between Anne and her women, where she seemed entirely ignorant about how a child was made, was invented as evidence to annul the marriage and that by this point Anne cannot possibly have learnt so much English, but I advanced my plot on the idea that the conversation was genuine, and that Anne had learnt that much English. She was a clever woman, and I think it entirely possible.

Others have put forth that this conversation meant Anne was in ignorance of what went on in the bedchamber between men and women, but I think this highly unlikely. Her mother would never have sent her away into marriage without some guidance on this matter, it would have been a dereliction of duty. Her upbringing in the court of women of Cleves, too, would have provided amble opportunity to see pregnant women and to witness labour, and I have no doubt Anne would have asked questions which would have been answered. Even if she had been in ignorance, her women would have told her what to expect on her wedding night. It is more likely, therefore, that Anne's answers on this matter were a subtle attempt to protect the King, who she probably thought was impotent, and to protect herself, since she would be blamed for not conceiving.

The code the sisters write in is my invention, there is no evidence this existed.

One other thing I invented is Anne's trip to Hever Castle. James Boleyn sold the property to the Crown on the 31st of December 1540, and it was not one of the properties initially given to Anna as her settlement. It is unlikely she would have visited so early, but I wanted her there for Cromwell's death, so I had her pay an investigative trip to the property to see if she liked it, which is not impossible.

I believe Anne of Cleves was a far more subtle and intelligent woman than history has given her credit for, as despite the fact that we all know now the flaws and faults of Henry VIII she has been vilified in our minds for being the wife he didn't want. That he rejected her has caused her to gain a reputation that I feel is undeserved, and in this series of books I would like to present the Anna I see when reading about her, a woman of grace, intelligence, understanding and subtlety so great that she has managed to elude many. And yet she is a woman who deserves to be better remembered. I hope I have done her justice in this book and will continue to do so as the series progresses.

# Thank You

…to so many people for helping me make this book possible… to my proofreader, Julia Gibbs, who gave me her time, her wonderful guidance and also her encouragement. To my family for their ongoing love and support. To my friend Petra. To my friend Nessa for her support and affection, and to another friend, Anne, who has done so much for me. To Sue and Annette, more friends who read my books and cheer me on. To Terry for getting me into writing and indie publishing in the first place. To Katie and Jooles, Macer, Pip, Linda, Fe, Pete and Heather, people there in times of trial. And to all my wonderful readers, who took a chance on an unknown author, and have followed my career and books since.

To those who have left reviews or contacted me by email or on social media, I give great thanks, as you have shown support for my career as an author, and enabled me to continue writing. Thank you for allowing me to live my dream.

Thank you to all of you; you'll never know how much you've helped me, but I know what I owe to you.

Gemma Lawrence
Wales
2024

## About The Author

I find people talking about themselves in the third person to be entirely unsettling, so, since this section is written by me, I will use my own voice rather than try to make you believe that another person is writing about me to make me sound terribly important.

I am an independent author, publishing my books by myself, with the help of my lovely proofreader. I left my day job in 2016 and am now a fully-fledged, full-time author, and proud to be so.

My passion for history began early in life. As a child I lived in Croydon, near London, and my schools were lucky enough to be close to such glorious places as Hampton Court and the Tower of London, allowing field trips to take us to those castles. I write historical fiction for the main part, but I also have a fascination with ghost stories and fantasy, and I hope this book was one you enjoyed. I want to divert you as readers, to please you with my writing and to have you join me on these adventures.

A book is nothing without a reader.

As to the rest of me, I am in my forties and live in Wales with a rescued cat (who often sits on my lap when I write, which can make typing more of a challenge). I studied Literature at University after I fell in love with books as a small child. When I was little, I could often be found nestled halfway up the stairs with a pile of books in my lap and my head lost in another world. There is nothing more satisfying to me than finding a new book I adore, to place next to the multitudes I own and love… and nothing more disappointing to me to find a book I am willing to never open again. I do hope that this book was not a disappointment to you. I loved writing it and I hope that showed through the pages.

If you would like to contact me, please do so. I can be found in quite a few places!

On Twitter, (I am not calling it X) I am @TudorTweep.

You can also find me on Instagram as tudorgram1500. I am new to Mastodon as G. Lawrence Tudor Tooter,

@TudorTweep@mastodonapp.uk, and Counter Social as TudorSocial1500.

On Facebook my page is just simply G. Lawrence, and on TikTok and Threads I am tudorgram1500, the same as Instagram. I've just joined Bluesky as G. Lawrence too. Often, I have a picture of the young Elizabeth I as my avatar, or there's me leaning up against a wall in Pembroke Castle.

I am also now writing on Substack, where my account is called G. Lawrence in the Book Nook. On there I publish articles, reviews, advice for other writers and I'm publishing a book there chapter by chapter each week. Join me there!

Via email, I am tudortweep@gmail.com a dedicated email account for my readers to reach me on. I'll try and reply within a few days.

Thank you for taking a risk with an unknown author and reading my book. I do hope now that you've read one, you'll want to read more. If you'd like to leave me a review, that would be very much appreciated also!

Gemma Lawrence
Wales
2024

Printed in Great Britain
by Amazon